MILO

LILY MORTON

Text Copyright© Lily Morton 2019

Book cover design by Natasha Snow Designs

www.natashasnowdesigns.com

Professional beta reading and formatting by Leslie Copeland, editing by Courtney Bassett www.lescourtauthorservices.com

This book is a work of fiction. Names, characters, places and incidents are products of the author's imagination, or are used fictitiously.

References to real people, events, organizations, establishments or locations are intended to provide a sense of authenticity and are used fictitiously. Any resemblance to actual events, locations, organizations, or persons living or dead is entirely coincidental.

All rights reserved. No part of this book may be reproduced, scanned or distributed in any printed or electronic form without permission, except for the use of brief quotations in a book review. Please purchase only authorized editions

The author acknowledges the copyrighted or trademarked status and trademark owners of the following products mentioned in this work of fiction: Vans, McDonalds, Converse, Volkswagen, Farmfoods, Savlon, Dammar Varnish, Burger King, Weebles, Heat Magazine, Levi's, Hallmark, Crayola, The Sun, Mills & Boon, Tie Rack, LEGO

All songs, song titles and lyrics mentioned in the novel are the property of the respective songwriters and copyright holders.

Warning

This book contains material that is intended for a mature, adult audience. It contains graphic language, explicit sexual content and adult situations.

CONTENT WARNING

This book deals with the aftermath of domestic abuse and as such includes scenes of it.

For my husband. Always.

"I cannot fix on the hour, or the spot, or the look or the words, which laid the foundation. It is too long ago. I was in the middle before I knew that I had begun."

Jane Austen
'Pride and Prejudice'

PROLOGUE

Until you're ready to leave, Lo, and not a second before.

Five Years Ago

Milo

I stand in the kitchen looking down at the mess of broken glass and the sluggish trail of red wine that's oozing from the shards like a bloody stream. My palms sweat, and I wipe them down the legs of the expensive black trousers he'd insisted I wear today. I catch a glimpse of myself in the shiny stainless-steel fridge and spare a split second to worry about the size of my arse in them, which had been the subject of his latest lecture. Then I go back to fretting over the bottle of wine I just broke.

"What the fuck?" comes the explosive voice from the doorway

and I can't stop the flinch that runs through my body. I wish I could, but the memory of the last time I broke something in his expensive flat is painful.

My boyfriend, Thomas, comes further into the room. He's dressed in skinny black jeans and a black V-neck t-shirt, the neckline so low I can practically see his ribs. With his golden hair shining he looks like an angel, but the way he can't disguise how pleased he is by my cowardly reaction is very far from angelic.

"What the hell have you done now?" he mutters, kicking the mess of glass to the side near the kitchen cupboard where I presume I'll be expected to clean it up later. "Can't you do anything properly?"

"I'm s-s-sorry," I mutter, feeling the words at the back of my throat like a massive lump that I can't swallow or spit out. They're just there, taunting me while I stutter.

"Oh, are y-y-you?" he taunts. "How s-s-sorry are you, Milo?"

"I'll c-c-clean it up," I manage to get out, bending to pick up the bigger shards of glass. He moves suddenly and I flinch again and then gasp as the forgotten glass bites into my palm. I look down dumbly to see the slice white against my skin for a brief second before blood starts to seep out.

"Shit!" he says, managing to sound both aggrieved and yet in some way horribly fond. "You can't do anything, can you? Come here, sweetheart. Let me clean it up." I pull my hand back from his grasp and he tuts disapprovingly. "Come on, Milo. The guests will be here soon. I haven't got time for this display of petulance. You and I both know that you won't clean it properly. Then you'll get an infection and we'll be at casualty before we know it. I haven't got the energy to waste on that performance."

He looks me up and down dismissively. "At least you're wearing what I suggested this time so you look at least halfway decent." He scowls at my hair, which at his request has been cut short. "You can get more cut off next time though. It's getting disgustingly out of control again."

He sighs in a long-suffering manner and I fight the impulse to apologise. "I really don't know why it's always me having to tell you what to do, Milo. You're so bloody hopeless. Like a fucking amoeba with no thoughts of your own. Happy to wallow around while I pay for everything."

He reaches out and pulls a loose strand of my hair. It's quick and surprisingly painful as is the vicious look on his face. "Get it all cut off," he mutters.

I try to pull back, but his grip on my hair tightens and it brings tears to my eyes. "I d-d-don't ..." I pause and take a deep breath the way my old speech therapist had told me to do and feel the now customary panic when it doesn't work and my voice won't come. Shit! What if this is permanent now? What if I've brought it back and it won't leave? Despite the panic, I force my words out like I'm taking an axe to them. "I don't want t-t-to ..."

"Don't want me t-t-to do what, you fucking imbecile? Help you? Well, excuse me for caring. Really, Milo, I don't know why the fuck I put up with your useless stammering incompetence. You used to be good in bed but even that's gone." He lets go of my hair and looks me up and down dismissively. "Gone the way of your l-l-looks and b-b-b-brain, I suppose."

"What the *fuck* is going on in here?"

The deep voice didn't come from me. We both spin around, and I gape at the sight of Niall in the doorway. My older brother's best friend stands there in jeans and a navy V-neck jumper, his blond hair messy and dishevelled around a face that at first showed disbelief but is now pretty quickly moving into absolute rage.

He looks extraordinarily bright at this moment, like he's under a spotlight, and I feel an intense pull towards him because he represents home and safety and everything that's been missing from my life since I met Thomas and at his behest abandoned everyone.

I want to move towards him so desperately but I can't make my feet move, so I do what I've learned through many hard and painful lessons over the last two years. I merge into the background and try to disappear. I've found that it's frighteningly easy to vanish from your own life.

Niall

The phone rings as I cross the road. I look down at the display and connect the call. "What do you want, Gideon?"

My best friend hesitates and then laughs. "How do you know I want anything?"

"It's like a sixth sense. Soon I'll be seeing dead people and sleeping in a tent on the floor."

"Well, at least I have all my own hair in this scenario, which cannot be said for Bruce Willis. And I know very well that if that tent was in the middle of a wet, muddy field, you'd be ecstatic."

I smile. No one knows me better than him. "I repeat, what do you want?"

"It's Milo."

I frown as I catch a note in his voice. "What's up with him?"

"I can't get hold of him."

"Well, that's not surprising. You were only saying the other day how he's living his best life with his new man."

"Yes, but normally he'll answer his phone. I've been ringing him for three days now and haven't managed to get him."

He sighs, and my pulse picks up. "Do you think there's anything wrong?"

The hesitation on the other end of the line confirms it, and my grip on my phone tightens as I think of Gideon's little brother. He's sweet and dreamy and, despite having a bad stutter when he was little, he's surprisingly sparky if pushed. He's as dear to me as my own brothers, and the thought of anything happening to him makes me feel a bit sick.

"You're not telling me something," I say with the certainty of someone who knows him inside out. "What is it?"

He sighs. "I don't know. It's just this boyfriend."

"What's wrong with him?"

"Nothing on paper. He's a successful artist, good-looking bloke, and well off. He just ..."

"What?"

"He pings my buttons," he mutters, and I feel the hairs on the back of my neck stand up. "He's very controlling. When I met him, he absolutely monopolized the conversation and wouldn't let Milo get a word in edgeways."

"How was Milo with that?"

"Accepting. Too accepting." He pauses. "You and I both know that although he stuttered as a kid, he's an opinionated little bugger underneath the shyness." I smile because Milo's ability to wind up Gideon when he was little was very endearing. The smile dies as he keeps talking. "And he put him down all the time. Subtle little digs that I soon put a stop to, but I didn't like the way Milo reacted."

"How was that?"

He pauses. "He *didn't* react, if that doesn't sound too weird. It was like he was so used to someone talking to him like shit that it hardly registered anymore."

"What do you want?" I say slowly. "I know it's something, Gideon. It's the only time you ring me."

There's a silence on the other end of the phone, but I know he'll ignore the barb of anger in my tone. He always does. Finally, he speaks, and I was right. His tone is even and logical. "I need you to go round to the flat."

"*Really?* That's not going to go down too well."

"See how it goes. Just check up on him and let me know how things are. I'm stuck in Romania and I'll get the fucking sack if I decide to leave the set. The director's already got it in for me."

"Could that be anything to do with the cheery warmth of your personality?" I murmur, hearing him laugh. I exhale loudly, feeling the sting of wanting to hurt him riding me under the skin. "So, you want me to leave the bloke I've got lined up for tonight and go to a complete stranger's flat and try to assess the state of your family's dirty laundry?"

"Please," he says. "For me."

This always works and he bloody knows it, and for a wild moment I want to reach through the phone and throttle him. Then I remember Milo and I know I can't. He's as much my little brother as he is Gideon's.

"Okay, I'll do it. Shoot me the address."

An hour later I stand outside the place where Milo is living. I look up and whistle. If his boyfriend's got a place here, he must have some money because property in Chelsea isn't cheap.

I try the front door and look around when I find it locked. Spying a rack of brass buttons next to little labels, I search for the name Thomas Dawley, but before I can press it the door opens and a lady appears holding the leads of four very lively Chihuahuas. Seizing the chance while she's distracted, I hold the door open for her and then slip inside the building.

Inside the lobby, it's hushed and smells of floor polish and the scent from a huge vase of gardenias. There's a concierge desk but it's empty with the seat pushed back as if the occupant has just gone somewhere, so I make straight for the bank of lifts. They whisk me upstairs with the quiet hush that money buys. Perish the thought that the machinery might disturb the wealthy people's minds.

I find the door of Milo's apartment easily and go to knock but pause as I hear raised voices from inside. I lean closer to the door, but when I rest my hand against the wood it falls open as it's on the latch.

I step inside. The flat is gorgeous with high ceilings and tall windows, but my attention is solely on the raised voices from the kitchen. I frown. Make that one raised voice and it isn't the low, soft tones of Milo.

The voice carries on, rising and falling in a hectoring fashion, and before I even know it my feet have carried me to the doorway where I pause, stunned by what I'm seeing.

Milo is leaning back into the kitchen cabinets, every muscle in his body seeming to scream that he'd be happy if he could seep into the wood behind him and disappear.

The last time I saw him he was full of life. His hair had been shiny and crazily long, but it had suited him. He's always had a quirky way of dressing that's somehow just him. Now, his hair is cut short and it's greasy and lank. He must also be a fucking stone lighter, and he could ill afford to lose a pound in the first place as he's naturally slender. His cheekbones are now juts of bone over hollowed cheeks.

He's talking to the other man who's towering over Milo's thin form, and I feel something twang in my chest when his stutter makes a reappearance. How the fuck has that come back? He'd worked so hard to get rid of it and I'd been so fucking proud of him when he largely succeeded. That spark in my chest catches light and rage fills me when his boyfriend Thomas mocks the stutter, laughing in Milo's face.

"What the *fuck* is going on in here?" I demand, my voice hoarse and deep in my throat. Milo jerks in surprise and Thomas spins around.

"Who the fuck are you?" he snaps. "How did you get in here?"

"Oh, you shouldn't be worried about that, mate," I growl. "You should be more concerned about the closeness of your face to my bloody fist. Who the fuck do you think you're talking to, you utter cunt?"

He immediately draws himself up but moves back slightly, which is a wise move in my opinion. "It's actually none of your business. This is my boyfriend and how I talk to him has got nothing to do with you."

"It's got everything to do with me, you piece of shit," I say indignantly. "He's my family." A curious look crosses Milo's face but then it's gone, and he resumes that desperately still position that small animals assume in the wild in the face of a predator. Rage spreads from my stomach to my chest, making my fingers tingle.

"Is this another of your brothers?" Thomas demands, looking at

Milo, his expression changing slightly and a flustered look coming over his face.

"He isn't my b-b-b ..." Milo starts to say but Thomas huffs impatiently and turns back to me.

"I'm so sorry," he says pseudo-charmingly. "I hate that you came in here and got the wrong impression." He must catch something in my expression because he hurriedly carries on. "Milo just cut himself and I was so worried that I lost my temper and–"

"You didn't let him finish," I say, and I can hear the outrage in my voice.

"What?"

"You didn't let him finish. You cut off what he was trying to say."

Incredibly, he laughs. "Well, we'd be here all day if I did that. Who's got that amount of time?"

I watch a red flush crawl over Milo's too-thin cheekbones and I've abruptly had enough. "I have," I say clearly, and before he can say anything else I reach out and punch Thomas neatly in the face. He makes a sound that's very similar to the one a weightlifter makes and slides down to the floor like an envelope coming through the letterbox, where he lies gasping and looking astonished.

I shake my head. "Now you've got plenty of time to listen to him," I say angrily. I step neatly over him and I'm at Milo's side in seconds. He immediately flinches and my throat hurts. "Easy," I say, automatically using the same calm and warm voice I use with sick dogs and horses and anything else that comes under my protection. He jerks as I grab his wrist.

"Easy," I say again roughly. "You're bleeding. Let me put your hand under water and get the glass off, Lo." The sound of his old childhood nickname trips off my tongue and he immediately relaxes a little bit. He lets me turn him and hold his hand under the cold flow of water. He immediately flinches and moves back instinctively, but I hush him and he stands acquiescently against me, letting me wash his hand then dry it off and inspect it.

Satisfied, I wrap it in a clean tea towel and step back. "Okay, Lo, go and get packed. Take everything." I look down at Thomas's prone figure and can practically feel the frown on my face. "You're not ever coming back to this bloody wanker."

Milo stirs, his big brown eyes looking up at me. "Are y-y-you telling me what to d-d-do?"

I wait him out quietly as he stumbles and trips over the words, remembering the lessons his mum and dad had taught me and Gideon years ago. No showing any impatience at all. I'd never understood that. Who could be impatient with Milo? The answer was, unfortunately, Gideon, who rather than wait him out would often answer for him instead.

Then his words hit me and I shake my head. He flinches back as if I'm cross with him and I repress the urge to step back onto Thomas's throat. Instead, I say gently, "No, I'm sorry. I think you've had enough of that. In my opinion, it would be best for you to leave the arsehole currently residing on the floor." I pause. "But if you want to stay, I'll abide by your decision." He raises an eyebrow and I smile wryly. "Okay, I won't abide silently." I look at him searchingly. "Well, shall we get your stuff?"

"Where w-w-will we go?"

I smile at him. "*Chi an Mor*. I'm staying with Silas, helping him to get the estate back in order. You remember Silas, don't you?" I think of the dark-haired and gentle man who's one of my best friends. He's spent most of his life looking after small creatures and his younger brother, and he's the perfect person to take Milo to. He nods slowly and I carry on. "You'll come back with me and stay there for a bit."

"H-H-How long?"

I can feel my smile turning gentle. "Until you're ready to leave, Lo, and not a second before."

He sleeps through the entire journey to Cornwall and I leave him alone, sneaking glances at him occasionally and noticing the dark shadows under his eyes like smudged paint, the length of his eyelashes, the thin wrists and the long, elegant hands. He's a grown man now but I can still see hints of the small boy who'd followed Gideon and me around the house so steadfastly, gracing me with his wide, warm smile whenever I'd been kind to him.

It's twilight when I pull up on the forecourt in front of the huge Elizabethan manor, and Milo stirs. For a second his eyelashes flutter wildly and his body goes extraordinarily still. With a pang, I realise that he can't work out where he is and is keeping still in case he's in trouble. I swallow hard.

"We're here," I say softly. He relaxes and opens his eyes, the warm brown seeming flecked with the purple of twilight. "And you're safe," I add firmly. "You'll *always* be safe with me."

The front door opens and Silas comes down the steps. Dressed in disreputable old jeans and a jumper with holes in it, he looks a little like a tramp, but you can't miss the kindness and strength in his face.

I get out and hear Milo slowly follow me.

"G-G-Good evening, L-Lord Ashworth," Milo mutters, his tall, thin body folded in slightly like his wings have been clipped. I throw my arm over his shoulders, feeling the delicate bones there and squeezing comfortingly.

Warmth crosses Silas's face and he shoots me a quick reassuring look that Milo misses. "It's Silas please, Milo," he says in the warm voice he uses with sick animals. He smiles at Milo. "Welcome to *Chi an Mor*. I want you to consider this as your home until you're ready to go again."

CHAPTER 1

Niall completely missed out on the memo that I'm a grown man now.

Five Years Later

Milo

I hear my best friend Oz's entourage before I see them. A cheerful whistle from him, the pattering of claws from his dog Chewwy on the wood floor, and the sound of a baby cooing. I smile and bend over the portrait in front of me and dip my swab into the solvent before rolling it delicately over the surface of the picture to remove the old layer of varnish. Slowly the old man's dark doublet lightens to a rich green and I nod in satisfaction.

A strand of my long hair escapes my ponytail and I hook it impatiently back over my ear, making a mental note to get it cut. I consider making another mental note not to forget the first one, but I know the likelihood is high that this time next month my hair will be even longer and more unmanageable until I approach a similarity to Mr. Twit.

The door creaks open and I hear Oz's sigh. "This room is fucking freezing, Milo."

Startled, I ask, "Is it?" I straighten up and hear my spine crack. Art conservation might sound glamorous, but it's actually low paid and quite hard on the body. I think people imagine a beautiful room full of exotic paintings when it's actually more likely to be working up a scaffold getting dirty in the cold and damp. As a consequence, I'm sure my spine is aging more rapidly than the rest of me. Currently, my body is twenty-seven and my spine is the same age as the pyramids.

He shakes his head. "I know you can be a bit absentminded, but surely even you've noticed the tell-tale signs of your breath in the air and your fingers dropping off from frostbite?"

"It's not that cold. It has to be cool in here, but I probably wouldn't notice anyway. Where I grew up, this is positively balmy."

"Did you grow up in the North Pole?"

I laugh and, stripping off my gloves, I hold out my hands for the baby he's carrying. "It's going to get even colder in a second when you open that window because of the solvent fumes in here. Anyway, give me my precious," I coo. "She hasn't seen her Uncle Milo in hours."

His mouth quirks but he hands the baby over quickly, watching me with an affectionate look on his sharp face. He opens the window, letting in the cold autumnal air, and settles his arse down on the old chair in the corner of my studio. He winces and immediately propels himself up. "Jesus. How old is this chair?"

"About the same age as my mother, I think," I say, settling his daughter, Cora, in my arms. She coos and reaches for me, her brown eyes warm and curious and her dark mop of hair an exclamation mark over her forehead.

"Well, it's time for it to go then," he mutters. "Jesus, that spring got luckier with me than Silas has managed for a few days."

I laugh. "Let's keep it. I'll make sure to sit in it and get a happy ending."

"You'd have more chance of a happy ending if you moved out of this room," he mutters, edging over to the portrait before recoiling slightly. "Bloody hell, is that a relation of my husband or a suspect in the Jack the Ripper case?"

I laugh and Cora startles slightly. I shush her and kiss the tiny fingers she holds up to my face. Moving next to him, I stare down at the picture. "He is a bit grim, isn't he?"

"Grim? Caligula was grim. This is a new and previously undiscovered level of malevolence." He cocks his head to one side. "Is it my imagination or do his eyes follow you when you move?"

I shake my head. "My remit isn't to judge. Instead, I reveal what has been previously hidden."

"While I'm sure that sounds romantic in your head, let's be realistic. You've actually just wiped dirt off a grumpy old git's face."

I laugh. "I'm so glad my time at art college wasn't wasted."

He looks searchingly at me and opens his mouth but then closes it again. I stare at him. "Oh my God, what were you going to say? It must be bad if it's made Oz Gallagher shut up."

He laughs, and I look affectionately at him. I know he's going to tell me the truth. Oz doesn't ever shy away from that. He's my best friend in the world and it comes as a shock to realise that I've only known him for a couple of years. He came here to *Chi an Mor* in all his wisecracking, sassy glory and proceeded to turn everyone's lives upside down. Footloose and fancy-free, he only intended to stay for a few months and ease the old house into opening to the general public. The best-laid plans always go wrong – or right – and now he's settled with his husband Silas, the current earl, and they have a beautiful seven-month-old daughter.

He clears his throat and looks at me, and I straighten from kissing Cora's forehead. "What?"

"I just think that you're actually a bit wasted here, Milo."

"Why?"

"Because you're so bloody talented. People from all over the country are starting to come here to consult with you, and rather than enjoying it you're stuck in a small, cold room wearing ugly gloves and hunched over a hideous painting. It's like something from a Dickens novel."

He pauses for breath and I try to relax my instinctive defensive shield. I don't need it with him.

He rubs my arm affectionately. "You're so clever and talented and no one sees it here apart from us, and you need more than that. You should be living it up and going to exotic parties. Mixing with artists and the bohemian crowd."

I swallow hard at the thought of the people that used to surround Thomas. "I don't think I'm cut out for a bohemian crowd. They sound quite noisy and tiring," I manage to say.

"Well, maybe look for a sub-branch. The whispering bohemians or something." I laugh, letting it flush away the horrible memory, and he smiles at me. "I'm not sure why you stay here, to be honest. It's a lovely place and my home, but you could be anywhere."

"I don't want to be anywhere else. *Chi an Mor* is my home too," I say quietly. "It's very pretty."

We both jump as there's a loud bang on the door and a familiar messy blond head appears. "What are the two of you doing up here?" he demands. "We're sending out for Chinese. What do you want?"

Oz grins at me. "Oh yes, he's very pretty indeed," he mutters. "But which of his parts are the prettiest?"

"Shut up." I feel my cheeks flush and hope it looks like it's the cold. I look at the man who's just appeared and sigh. Niall Fawcett. Estate manager of *Chi an Mor*. I've known him all my life, as in his teenage years he practically lived with us. He's my brother's best friend and the man I crushed on for years.

He's gorgeous. Tall with wide shoulders, narrow hips, and legs that go on for days. With a head of shiny white-blond hair that looks fashionably messy and piercing blue eyes, he looks more like a Nordic model than an estate manager. He was the subject of many of my wet dreams when I was a teenager, which is slightly awkward, but it needn't be for one very good reason.

"It's bloody cold in here," he says, coming into the room fully and striding over to the radiator. "Jesus," he mutters, standing up and coming over to me. "The radiator's out." I swallow hard as he grabs my hands. "Fucking hell, Lo, your hands are freezing. You'll make yourself ill again. You've only just got over that flu you had a couple of months ago." He ruffles my hair affectionately, sending strands of it falling messily out of my ponytail.

Yes, that is the reason why it's not awkward. Niall completely missed out on the memo that I'm a grown man now and not the small, nervous child who shadowed his footsteps through the long school summer holidays or even the damaged man he brought back here. He treats me like I'm seven and although I know the reason and adore him for it, it's still fucking aggravating.

I pull my hands back, not missing the swift frown he gives. "I'm fine," I say shortly. "You make me sound like something from a Bronte novel."

"Which one would you be?" he asks.

I arch my eyebrow. "Read many of them, have you, Niall?"

He flushes slightly. "I do read, you know."

"The weather reports, mainly," Oz says tartly.

"They're very educational."

"Only if you're interested in hot air and cold fronts."

He laughs. "That sounds like the title of your autobiography, Ozzy."

"Oh, fuck off," my friend mutters, shoving Niall but not managing to move him an inch. Niall ignores him and looks back at me.

"Food," he says succinctly. "You've been up here all day and Maggie says you haven't eaten anything."

"Oh my God, you're spying on me using Maggie."

He raises one very arrogant eyebrow. "Spying is such a common word, Milo. Let's call it overseeing."

"Well, stop all the seeing over," I say crossly. "I'll eat when I'm ready and not a second before."

He shoots a quick look at me which for a second almost looks proud but then it vanishes, no doubt because I just sounded like a sulky seven-year-old.

"I'll order you a sweet and sour chicken," he says decisively. "You always eat that like it's going out of fashion."

I open my mouth but it's too late to blast him as he smiles at Cora in my arms. It's far too warm and potent this close up and I swallow hard, seeing Oz grinning out of the corner of my eye.

"How's my precious?" Niall coos. "Did she miss her Uncle Niall? Did she?"

Oz and I exchange shakes of our heads, but Cora is a lot less discriminating. She fucking loves Niall, and whenever he's in the room she gets agitated and waves all her arms and legs trying to get his attention. I gape as he removes her adeptly from my arms.

"Let's go and get some food, Cora Bora," he says, kissing the tiny tip of her nose and making her go briefly cross-eyed. "If I take you downstairs the silly boy will follow."

"That had better not be me," Oz says somewhat menacingly, but Niall just laughs and exits the room.

I fold my arms. "I'm not eating just because he says I am," I say crossly. At that moment my stomach gives a massive grumble that's loud in the quiet room. Oz raises his eyebrow and I huff. "I'll eat because I'm hungry and not because the Lord and Master orders me to."

He shakes his head. "Fascinating as this latest development in your and Niall's relationship is, I'm hungry and knackered because Cora woke me up twice in the night."

"What development? We haven't got a relationship to develop," I splutter.

He pats my shoulder happily. "You know denial isn't just a river in Egypt, don't you?"

"Where are you getting these lines from?"

He laughs and drags me to the door. "I think Mark Twain said it first, but I'm a lot prettier than him. I'm just saying that I like this pert side of you and I think Niall does too."

I shake my head. "I'm the next best thing to a little brother that he's got. It's practically built into the job description that I get irritated by him. He just enjoys winding me up."

"I think he enjoys the sassiness from you most of all," he murmurs. "He loves it."

Old memories strike with the force of a blow and I flinch slightly. "Yes, well, he's got his reasons for feeling like that and he's more than earned them."

His frown follows me out of the room but as normal he doesn't push. However, the time is approaching when I know I'll have to confide in him or he'll keep pushing Niall at me, unaware of why it's never going to happen.

～

Later that evening I button up my coat before stepping out of the front door. The wind hits me instantly, grabbing at my hair and scarf and trying to tangle them together.

I pause for a second to admire the sight of *Chi an Mor* in autumn. To most people, the Elizabethan manor house is at its best in the summer when it seems to glow honey gold against the blue skies. Not me. I love it best in autumn and winter when the warm stone stands as a fixed point in a landscape dominated by the changing seasons.

Tonight it's wild. The trees dance and bend, sending wild shadows across the grounds and rain splatters on my face. Seagulls ride on the wind calling joyously to each other.

I set off on the path that will lead me down to the sea. The cove will be wild in this wind and I love that more than anything. The waves crashing onto the shore, the salt-wet wind in my face. It makes me feel more alive than I have in years.

The voice calling my name is flattened by the wind and it's only the third shout of "Milo" that makes me comprehend. I turn to see Oz speed walking towards me with the dogs Chewwy and Boris at his heels. As I wait, he pushes his arm into his coat as it flaps behind him like it's trying to escape. "Are you okay?" I ask. "You look in a rush."

"I had to catch you," he gasps, coming to a stop in front of me.

"Why?"

"I wanted to say sorry."

"What are you sorry for?" The incredulity is clear in my voice and he gives me a sheepish smile.

"For going on at you earlier. It's not my business if you want to stay here, and I never want to make you uncomfortable."

My lip twitches. "Did Silas tell you off?"

"No," he immediately scoffs before sagging. "Totally. But in that really gentle, kind way he has that prevents me from telling him to fuck off."

I laugh. "Ah, marriage. It's a constant torment."

He smiles and steps into me, hugging me tight for a second. "I'm sorry anyway," he whispers. "Personally, I'd be happy if you stayed here forever because I love you loads."

"I love you too," I whisper.

He steps back. "But because I love you, I want the best for you, and that might not be what makes me happy." He sighs and scuffs his feet across the sand. "I guess I just don't understand what keeps you here, and I know it's not all Niall."

I open my mouth to refute that any bit of it is about him, but I can't, so instead I say what I've been dreading doing for ages.

"*Chi an Mor* is a bit of a sanctuary for me. A few years ago, I was in a really bad way and Silas took me in." I laugh humourlessly before reaching into my coat pocket for my inhaler. Taking a puff, I put it back and continue. "He said he wanted me to stay because he had hundreds of pictures that needed restoring. He was telling the truth." I smile. "It's just that they're all of his really hideous ancestors and he couldn't have cared less if he ever saw their faces again. Then he spent a year trying to give me a career which would entail me actually talking to people. The only problem with that was that he apprenticed me with you and you talk enough for ten people, so eventually he let me go back to the silence and my paintings."

He bangs me in the ribs with his sharp elbow and I laugh, but his face softens the way it always does when he talks about his husband. "He's a kind man."

I nod. "And generous." I sigh. "I hoped I'd never have to tell you this because honestly I don't come out of it well and I ... I rather like the way you view me as sassy."

"You're a lot more than that," he says fiercely. "And nothing you tell me will change the opinion I have of you now as one of my best friends. *Nothing.*" He pauses. "Unless you did something really heinous like murder Silas's mother."

"I don't think that would be heinous so much as totally justifiable," I say wryly. "But no, she lives and breathes on a golf course with her husband Martin somewhere."

He shudders. "Rather her husband than us, and let's hope the golf course is very far away."

I gesture rather awkwardly. "Let's walk and talk." It will be easier to talk if I don't have to look at him.

He falls into step next to me as we walk the sands, the wind tearing at our clothes but the rocks around us neutering the noise so we can talk.

"I've told you before that I had a stutter when I was little?" I say, and he nods. I shake my head. "It was horrible. I fell and hit my head when I was five. Before that, I was apparently very loud, but afterward ..." I shudder. "It was horrible. I would open my mouth and I'd know exactly what I wanted to say, but it was like something was strangling me. You hear people saying the words are stuck in their throat, but it was literally what happened to me. They'd almost choke me and meanwhile, while I stuttered and stammered, the person opposite me would be looking at me like I was a fucking freak. After a bit, I learned to be self-conscious. I learned to hide myself in full view, to shrink into the room so people wouldn't have to look at me like that."

"Did you have a speech therapist?"

I nod. "So many. Some crap, but in the end, I got a good one. I learned to talk more softly than I had been because it makes it easier to get my words out. But it also made me even more invisible somehow. However, the worst of it slowly disappeared and when I was eighteen, I went to art college. I felt so much better in myself at that point, but my parents still didn't want me to go. They were a bit overprotective and they worried about my mental state, but I was determined."

"Did you enjoy it?"

I smile. "Of course. And it was wonderful. I made good friends and I enjoyed the classes. Although I loved painting, I wasn't that good, but I found that I really loved restoration and I was good at that. Enough to get an apprenticeship at a really prestigious museum and gallery in London. My confidence was high ... and then I met Thomas."

"I somehow feel that this merits the *Jaws* theme tune."

I sigh and laugh. "All four films' worth, including the really shitty last two." I shrug. "It's a fairly common story. He was an artist. Extremely talented and temperamental and a bit of a darling of the art world. Very up and coming. He was gorgeous, and for the life of me I couldn't understand why he wanted me."

"Have you looked at yourself, Milo?"

I shake my head. "Anyway, he totally swept me off my feet. I was in love for the first time in my life and it was incredibly intense. He moved me in with him after a few weeks and we were together for a couple of years. He wouldn't let me get out of bed for the first month." I pause at that thought and shudder slightly before going on. "He was very popular. He was invited everywhere and I went with him, and it was like he'd sprinkled magic dust on me because I became popular too. I thought life couldn't get any better."

"What happened?"

I sigh. "He was incredibly intense. He wanted my attention all the time. Sulked like a child if he didn't get it. He had this way of monopolizing you and making you feel like it was because you were incredibly important to him. Gradually I lost contact with my friends and I lost track of my apprenticeship too. I'd try to get up for work, but we'd be hungover and he'd fuck me and before I knew it, it was four in the afternoon and I had another irate phone call from work which I'd forget about by going to another party. I got the boot eventually, and who can blame them. He just laughed, opened a bottle of champagne and said we'd celebrate because now I was all his."

"Oh no."

"Oh no, indeed. From that moment he changed. He'd switch moods so quickly. He'd be so possessive. Couldn't bear anyone to talk to me. Couldn't bear my attention to be away from him. Then the next minute he'd belittle me. Tell me how ugly I was, how stupid. How I was worthless and no one would ever want me." I shake my head. "My stutter came back for the first time and nothing I tried that had worked before, worked again. He'd mock me all the time in front of his friends and they'd join in. If I ate, he'd tell me how fat I was. I lost a stone because my throat would close up whenever I tried to eat." I shoot him a look. "It's utterly pathetic. Very far from strong and sassy."

"Don't say that," he says fiercely. "You are strong. If you got through that then you're the strongest person I know."

I huff. "Not that strong. A real man would have told him to fuck off. Not taken it and stuttered while I was doing it."

He comes to a stop and drags me round to face him and I realise that he's very angry. "A *real man*? Can you hear that? What is a real man, Milo? I'll tell you what a real man is. He's someone kind and generous and loving. Someone who has had his spirit crushed yet gets back up and carries on making ugly things beautiful." I swallow hard and he hugs me. "Tell me something awful happened to him?"

"You could say that," I say wryly. "Hurricane Niall came calling."

"Oh my God, tell me," he breathes, and I grin. It's the first time I've ever smiled about this, but it lasts all the way through my telling of Niall's rescue.

"It was like when you open your windows in a stuffy room and the wind blows in and cleans everything," I muse. "He was like that. A fresh, clean breeze. He brought me back here, moved me into the rooms he was in and basically nursed me back. He never made me do anything, but somehow I did exactly what he wanted. You know Niall." Oz smiles. "He listened," I say softly. "Even though it must have been fucking torturous because everything I said took an hour. He listened and never displayed an ounce of impatience, and he made me get the poison out. Then one day he decided things had to change."

I think back to the memory and smile, but it's bittersweet because it underscores how pathetic I was.

I come awake when the curtains in my bedroom are swished back by an energetic hand. I squint through the dazzling light to see who is standing in my bedroom and then groan. It's Niall. He looks full of life and very awake, dressed in jeans and a thick, black jumper. With his face flushed from the wind outside, it's obvious that he's been at work already. I peek at the clock and wince. Probably for a while now because it's eleven o'clock in the morning.

"Rise and shine, Sleeping Beauty, and let down your lovely locks," he says, his rich deep voice full of amusement.

"You're mixing up your f-f-fairy tales," I say slowly.

"I don't think stories, where some silly bint lets a total stranger use

her preternaturally long hair in order to gain access to her locked home, are necessarily big on realisation," he offers.

I fall back against the pillow and groan pitifully in the hope that he'll leave me alone. It doesn't work. It never has since I came here months ago. In all that time, he's badgered and pushed me until I could scream. When I got to that point but subsided, he always looked disappointed and then went right back to pushing me.

First, it was speech therapists and counsellors who were shoved my way. Silas and Niall had worked as a team, Silas easing the way with me using sweet words of reassurance and then Niall badgering the professionals until they agreed to see me immediately just to get him off their backs. I know they've done some good but God, it's been hard, and at times it's seemed impossible.

Niall chose food as his next battleground. He dedicated himself to finding out my favourite foods, and when Mrs. Granger couldn't manage them he cooked them himself, coming in from work and serving up rich stews and cottage pies and custard tarts. God knows where he gets his energy from, but I wish I could find the source because some days I've felt too tired to even get out of bed.

It's on these days that he's been at his sweetest. He'd sit patiently waiting for me to eat breakfast with that amiable smile on his face which somehow made me eat, and then he'd bundle me up and take me out for long walks with him all over the estate. Or, on the days when I was too tired to move, he'd put me in the car and take me with him as he motored all over the estate checking the progress of jobs and calling in on the estate tenants.

I'd sit quietly with him, listening to his deep voice discussing business while eating whatever piece of cake had been thrust on me, my cheeks glowing from the wind and cold. And slowly I found that I could digest food again once Thomas's glowering presence had been replaced by Niall's steely sweetness.

I sit up when he moves around the bedroom. "What are you doing?" The strength in my voice is thrilling, but I hold it close to my chest in silly superstition just in case it makes my stutter come back.

"I'm getting your clothes, dearest," he says, throwing some jeans and an old sweater of his onto the bed. It's one I've been wearing all the time because the comforting bigness of it clings to my body, offering warmth and a phantom gust of his scent. I flush, suddenly more aware of him than I've been in the years since I had my teenage crush on him. That had been broken abruptly when I was seventeen and the scales had fallen from my eyes, and I sincerely hope I'm not going to start it all over again. It's the last thing I need after Thomas.

That's a sobering enough thought to get me out of bed and it's reinforced when I catch sight of myself in the mirror, because really, why on earth would Niall look twice at me anyway? I'm still scrawny thin, although I've filled out a bit, and my wavy hair is the longest it's been since I moved in with Thomas.

I raise my hand to push the messy waves away.

"What's up?" he asks, ever sensitive to what I'm thinking.

"Maybe I should cut my hair."

"Why?"

"Thomas said I should. He said it was ugly when it was long."

His eyes narrow but that's the only sign of his agitation. "Well, if that turd said you should cut it then it's obviously an indication to me that you should grow it so long you could plait your toes in it."

Unbidden I laugh, and his eyes lose their chilly coolness at the mention of Thomas and warm as they look at me. "Cut it or don't cut it," he says steadily. "It's your hair and your body, Lo. Do what you want to do with it."

I offer him a small smile and settle for pulling some of it off my face in a topknot before following him out of the room. I traipse after him down the corridor outside and frown as he starts up the staircase that leads to the first floor of the attic rooms. "Where are we going? I thought we were going out for a walk."

He looks back, his blue eyes almost navy in the dim light. "Nope. I have something to show you."

"Oh God, it's not p-p-porn, is it?"

He laughs, the sound rich and warm in the stairway. "No. That's why God invented computers and locked doors." He pauses. "And socks." I laugh, and he gestures to me. "Come on, I'll show you."

Intrigued, I follow him up until we stand outside a white painted door. "Okay," he says, breathing in deeply which is the only sign of nerves about him. He throws open the door and gestures me in. "After you."

I stare at him and wander into the room only to stop dead. "Niall," I breathe. "What is this?"

"It's your workroom," he says steadily. "Where you can start restoring pictures again."

I stare around the room with the large window letting in tons of light. My glance skips over the huge table with the expensive-looking microscope on it, the easel in the window and the table next to it on which are set pots full of wooden sticks and cotton-wool swabs. The floor-to-ceiling cupboards are open showing oil paints, their colours jewel bright in the glass bottles. I inhale and already I can smell varnish on the air.

I notice a picture on the easel and walk over to it. "Jesus," I say instinctively. It's an oil painting of an old man, but that's as far as I can say because the picture is darkened by layers of grime. However, it doesn't quite manage to dim the malevolence that dances in the old man's eyes.

He nods. "I know. Apparently, it's one of Silas's forebears. If he's anything like Silas's father you'll probably be sorry if you bring him into the light, but then art restorers can't be picky."

I turn to him. "You must have spent a fortune on this. How did you know what to get?"

"I made a few calls," he says airily, and I know instantly that he's made dozens of calls and probably badgered the life out of people. Niall is relentless if he's doing something for someone he cares about. I know I come under that remit because of Gideon, which is a sharp splinter that lodges under my skin.

"Why have you d-d-done this?" I whisper.

His eyes soften. "Because it's what you're good at, Lo. You always *used to find beauty in everything. You just forgot how to do it for a while when you were living with ugliness. I think you need this for your soul." He flushes as if he's startled himself then smiles and ruffles my hair. "Besides, you'll be doing Silas a huge favour. He's got fucking tons of these ugly old buggers lying around."*

I stare at him. He knows I'll do it because it will please him and it's a chance to do a favour for Silas who's given me everything and taken nothing in return. However, I wish passionately that for once I didn't need this. That just for once Niall wouldn't have to rescue me and take care of me, because we seem to be locked in these roles now and nothing will ever change.

I come back to the now and shrug. "And that's how Niall dragged me back into the land of the living."

Oz laughs but there's a softness to his face. "And that was it?"

I nod. "It wasn't easy. I went to speech therapy and saw the therapist they found for me, but my real salvation was that picture. I swore and cried at the bloody thing, but it was my way back and I took it." I pause. "Although thinking of the ancestor I discovered under the dirt, I think everyone might have wished that I hadn't bothered."

He stops and hugs me, his smaller body strong and warm. "I love you, Milo," he says fiercely. "And nothing will ever change it." He pauses. "Niall's actually getting easier to love the more stories you tell me about him."

"I don't love him," I say sharply and shake my head emphatically when he looks at me. "I know you think there's something between us, but there isn't. I'm not what he's looking for. He goes for confident people who are the life and soul of the party. He thinks of me as a little brother. Someone to look after and watch over all the time. Someone a bit pathetic who needs rescuing."

He opens his mouth but the knowledge that he can't argue with this statement is plain in his face along with a tiny hint of pity, so I rush on. "I don't want rescuing. I don't ever want that to happen again. I won't do anything anymore unless I can see the way it's going to be. I don't like surprises. The next time I go out with someone, I want them to be calm and easy-going. I spent too long being swept along by the force of someone's will to want to go back. I need a clear, safe, and calm path."

I look out to sea and the red sky and nod to emphasise my point. He looks at me for a long second but then, to my relief, he nods. We walk silently for a few minutes, but my words still seem to hover on the breeze like smoke.

CHAPTER 2

You want to leave a baby with me? Have you gone fucking mental?

Milo

I come awake that night suddenly and with a gasp as I realise that someone is in my room.

"Sorry." Silas's voice is loud in the quiet. "Sorry to wake you up, Milo, but it's an emergency."

I reach over and switch on the bedside lamp and the two of us hiss and shield our eyes for a second. When I uncover them, I cast a quick look at the clock. "What's the matter?" I ask slowly. "It's three in the morning." Then his words sink in and I bolt upright. "What emergency? Is it Cora?"

He shakes his head immediately. "No, calm down. It's Oz's mum. She's fallen and broken her hip."

"How did she do that?"

"Rollerblading, for God's sake." Oz's voice comes from the doorway and I look up to see him bleary-eyed and dishevelled, dressed in jeans and a crumpled t-shirt and hoody. He's holding Cora and doing that slight side-to-side sway that I've noticed most people do automatically when they're holding a baby. Anything to stop them from potentially crying.

"Is your mum okay?"

Oz nods. "I've spoken to her. She's in pain, obviously, but she's in hospital. They're waiting to see the surgeon in the morning to discuss the options."

I straighten up, pulling my tangled hair away from my face. "So, you're obviously going to her. That's fine. We can manage here."

Silas shakes his head. "It's not quite that simple."

"Why?"

Oz comes nearer the bed. "We can't take Cora with us. I want to, but Silas isn't keen on exposing her to a hospital and all those germs. She's just got over that horrible cold."

"Oh, okay," I say slowly. "So who are you leaving her with ...?" My words trail off as the two of them look straight at me. "Oh my God," I say slowly but any other words trail away as heavy footsteps sound on the attic steps outside and Niall appears in the doorway.

He's rumpled like Oz and wearing pyjama shorts, battered old motorcycle boots, and an ancient-looking hoody, but unlike the rest of us he actually looks rested and alert. "What's up?" he says deeply. "You said you needed me and it was urgent." He looks at the three of us with Oz and Silas grouped around the bed with me in it and blinks. "Okay. If you're thinking of a threesome, I'd totally leave Cora out of the room."

I shake my head.

"You're disgusting," Oz mutters but it's in a slightly admiring tone. He and Niall always spark off each other.

"I know," he says happily before his eyes take me in. I self-consciously scrub my hands through my hair, wishing it was tied back. His face darkens. "Is the urgency you, Lo? Are you okay?"

"I'm fine," I mutter, grabbing my hand back that he's just seized.

"It's my mum," Oz interjects. "She's fallen and broken her hip and Silas and I need to go to her."

He stands upright, his notorious calmness in a crisis snapping into place. "Of course you do. What do you need?"

Silas pats his arm. "We need to go to London tonight so we can be there when she sees the surgeon. I'm not sure when we'll be back, but Oz is intending on bringing her back with us." He pauses. "Oh, and we need to leave Cora with you and Milo."

Niall's calmness in a crisis abruptly leaves and he gulps with his eyes bulging. "You want to leave a baby with me? Have you gone fucking mental?"

"And Milo."

He shakes his head and my hands clench on the sheets at the dismissive gesture. Then I jerk at his next words. "Milo will be fine. It's me you should be worried about."

"You love Cora. You're really good with her," Silas soothes.

"I'm good at carrying her from one room to the other and then giving her back to one of the three of you. I'm practically an expert at that, but it's not exactly child rearing."

"You're not rearing her," Oz says smartly. "If we were intending to be gone that long, she'd probably be better off with a pack of wolves than you. She'd certainly end up with more social graces." He shrugs. "But short-term is fine."

Niall's eyes narrow. "How is it that the massive favours you ask from me always manage to sound like insults?"

Oz's mouth quirks. "It's a gift."

Niall shakes his head. "I don't know. Talk me through it. What if she cries and needs you? What if I break her?"

Then they're off, all three talking loudly while I sit quietly with Cora in my arms when Oz hands her to me so he can pace. It's hardly worth me getting involved. When the personalities are this loud and vibrant, I tend to sink into the background a bit more and I always worry about raising my voice because that's when the stutter came back in the past. I look down at Cora's tiny face, her eyes as clear and lively as a little squirrel, and I send one finger dancing through her soft, thick hair.

Becoming aware that the voices have stopped, I look up to find them all staring at me. "What?"

Niall smiles. It's a fond, warm smile that still has the power to make my heart skip a bit. "I said what do you think?"

I swallow. "About what?"

He blinks. "I mean, do you think we can do it? If you say we can manage, I'll go along with you."

"*Me*? You'll listen to me?"

"Yes. You. Who else?"

"Who knows?" I mutter. I look down at the baby and then back at them. "Of course we'll manage," I say quietly. "I know how to do bottles and what you're giving her to wean her, so she'll be fed. I'll move into your apartment so Cora has familiar surroundings. She can come around with me during the day. I'll use the sling that Oz has." I think hard. "I'll stop restoring the Hamilton portrait though. I don't think the fumes will be good for her. I'll do your job instead, Oz, which shouldn't present any problems since Silas spent a year trying to make me into a house manager."

"You'd have been good at it," Silas says loyally but I shake my head.

"I'm better with pictures. They don't talk back."

"Not something that could ever be said about Oz," Niall muses. "Any jobs left for me?" His tone is wry but his eyes look proud, which makes me squirm a little.

"Maggie's away on holiday next week, so you can cook." Then Oz, Silas, and I groan. "No, ignore that," I say quickly. "We'll have takeaway." Niall sniffs but doesn't correct us, which he couldn't anyway. He's a fantastic but very erratic cook. I don't know whether it's because he's so busy with his phone going all the time and people wanting his attention, or whether he gets distracted, but his meals can be either amazing or so dreadful you swear off food for a few days.

I look up at him. "You've got enough on your plate this week," I say quietly. "Aren't you repairing the walls in the bottom field?"

His eyes sharpen as his brain almost visibly runs through his itinerary before he nods. "Fair enough. I'll do my bit around the house, though, and you'll ring me if you need anything. I'll tell Barb that you're to be patched through wherever we are, no matter what."

I nod and he grins. "Okay, we're sorted."

"Just like that?" Silas asks and Niall frowns.

"Milo's organised it. You need to start paying more attention." His face softens. "Take Oz and go. Wish your mum all the best from us and don't worry about a thing."

Oz looks at Cora in my arms and the war between his worlds is obvious in his eyes. "Don't worry," I say quietly. "She'll be fine. Ring whenever you want, and we can Skype so she can hear your voice."

He nods and I get up and troop after them, holding Cora tight. Within half an hour they're packed and ready and after several pauses, while they kiss Cora, Niall and I stand on the steps of the house and watch their taillights disappear down the drive.

Silence falls for a second until he stirs. "Well?" he says meditatively.

"Shit," I mutter.

He looks at the disappearing car. "Yep, that's what I wanted to say too."

∽

The next morning, I sit in the kitchen looking thoughtfully at Cora. She's sitting in her high chair with a very stubborn look on her face. I look down at the breakfast of mashed-up Weetabix. "Look, I know it isn't the best thing and you'd rather have milk, but you can't have that forever and really, I think you'd be bored if you did."

She yawns, and I seize the opportunity to stick the spoon full of the disgusting mixture in her mouth. For a second I think I've triumphed, but then she pokes her tongue out and the food neatly reappears. 'Okay, I know you think you've won, but this is a battle that no child triumphs in. All babies are weaned." I look at her. "*All* babies," I emphasise.

For a second she stares at me, her little topknot bobbing and her eyes big and wide. Then she screws up her mouth and starts to cry.

"Oh dear," I soothe, mopping her face. "I know how you're feeling. I like strawberry Pop-Tarts and chocolate milkshakes, but I can't eat that all the time."

"I can't believe you eat that at any time," an amused voice comes from the door.

Cora immediately brightens. She's a sunny child and easily distracted but no more than with Niall. She holds up her arms imploringly and I tut.

"You'd think I'd kept her captive on an island for fifteen years, not in a high chair for a few minutes."

He looks at the bowl in front of me. "I'd have opted for the island myself," he says with a moue of disgust. "Can't you give her something else?"

"What, like bacon and eggs? Or maybe steak and chips?"

He shoots me a slightly startled look, the way he always does when I say something that isn't meek and quiet. It irritates me like a splinter stuck in my skin. Makes me want to say more. Really push his buttons. I mentally shake my head at myself and reach out to try another spoonful as he moves to the counter where the coffee machine sits.

"Do you want one?" he asks.

I shake my head, my gaze focused on Cora's tiny mouth which is squeezed up into a teeny pout. The coffee machine whirs and bangs as I push the spoon at her. "Come on, baby," I croon. "Be good for me."

Niall chuckles. "I've said that a few times in my life," he announces, throwing himself down into the chair opposite me and next to Cora. He drops a kiss on her head and grabs the newspaper, unfolding it with a snap.

I shake my head. "You're disgusting."

He nods happily. "You know it." He takes a sip of his coffee and looks at Cora. "Weetabix is very nice," he informs her in a solemn tone. "And you are not winning with us. We may be cool uncles but by God, we're going to wean you before your small and annoyingly know-it-all daddy gets back."

I laugh. "That's a mission statement if ever I heard one."

He grins at me. "I do like a challenge."

They're innocuous words spoken with no subtext but for some reason, my head shoots up and our eyes lock.

I pull my gaze away. "You really do," I say. Then I smile. "Do you remember when you tried to teach me how to ride a bike? Now, that was a real challenge. I ended up going backwards and breaking one of your toes." I throw my head back and laugh at the thought and it's surprising. A deep, big laugh like the ones I used to give before Thomas.

He doesn't laugh but instead looks at me for a long, stretching moment, and his brow creases almost in shock as if he's seen a ghost. My laughter dies away, leaving us sitting in a strained silence that seems to linger and stretch like candyfloss unravelling in a string. He makes no attempt to break it but just looks at me with his eyes dark and mysterious.

I clear my throat awkwardly. "You okay?" I ask, and my voice is husky and sounds like I've never used it before.

I feel a blush starting up on my cheeks and he jerks as if I've wakened him from a dream. We stare at each other for long seconds and he has the most peculiar expression on his face. I can identify shock but nothing else. Then it clears and he laughs. It sounds slightly shaky to my ears, but I can't detect anything other than a slight awkwardness when I look at him.

"I certainly am," he says, his voice slightly deeper than normal. I swallow hard as he reaches across the table but he merely plucks the spoon from me. "Let's have a go," he says and turns to Cora.

Silence reigns for a moment, only broken by the radio in the background and the sound of Cora spitting every spoonful of food back. I get up and wander over to the teapot to pour myself some more tea. Once done, I lean against the counter and watch Niall as he tries to coax food into the truculent baby's mouth. His hand looks massive on the tiny spoon and he towers over Cora, but the power is definitely reversed in this scenario as once again he removes the spoon from her mouth and, with a slightly triumphant air, Cora spits it straight back out. I turn and switch the kettle on.

He looks up and shakes his head when he sees the bottle I'm getting from the fridge. "Giving up already? For shame, Milo."

I smile. "You will too because any minute she's going to get really hungry and start crying at a decibel level that could be heard in Australia." I shake my head. "Tiny battles, one at a time, and always do it when she's hungry and not starving. That way she'll get used to it quickly and mealtimes won't be associated with suffering."

"How do you know this stuff?"

I shrug. "Oz has read so many baby books he should take out shares in Penguin Books. I listen when he talks, and it also tends to go in like osmosis."

He sips his coffee and watches as I squirt the bottle on my inner arm to test the heat. "You're very good at it." He pauses as if thinking hard. "Do you want children?"

I can't help my startled laugh as I walk towards Cora. She spots the bottle and immediately bounces in her chair like a baby bird in the nest. I unstrap her and, cradling her in one arm, I sit down. Seeing that I have my hands full, he immediately reaches over and takes off the top of the bottle for me. I smile my thanks and for some reason, he looks awkward, his cheeks flushing.

I stare at him as I feed Cora the nipple of the bottle and she settles heavy against me. "You alright?" I ask.

He nods quickly. "You never answered my question," he says abruptly.

I jerk and whisper my sorry as Cora loses the bottle and gives me an accusing look. Settling her again, I look back at him. "Do I want children?" I shake my head. "No, I don't think I'd be very good."

"Why? You're amazing with her."

I shrug. "Thank you." I sigh. "I've been so fucked up for years and I don't think that's a very good thing in a parent. They need someone confident and sure of themselves."

"Bollocks," he says, and there's a cross note in his voice. "You're perfect. So you had a stutter and had bad taste in the partner you picked. So fucking what? Those things don't matter. What does matter is that you're warm and funny and you really listen to people. You bloody care and that's in short supply in this world. I also happen to think that you're plenty fierce when it matters to you. A baby would be very lucky to have you in his or her corner."

I stare at him with my mouth open and he flushes, looking extremely awkward. It's such a rare sight that I relish it without knowing why. Finally, I stir. "Thank you."

He shrugs, reaching for his coffee and picking the newspaper back up. He then starts to discuss world events with a slightly feverish determination. I take part, but I can't help the small glances I give him as I sit in the sunlit kitchen with Cora's weight and baby smell surrounding me. It's why I'm able to catch the quick glances he keeps giving me too. What is happening right now?

∽

I'm no nearer an explanation by night time. The day has been spent walking the house with the housekeeper as we prepare to close down for the winter. Silas only opens *Chi an Mor* for six months of the year and for the rest of the time the house is closed to the general public. It's a magic time when the place seems to return to its true self. Silence falls, and instead of people talking and laughing there is the sound of the sea and the wind in the trees.

However, this year we won't have so much quiet as a film crew is using the house to film a fantasy TV series. It's the second time they've done it, and I know Oz and Silas are hoping that it's popular enough to get the rest of the books they're based on filmed. The books are a huge success and the TV series has brought a lot of visitors to the house, so the shop regularly sells out of memorabilia.

So for the next few weeks, rather than shutting the house up for the autumn, Polly, the housekeeper, and I will be going around with a list that's longer than my body of what needs to be done before the film crew arrives in a month. Consequently, I'm tired, dirty, aching, and looking forward to a nice bath and maybe a takeaway.

Cora has been an angel. She's used to being carted all over the house by Oz and she loves people. Any people. She'd, therefore, sat happily in the sling attached to me looking out at everyone like a tiny queen.

I haven't seen Niall at all after the strange episode this morning. He strode out muttering that he'd be on the bottom field if I needed him, and he didn't even come back for lunch, which he usually manages to do. I frown as I look down at Cora as we move through the lounge on our way to the bathroom to give her a bath.

"Don't tell anyone," I whisper to her. "But I actually missed him today. I know he's forceful and arrogant, but I do like his company. Do you think that's silly?"

She stares back at me and bats my lip with a tiny fist. I grab it and kiss it and she chortles, giving me a wide, gummy smile.

"Okay," I say briskly. "We'll give you a lovely bath. And then it's a nice bottle and bed. What do you think?" She stares at me and I nod and make my eyes wide in an exaggerated fashion that I've learned babies like. "You'll be such a lovely clean girl and maybe Niall will come to see you before bedtime." I sigh. "I'm not mentioning him again, Cora. Stop me if I do because before you know it, I'll be making myself a fool over him like I'm thirteen again."

I shudder at the memory of my crush. "God, it's embarrassing looking back on that," I say. "Push it away, Milo."

I shove the bathroom door open and stop. "Does it seem cold in here to you?"

Obviously, she doesn't answer so I stride over to the radiator and, juggling her on my hip, I reach out and touch it. It's stone cold.

"What the hell?" I whisper. I think back to the radiator not working in my workroom and, now I come to think of it, the lounge had been cold in the apartment. I'd dismissed it as Silas and Oz thinking of the bills they'd have if they heated an empty apartment, but maybe it's not that.

I exit the bathroom and try the radiator in Cora's room. It's ice-cold too. A horrible thought occurs to me and, retracing my steps to the bathroom, I turn the hot tap on. Letting it run for a second, I stick my fingers under the flow of water and pull back with a hiss. It's freezing.

"Shit!" I say.

Cora chuckles and I look down at her and shake my head. "You didn't hear that, and you definitely are not going to make it your first word." She stares back at me and I cuddle her close. "Well, Cora Bora, the heating's broken. Shall we go and try and get the boiler to work or shall we ring Niall?"

She kicks her legs at the sound of his name and I kiss her forehead, inhaling the faint scent of baby shampoo.

"Maybe he'll repair it shirtless." I shake myself. "Stop it, Milo."

Pulling my phone out, I press the button to ring him. The phone rings for a few seconds before his deep voice comes over the line, making me shiver slightly. "Lo," he says quickly. "Everything okay?"

"Not really," I sigh. "The heating's off and the water's cold. I think the boiler's broken down again."

"Shit," he mutters. "I told Silas he needed a new one and it was a priority before winter."

"I think paying the gas bill was more of a priority."

He sighs. "Okay, I'll be five minutes. I'm out by the lake."

"You're still working?"

He chuckles. "Always."

"I'd try and do it myself, but I think we all remember the time I tried to put that flatpack bed together."

He groans. "I remember it vividly. You ended up with a load of screws that you hadn't used, and when Silas got in the bed it collapsed and nearly broke his legs. Let's not do that again. It wasn't a fun moment. Anyway, you've got Cora. I don't want you poking around on that thing when you're looking after her."

I try to dispel the sense of warmth I get when he goes protective. I think of how Thomas had started like that and the warm feeling disappears.

"I could do it though," I say a bit too forcefully.

There's a startled silence for a second. When he speaks next I can hear the warmth. "Milo, I think you can do anything you put your mind to."

My feathers settle down again. "Okay. Just so we're both on the same page. I don't need you riding in like a knight to the rescue."

I don't know where this aggression is coming from, but predictably he chuckles. "I would totally have the biggest and best armour."

"Size isn't everything," I say tartly.

"Baby, who told you that?"

His voice is deep and rich and filled with laughter and something that sounds very much like heat, making me swallow hard. "Never mind. I'll be here," I say and end the call on his laughter. I look down at Cora and groan. "*I'll be here*. Where else would I bloody be?"

An hour and a half later there definitely aren't any signs of humour about him. "Motherfucker," he hisses as he fiddles with the recalcitrant boiler.

"Language," I say primly, and he grunts.

I watch him, trying not to dwell on how gorgeous he looks. He's dressed in his comfortable working clothes of jeans and a white long-sleeved t-shirt over which he's slung on a denim jacket and on top a red and blue plaid padded shirt jacket. He's wearing old work boots and his hair is messy, but he looks like a runway model as normal. I take a second look. A lumberjack runway model.

"Any good?" he asks, and I jerk back to reality and put my hand on the radiator for a long minute.

"No," I finally say apologetically.

He straightens up and stretches with a grunt. "I give up. The bloody thing's fucked. We'll have to get someone out to it."

"How much is this going to cost Silas?" I ask worriedly.

He scrubs his hands over his face, leaving a dirty streak down one chiselled cheekbone. "I've got a friend who'll come and look at it. He'll give us mate's rates. But it's got to be done now, particularly as the film company is coming in a month."

I nod. "Well, Cora and I will be fine. It's only October. It's not even that cold yet."

"There's a frost coming tonight, Lo."

I don't question him. Niall has a countryman's native instinct for weather and tides and anything to do with the earth. He's always right.

He shakes his head. "You can't stay here with Cora. It'll be too cold."

"Hotel?"

He looks askance. "No, of course not." He stares into space, obviously thinking hard. "Maggie's away now so that only leaves Sarah and Michael who live in. They'll more than likely go and stay with the Thompsons in their cottage and you'll come and stay with me."

"I can't do that," I say, panicked.

"Why?"

I can't say I don't want to be in close quarters with someone who, no matter what I do, I'm still attracted to. At some point, he'll notice and I'll die of embarrassment. I stall for time by shrugging. "She's got so much stuff."

"She'll have as much stuff at my house as in a hotel and I've got a big car. We'll get it all packed up and then the two of you are coming back with me." He laughs. "I can detect your enthusiasm from here, Milo. It's making me almost embarrassed by how much you want to be in my home."

I shake my head. "Well, it's only for a night."

He grins. "Probably a few nights, babe. It's Friday and he's away for the week."

"Shit!"

"Language," he says primly.

CHAPTER 3

He's never been attracted to me before, so why would he start now?

Milo

An hour later we set off down the long drive leading away from the house. Niall stirs in his seat. "You sure we've got everything?" he grumbles. "Or will we have to go back and start moving the heavy furniture out?"

I snort and look back to check on Cora in her car seat, but she's already sleeping. Oz swears by the car, and I know he and Silas used to take her out in it a few times a night in the early days so she'd sleep.

"Babies need lots of things," I murmur. "Time was when Oz and I went out he'd just have his diary and wallet. Now he has bags and car seats and stuff. Lots and lots of stuff."

"Starman" by David Bowie plays on the radio and trees throw

their shadows into the car as he navigates the twists and turns of the long, gravelled drive. He slows, and I look up to see his house appear. In the past, the Dower House was used for the dowagers of the family who upon their husband's death would relinquish the main house to the heir and retire, usually in luxury to this house in the grounds.

Niall moved into the Dower House on the estate last year, claiming he'd be catching family if he stayed any longer. However, he still makes his way up to the main house for meals and coffee.

With a quick stop to open the five-bar gate we pull up on the forecourt in front of the house, and I look up at it curiously. It's made of the same honey-coloured stone as the main house but was built at a later date, and it's utterly charming. It seems to belong in its setting of the woods like a fairy-tale cottage, and the architect obviously played up to that with its gables and tall chimney stacks. It seems to flow over the space it occupies and its mullioned windows with their leaded lights twinkle cheerily in the moonlight.

We leave the car, and he saunters off to open the front door while I retrieve Cora's car seat. I look at him as he comes towards me. "I'm looking forward to seeing inside," I say as he grabs the changing bag and Cora's Moses basket. "Last time I saw it, it resembled something that Miss Haversham might have been comfortable in."

He looks startled. "You could have come round at any time."

I break in quickly, feeling awkward because I sounded like I'd been angling for an invite and was piqued at not getting one. "Doesn't matter. I was just curious. You know how I like those house renovation programmes."

"You and old people," he mutters. "What you find interesting in someone else's house is beyond me. The only home I'm interested in is my own."

"You have no soul or imagination." I follow him into the hallway and look round. "Wow. This is lovely."

The hallway has a floor made of aged flagstones which seem to be harmoniously mismatched, and the beams and woodwork have been sandblasted back to their natural pine. It's warm and welcoming.

He smiles at me. "Have a walk around while I get the rest of the stuff."

"Oh, I'll help you," I say hurriedly, but he shakes his head.

"Keep moving around. It might make her stay asleep and that's our most important mission tonight, comrade."

I shake my head but when he disappears outside again, I take his invitation. Carrying Cora in her car seat, I wander up a set of steps and into a wide, white-painted lounge with more sandblasted beams. Two large sofas in a French grey material sit opposite each other with a low coffee table in front of them, on which is a huge pile of unopened mail and a couple of newspapers obviously abandoned mid-read. Adjacent to the sofas is a large fireplace with a driftwood mantlepiece and there's a set of French doors at one end which obviously leads out into the garden. I wander over and peer out but it's too dark to see much apart from a stone patio area.

I retrace my steps and find his study next. That too is painted white with bookcases and a table over which there is splayed a big pile of maps. A huge old desk sits in the middle of the room that is so big I can't see how they got it through the door. I wonder fancifully if the house was built around it. The desk is piled high with more mail and maps. I inhale the scent of his sweet woody aftershave and close the door behind me. I turn and jump when I find a pretty little tabby cat sitting in the hallway and staring at me.

"Hey, puss," I say softly so I don't wake Cora. "I wasn't aware that Niall had a cat. Aren't you pretty?" I reach out to pet her but just as I get close, she hisses and swipes at my fingers with her paw before darting off.

"Bye," I say faintly. "Nice to meet you."

I wander down the corridor, poking my head into more rooms and finding a downstairs toilet and a dining room, painted grey. It has a table big enough to seat ten, and pulled neatly up to it are ten chairs upholstered in an expensive cream fabric. I shake my head and move on.

The last room is the kitchen, and he finds me standing in there when he comes back in.

"I've just met your cat," I say cheerfully. "I wasn't aware that you had a pet, let alone such a psychopathic one. How very cute."

He flushes, and I watch the red flow over his cheeks with glee. "Yes, well, I found her in the woods when she was a kitten and I couldn't leave her out there," he mutters. "I kept trying to give her to people who wanted a cat, but she's never been very sociable and they never seemed to warm to her after she removed the top layer of their epidermis."

As if she knows that we're talking about her, the cat wanders in. "Hey, Dotty," he coos, smiling widely at her. The cat immediately moves towards him, making little chirruping noises. It's quite adorable and I immediately want to check that we haven't moved into an alternate timeline because nothing about Niall has ever screamed house in the woods and pet cat.

I settle for more winding up. "*Dotty?* Your cat is called Dotty?"

He scratches his head, looking slightly embarrassed. "My grandmother was called Dotty."

"Was she actually christened that?"

"Well, she was Dorothy by birth but then she took off all her clothes and streaked through the house naked when the vicar was taking tea, and my father said she was quite dotty. The name stuck." I laugh and he grins at me. "She was quite vicious too, like feline Dotty."

"Not with you," I say, watching as he bends and Dotty butts his hand demanding cuddles.

"Let's not talk about her," he says quickly as she puts her paws on his knees and reaches up to kiss his chin. "Let's talk about war or poverty or famine."

"That's so adorable, Niall." I reach for my phone. "I must get a picture for Oz."

"If your finger moves on that button, I'll murder you and let Dotty eat your remains."

I blink. "Okay, that's very explicit." I look around the kitchen. "I think this room might just be my favourite part of the house."

It's a large room big enough to have an old pine table and chairs at one end by another set of French doors and still have room for lots of cabinets. It's obviously had a lot of money spent on it. The cream cabinets sparkle and the wooden worktop gleams in the light and echoes the sandblasted beams above. There's a breakfast bar at one end with two cream leather bar stools pulled up to it and a coffee machine that looks like it could run the control tower at Heathrow Airport. The walls are painted that French grey again and I wonder if he had a job lot of the paint, because so far the only colours I've seen are white and grey and one of them is a shade.

My heart cries out for some colour, but then I remember his horrified reaction to my colour choices in the attic and I grin at him. For some reason, his step falters but he recovers and looks around contemplatively at his room. "It's nice. You know I like nice things."

I laugh. "I know the main house makes you twitch."

He shakes his head. "All those really old ornaments and pictures. Makes my skin itch. I like things plain."

I rest Cora's seat on the floor and stretch. "I can tell that from the colours. This is a really lovely house though," I say quickly, afraid that I've offended him. "I'm just not sure if I'd have gone this far with the renovations." I come out of my stretch to find him staring at me, or more precisely at the slip of skin showing where my t-shirt has ridden up. Feeling slightly self-conscious, I pull it down, and the movement seems to recall him.

He jerks and appears to pull his mind back. "Why wouldn't you have gone this far?"

"Well, it's not your house so I'm surprised you've spent so much money on it. You may scoff at my home programmes, but it means that I now know quality when I see it and how much that quality costs."

"Not mine?" He sounds astonished.

I run my fingers through my hair, feeling embarrassed. "Well, it belongs to Silas and it'll revert back to him at some point."

He shakes his head. "It is mine. Silas gave it to me when I came back here."

I gape at him. "He *gave* you this?"

He grins and switches the kettle on, bending down to pet Dotty as he does so. "Yes, he gave it to me. Deeds and everything." He takes two mint-green mugs down from a cupboard and indicates a basket of different teas. "Pick one."

I stare at him. "You have flavoured tea?"

"That sounded like the sort of voice you'd use to state that I have men chained in my basement."

"That would have been slightly more believable than you drinking peppermint tea," I say dourly, and he gives a snort of laughter. I hush him as Cora stirs. We both stand still with bated breath as she stretches her little arms, extending them from her body, but then she smacks her lips and settles back into sleep. We both relax and grin at each other.

Dotty pads over to her and sits staring at her enigmatically.

"She hated me on first sight. Do you think she'll be okay with her?" I ask worriedly and then stare as the cat rubs against Cora's foot and licks her toes. "Oh okay, just me then," I say crossly. Niall grins and, taking the cup he offers me, I slide onto the stool at the breakfast bar. "So, he just gave you the house?" I ask, returning to the subject.

He runs his fingers through his hair, looking slightly awkward. "Yes, against all my objections. I didn't want anything from him. Silas is my best friend and he needed me. The estate was terrible when he inherited. I remember us coming here after the will had been read and his brother had gone back to London. It was shocking. The whole place looked like it had been abandoned in time. His father hadn't done any restoration for years and the tenants' cottages were falling apart. And he'd left him no money to do anything." His expression darkens. "Old bastard." He shrugs. "I had a really good job lined up in Norfolk but I couldn't leave him with all that, so I stayed."

"For free, I bet."

He looks slightly embarrassed. "Just room and food for a few years until he got more on his feet." He shudders slightly. "Which wasn't a good deal when you remember how bad Mrs. Granger was at cooking."

"I never understood everyone's objections to her food. I know her cakes are legendary, but her day-to-day cooking seemed okay to me."

"That's because you have some sort of iron lining your stomach from your childhood spent eating Derry's food." He smiles at the thought of our old cook. "Anyway, I stayed."

"But surely you've got your family and the house in Norfolk to consider?"

Niall is the third son of a Norfolk landowner and although his elder brother manages the family business Niall still has a share in it, and when his father died he left him a big Georgian house in Norfolk.

He shakes his head and smirks. "I sold the house back to my brother, which enabled me to decorate this place in the décor you so obviously approve of."

I sniff, thinking of the grey and white. "I'm not sure about that," I mutter. I look up at him. "Did you not want to go home to your family?"

He shakes his head and looks slightly abashed. "No. Don't get me wrong. I love them and I always will, but somehow this place feels more like home. I don't know why, but I'm happy here. I don't want to move." I open my mouth to agree with him, but he jumps up and takes the cups over to the sink. "Anyway," he says briskly. "Silas insisted on deeding the house to me. Said as far as he was concerned, I could stay forever. And let's face it, estate managing here is a fucking job for life."

I smile. The two of them were roommates all through boarding school and uni and Niall is closer to Silas than anyone else. My mood darkens. Apart from my brother. He's certainly close to him. The thought makes me wince, but I chase my frown away when I see him watching me with a peculiar expression on his face.

I stand up quickly. "Let's get Cora settled and bathed. I'm knackered."

He nods and follows me obediently like a very large dog.

∼

I don't know whether it's being so close to him and alone together or whether it's because I'm unsettled but that night I can't sleep for ages, and when I do finally close my eyes I dream about the moment when I was seventeen and he accidentally broke my heart.

The car pulls up outside my house and my mum turns to look at me. "Are you sure you're going to be okay, darling? I hate leaving you when you're feeling poorly."

"I-I-I'm fine," I say and pause to take a breath through my nose and out of my mouth the way Sheila the speech therapist has been teaching me. When I feel calm and like the words aren't strangling me, I smile at her. "I'll be fine. I don't want you to can-cancel the trip. It's just a cold."

"Well, if you're sure." She smiles and strokes a piece of hair back from my forehead. I want to point out that I'm not five anymore, but I don't want to hurt her feelings and I also don't think I'd get all those words out before the weekend is over. "Anyway," she says happily. "Gideon and Niall are visiting for the weekend for a school reunion, so I'll tell them to watch you."

"Mum," I immediately whine, feeling red heat on my cheeks. "P-P-Please don't do that."

"We'll miss the ferry, Monica," my father says quickly. "Let him go. He'll be fine."

I shoot him a grateful grin which he acknowledges with a wink, and I get out quickly before she can change her mind. Waving to them, I watch them go before turning to the house, nerves spinning in my stomach and making me feel sweaty.

Niall is in there and I've got all weekend with him. I know Gideon will whinge about it but I'm sure Niall won't. He's always so nice to me. He's very calm, and when my brother gets cross with my halting speech, he shuts him up. Last month he'd told him to fuck off if he couldn't be patient. I'd glowed while Gideon had glowered.

I walk up the path to the front door of the Georgian house, seeing Niall's battered old Volkswagen Polo parked near the garage. I feel warmth in my cheeks and my groin. That part is very new. I've always loved Niall. He's been my brother's best friend since my brother left for boarding school when he was seven. Niall usually came back to stay for a few days with us in the school holidays and as a little boy, I followed them around like a puppy. I flush at the thought of how silly I must have looked, but he never treated me like that. Instead, he'd been kind and interested and with him, my stutter has always eased a bit.

However, this last year I haven't noticed his kindness but how gorgeous he is. Tall and white-blond, his hair is cropped close to his head, showing off the denim-blue colour of his almond-shaped eyes with their long, curling lashes. He's also long-legged and walks like a panther I'd seen once on a wildlife programme. His looks do funny things to me and I'd been mortified when my first wet dream had been about him, waking me up in a tumble of wet sheets and heavy heartbeats.

Lately, I've become sneakier in my desire to spend time with him on the rare occasions I've seen him, affecting disinterest when he speaks to me. But I'd seized the chance for a full weekend with him alone apart from my brother by pretending to have a bad headache. I smile. Mission accomplished. Hugging the knowledge that I'll see him in a few minutes, I let myself into the house.

It's quiet and feels empty and I frown. I wonder whether they've gone to the pub. I hope so because when he's had a few drinks he's very affectionate, slinging his arm around my shoulders and ruffling my hair.

I'm looking around, wondering what I should be doing when they get back that displays me to my best advantage, when I hear a thump from upstairs and a hoarse laugh that I recognise as belonging to Niall.

I start up the stairs but something tells me to be quiet, so instead of shouting my presence I ease up the steps, avoiding the creaky one in the middle. There's a short groan and another of Niall's laughs and I realise they're in Gideon's bedroom. I frown, removing my hands from my pockets and wiping the sweaty palms against my jeans.

I start down the landing towards the open bedroom door. The noises are louder now. Sighs and groans and a rhythmic creak of bedsprings. I scuff my Vans along the carpet as if to stop myself from reaching the open doorway, all haste gone now and replaced with dread. However, I arrive at the door and when I peep in I draw in a shocked breath, the scene etched in my brain like it's been burnt there.

Gideon is lying on the bed completely naked. He doesn't spot me because his head is thrown back, and he's the source of the gasps and groans because between his legs is Niall. He's propping his weight on his arms as if he's doing press-ups and he's thrusting into my brother so hard that the slap of the flesh echoes around the room. His backside clenches as he moves. He's staring down at Gideon, his eyes slitted and lazy and a film of sweat over him. His gaze is intent and hot and his movements rough and forceful in a way that makes my balls draw up and my belly hurt.

I can't move, held captive by the sheer hotness of the scene. It'd obviously be hotter if it weren't my brother underneath him, but even so, I'm seventeen and Niall is naked, so I watch with a hard cock and a broken heart as they shudder and groan together.

I wake up with a start, my breath coming fast, and once again my cock is hard at the thought of Niall. I shake my head. I don't think at seventeen I ever thought he'd want me in return any more than I do at twenty-seven. Why would he? My brother is gorgeous and witty, and even as a teenager he already had that extra elusive something about him that had made him a star. Niall would never have looked at me.

I'd just wanted to be close to him at the time. However, they never knew I'd been there. I slipped downstairs and went to stay with a friend for the weekend but after that, I'd removed myself from his presence whenever I could. At first, he'd been puzzled and almost hurt, but he was a grown man so he soon forgot.

I lie still for a few minutes just breathing and trying to get back to the state of mind I'd arrived at a few weeks ago when I'd realised that I was drifting along through the days waiting for him to finally see me. It had coincided with a weekend when he'd gone away with my brother who he still fucks. I'd watched them through a window laughing together all bright and confident, and the next morning I'd woken up with the realisation that he would never be mine. I'd made the resolution that I would move on and try and find someone of my own. Someone kind and quiet like me. Staying here alone with Niall might be bad for this plan, but I'm determined to stick to it.

I don't know how long I lie in bed thinking, but the silence of the room suddenly drags me into the now. It's too quiet. When I went to sleep, I was lulled by Cora's tiny snores and snuffles. Now, there's nothing. I jump up with my nerves jangling and my heart pounding and race over to the Moses basket tucked neatly in the corner of the room, only to sag with relief when I find it empty.

I look around wildly and then stop and laugh. It sounds loud in the room, but what the fuck was I thinking? Did I imagine her rolling out of bed and going out for a coffee? There is another person in the house with me who must have her.

I move towards the door only to stop dead as a mortifying thought hits me. Niall came in to get her while I was dreaming about him. I rub my hands down my face and groan. I hope I wasn't talking in my sleep, which has been known to happen. It's as if in dreams my mouth lets all of the unsaid things out.

I take a deep breath and shake my head. Not going there. Resolved, if still somewhat embarrassed, I move over to his bedroom but the room is empty. I sneak a look around. Decorated in shades of white and grey (of course), it's a big room that looks down onto endless fields. The window is ajar, letting in a cool breeze that disturbs the curtains and sends them billowing. I smile because Niall always has to have a window open when he sleeps, no matter how fucking cold it is outside. It's as if he's so at home outdoors he feels trapped under a roof and hemmed in by bricks and mortar.

The bed is huge and rumpled, the duvet flung back as if he'd got up in a hurry. I breathe in the sweet woody scent of his aftershave and back out of the room. Padding down the stairs, I become aware of the faint sound of music coming from the kitchen and a light shining from there, laying warm stripes over the hallway.

I edge to the door intending to make a smart remark about baby-napping but instead, I stand stock-still. Ed Sheeran's "Perfect" is playing softly on the Bluetooth speaker, the whimsical and almost folksy music seeming to suit the hush of the house, and Niall is standing in the middle of the kitchen lit by the downlighters on the cabinets. He's shirtless and wearing only a plaid pair of pyjama shorts that hang low, clinging to the swell of his arse. The light gilds him as if he's been colour-washed in pale gold paint. It shows off the wide expanse of his lightly haired chest and the length of his legs. His bare feet are long and narrow and his arms bulge with muscles, as does his torso, celebrating the amount of physical work this man does every day.

Held to his chest, Cora looks as tiny as a little doll. Wrapped in her dinosaur-patterned sheet, she has one small hand wrapped up in a hank of his golden hair and she's staring at him as he sways to the sweet song and croons the lyrics. I watch her eyes blink heavily a few times as she fights sleep.

He smiles happily down at her. All of the energy that he seems to thrum with during the day is muted now, held at bay in the stillness of the night. He seems softer somehow, like his hard edges have melted away, and against my will, I sigh. If only he was like this all the time, he'd be so much more approachable. Instead, he's forceful and confident and makes me feel a little bit less.

However, he must catch the sigh because his head shoots up. When he sees me, he smiles, but it dies as he looks down my body. It's a slow, long slide of his eyes and I feel self-conscious in my old yoga leggings and washed-out, tight Mr. Messy t-shirt that my brother bought me years ago. I don't look like him. My skin is pale and I'm thin rather than muscled and golden. My hair is loose around my shoulders and doubtless makes me look like a scarecrow.

I shake my head impatiently at the silliness of my thoughts. This is me and Niall. He's never been attracted to me before, so why would he start now?

I make myself smile at him. "Ed Sheeran. Really, Niall?"

The slow darkness of his gaze clears and he blinks before looking almost embarrassed.

"It was the only bloody thing she'd settle down to. Do you think Oz or Silas play it to her?"

I shrug. "God knows. Knowing Oz's taste, it'd be more likely to be Slipknot."

He grins. "Well, the ginger singer did it tonight. All hail, King Ed."

I laugh. "Did she wake you up? Because I never heard a peep."

He shakes his head. "She'd just started fussing when I heard her. You were sleeping heavily." I blush fiercely and want to hold my hands up to my cheeks. His gaze sharpens but he neatly sidesteps the landmine. "I thought I'd let you sleep. You'll have her all day. It seems only fair for me to do my bit."

I pad over to the kettle and switch it on to make tea now that I'm awake. "Actually, while I think of it, there might be a morning when I'll need you to have her. Is that okay?"

He nods. "Of course. Let me know, or better yet, tell Barb. She'll remind me." Barb is his grey-haired, take-no-nonsense secretary. She keeps all the estate staff in check and has a mind like a steel trap. He looks curiously at me. "What are you doing?"

I fiddle with the kettle. "Simeon Frith is visiting. He's got some pictures that he wants me to look at with a view to restoring them. I told him I don't travel much so he's coming here. It's taken so long to arrange it that it would be terrible to try and cancel."

He looks at me thoughtfully. "Is that the bloke from the night we had Shakespeare by the lake?"

I nod. Oz had started these highly successful evenings last year. The cast descends on us and performs the play in return for lodging at the house. Visitors bring their own picnics and sit out under the stars. So far they've been huge successes, mainly because the English weather has obliged us. I'd met Simeon at one of them. He's an art collector, a very successful man in his late thirties. I'd enjoyed talking with him immensely once I'd overcome my shyness, and I'm looking forward to seeing him again.

Niall's eyes sharpen. "That's the one who spent the whole night ignoring the play and slobbering over you?"

I frown. "There was no dribble involved. Ugh, that's horrid."

His gaze turns inward. "I don't know. There've definitely been occasions when I've slobbered very pleasurably."

I have an instant vision of him choking on a man's cock and turn scarlet. Luckily the kettle switches off and I turn away, busying myself making some chamomile tea, but I can feel his gaze hot on the side of my face.

I turn back to him, startling slightly because just for a second he seems to have been looking at my arse with a hungry expression on his face, but it slides away instantly so I dismiss the suspicion. He rocks Cora, still swaying slightly to the song, and I put his tea on the table.

"Why is he coming here?" he asks abruptly.

For a second I don't have a clue what he's talking about. Then I remember. Simeon.

"Well, he'll want to accompany his art. There's a lot of money involved."

"And he's doing that himself? Don't bigwigs like him bring their entourage with him to wipe his brow, bring him champagne, and separate the red Skittles from the other colours?"

I shake my head, a smile playing on my lips. "I think that was the Roman Empire you're talking about. Either that or Mariah Carey."

He grins suddenly, the sunny warmth of his smile lighting his face. I feel happy inside when I make him smile. I dismiss that thought instantly and sip my tea. "He said he wanted to talk some more with me," I mumble.

His lips purse. "We do have phones for that," he says primly. His gaze sharpens. "I'm not sure I want–" he starts to say and trails off.

"Not sure you what?"

He jumps as if he's drifted off into his own thoughts. I look at him sympathetically. He must be tired. He works so hard.

He shakes his head. "Nothing," he says. "I'm just being silly."

The conversation moves on, but later when I lie in bed, I wonder what he was going to say about Simeon. I also wonder about what the skin on his chest would feel like under my fingers and tongue before I make myself stop.

CHAPTER 4

I can't stuff this Jack back into his box.

Niall

I have my hands full of dead tree branches when Frank, one of my men, ambles up. "You're needed, Niall."

"Needed for what?" I grunt, pulling the mass of the branches that we've just sawn down from a copse of trees and feeling them give slightly. "Am I needed to help Phil find the bottom of his tea flask?"

He laughs. "Now, you know he doesn't start the day well without three cups."

"I know and have the scars to prove it." I pull again. "Motherfucking things. What the hell are they stuck on?" I look up. "Tell me they're stuck on Phil's inert tea-less body and I'll cheer the hell up."

"Get out of the way, lad," he says, shoving me politely to the side. He nods over to the fence lining the field. "You've got visitors."

I look up, shielding my eyes against the autumn sun which is lying low. Then I straighten so quickly I nearly fall over. "Shit!" I mutter.

Frank grins and releases the hand that's just saved me from going arse over tit. "Bit eager, boss."

"Shut up," I grumble. "It's my goddaughter."

He sticks his tongue in his cheek, obviously trying not to laugh. "Aye, of course. Your goddaughter. Well, you'd best be getting over there quick or that good-looking lad will take your goddaughter away."

"Fuck off," I mutter and walk off, hearing his laughter behind me. I try not to smile when the laughter turns to a groan as he too tries to clear the branches. I look up and see Milo leaning on the fence.

He's wearing old holey jeans and mid-calf lace-up boots with a red and white t-shirt and buttoned-up cardigan and over the top, he's slung an old grey canvas jacket. It should look ridiculous, but he has an unerring sense of style so that whatever he puts on looks right. He's windswept and rumpled, his pale sharp cheekbones dusted with red which seems to echo the shade of the leaves all around. It's like he's a chameleon taking on the colours from the land that I love so much, making him one with it.

I shake my head of the flowery thoughts and pull off my thick work gloves before wedging them in the back pockets of my jeans. I eye his deep brown hair which is tied up in some sort of messy bun arrangement which I shouldn't find as charming as I definitely do, judging from the tightness in my jeans.

I sigh and swear under my breath. *Why now?* Why has the fucking universe decided to screw with me now by making me suddenly notice how fucking lovely he is? I've gone years looking on him as a younger brother. Someone I owed the same loyalty and kindness to as I do my own siblings. Maybe more because something about Milo has always just simply called to me and touched a soft spot inside me that nobody has ever reached before.

I've watched over him all these years and felt this strange protectiveness towards him. He's always just seemed so brave to me, coping with his nerves and stutter in such a dignified and stalwart way. Gideon had always found it incomprehensible how soft I was towards his brother, why I welcomed him around us.

The simple truth is that I like his wit, intelligence, and sharpness. Others seemed to miss it, seeing him as being stupid just because he stammered. Even now people see the hunched shoulders to hide his height, his blushes and the frequent pauses and hitches in his speech, and they classify him as needing protection. They never seem to see what I do. The flash of his eyes when someone is rude, the humour shining clear in those brown depths that he doesn't share easily. They don't stick around long enough to get through the stammer to hear the caustic wit that lies beneath.

After I'd brought him home with me to *Chi an Mor,* I watched over him carefully and noted the way he slowly came back to life like a plant sending shoots up through the cold ground. I'd annotated the life coming back into his eyes, the gradual cessation of his stammer and the way he unfurled a bit more every day, coming out from his shell like a rather gawky tortoise after hibernation.

I'd managed to see all that and keep him as a little brother until the other day when he laughed at something he'd said and I'd looked at him. *Really* looked at him. And as if for the first time I saw the sheen in his brown hair that's the colour of muscovado sugar. I'd taken in the chocolate-button brown of his eyes with their thick lashes, the sharp bones of his face, the full pink lips, and the shy warmth of him.

I'd blinked and said something facetious, hoping that the heavy beating of my heart was just breathlessness but knowing that the stiffness of my dick belied this.

Ever since then it's like a lid's been taken off a secret and I can't go back. I can't stuff this Jack back into his box. He doesn't fit anymore; the way Milo doesn't fit my preconceptions. I've tried to ignore it because the whole fucking scenario is like something from *Hollyoaks.* I've slept with his brother, for fuck's sake. I slept with him a few months ago before all this started. How can I move on straight from him to his younger brother who I remember playing with his toys? I shake my head. *Get a fucking grip.*

At that moment he looks up and sees me coming towards him and he smiles. His smiles always look slightly mysterious to me, like secrets are resting on those lips. I wonder if I kissed them if I could suck those secrets into my mouth the way I'd suck on those full pouty lips. Take his smile into me the way I'd take his breath and spit. My step falters and I stutter in a breath, and he straightens with a puzzled frown.

That right there is my salvation because it would never occur to diffident Milo that as I cross this field, I'm thinking of fucking him. He'd never believe it, the way he'd never believe that the rich arsehole coming to visit him wants more than his opinion on some poxy paintings.

I should seize this unawareness and move onwards, the way I've always done. Good sex and on to the next, my life has a simple rhythm that I love. Good friends, family, food, a nice house, and a hot, willing body whenever I want. Life is great and complicating things with Milo could be disastrous, not least because of what I could do to him. He has a need for security and stability that's written all over him. I would trample that underneath my feet as I walk away, the way I always do, and I can't do that to him. He means too much to me, this shy, gentle boy who I've known for so many years.

Resolved, I clear my expression as I reach him. "What are you doing here?" I say far too heartily, but he ignores it, giving me one of his wide smiles.

"We came for a visit. Cora needed some fresh air, so we've been for a walk."

I smile because Milo's love of walking is legendary. He seemed to get a taste for it when I used to drag him all over the estate as a way of getting him out of the house, and now he'll walk happily for miles in any weather. I'll often see him about the estate and wish that I could join him and walk together again, listening to his quiet voice and making him laugh, loving the sight of that half-cautious smile spreading over his face.

I look down at the baby cocooned in a sling held close to Milo's torso so the only things that can be seen are her bright button eyes and rosy cheeks and a cute little red bobble hat. I reach out to trail my fingers down her soft downy cheek and subtly inhale the scent of baby shampoo that clings to him along with his own warm scent of lemon and rosemary that always makes him smell a bit like an herb garden in summer.

Cora coos and wriggles frantically as she manages to extract one tiny hand in a little red mitten and waves it at me. I lean down and grab it, making munching noises on her fingers while she chuckles.

I look up and still at the intent look on his face and for a long second, we stare at each other until the sounds of the chainsaw and the men shouting in the background fade away so there's just us and the gentle soughing of the wind through the trees.

I shake my head to clear it and search for a topic of conversation that doesn't include the opening of, 'I'd like to push you against that tree over there and stuff you full of my cock.' I look down at the fabric baby carrier and find it.

"What is this?" I huff.

"It's a baby sling," he says patiently.

The slight hitch in his speech is barely noticeable now but I still hear it. He doesn't stammer much anymore which is a testament to all of the work he's done with speech therapists, but if you listen carefully you can still hear the indrawn breaths and hesitations. I like it because it's so him. Such a subtle, barely there symptom of something a quiet man has striven so hard to conceal, yet it's as much a part of him as his expressive eyes and herby scent. It gives me a feeling of privilege that I know him so well that I can tell.

I shake my head, pulling myself back to the conversation as he looks at me, waiting with his lip quirked. "You're carrying my goddaughter around in something that looks like it came from fucking Tie Rack. It surely can't be safe."

"She's my goddaughter too," he says patiently. "And yes, it's perfectly safe. You're just overprotective."

Not just of her, I think, staring at his pale, eager face. *Shit!*

I think hard for something to say that doesn't involve my tongue hanging out and grunting, seeing as I seem to revert to being a caveman around him at the moment. An image comes into my head of him doing yoga the other day. He'd been lying on a mat in the lounge with Cora in her bouncy seat. She'd been utterly fascinated, and I can't blame her. I've never seen anyone move so gracefully and have such a command over his body as he contorted himself into position after position. His lean body had been corded with muscle and dusted in sweat and had formed the basis for a massive wank session that I'm ashamed to admit I had in the shower afterward.

At the time he'd blushed when he saw me watching and explained that he'd taken it up because the breathing involved helps him with his speech.

I look into his warm brown eyes that are watching me curiously as his hand pats and soothes Cora's back, and a curious longing comes over me. I want to be involved in his life. Not in an overprotective big brother way but in the way a man has if he's interested in him. I don't just want to tease and joke with him anymore. I want to know him in a way that no one else does. I want to know what thoughts flash through his head and for him to speak them to me when he won't do that for anyone else. I want to be in his life in a way I've never wanted to do with any other man, even his brother.

I find myself opening my mouth and words fly out unconsidered or censored. "Will you teach me how to do yoga?"

There's a stunned silence for a second and myriad thoughts flash across his face before he settles on amusement. I swallow hard.

"Why?" he asks, as well he should.

"Erm." I think hard. I can't say what I really want. He wouldn't believe me and there's no point anyway because it can never go anywhere. I'm just infatuated with him at the moment because it's novel. I've never been attracted to anyone I've really known other than Gideon. The fact that this is his brother and it's like the plot of a Mills and Boon book means I know it won't come to anything. But still, there's this yearning inside me that I've never felt before to know this fey-looking man in front of me.

I realise that he's still waiting for me to speak and flush. "Erm. I'm just a bit stressed at the moment. I ache all over and I've heard that yoga can help with that."

His face immediately clouds with concern. "Of course I will," he says hurriedly. "And you know if you're stressed you can always talk to me. I'm not sure how much help I'll be, but if I can help you in any way you know I will in a heartbeat."

I feel so fucking bad at this moment and equally warm inside at the feeling that he cares enough for me to react like that. But then I remind myself that he's the reason I'm stressed anyway, so we can do yoga together, goddammit.

I have a strange feeling that I'm setting myself on the road to being truly fucked over this man, and pretty soon I won't be able to turn back.

Milo

I stir the minestrone soup in the big pot on the stove and switch the phone over to my other ear. "So, how's your mum?"

Oz sighs. "She's fine. She's in really good spirits and the operation went well."

"So why the heavy breathing?"

"Because she's insisting on staying in London. She says all her friends and her sister are here and the hospital is in easy reach."

"She has got a point."

He sighs again. "I know that. She always does have a point." I smile at the thought of his small, fiery mother. "It's just I want to look after her at home."

"But that's what *you* want," I say softly. "It's not really about that, is it?"

"I know." There's a silence and I wonder whether I've offended him. "You're right," he says. "You're always right."

"Well, not always."

"Mostly."

"I'll settle for that." He laughs. "So, when will you be back?" I ask hesitantly.

"As soon as she's out of the hospital and settled. Silas is coordinating with them so we can make sure she's all set at home. We can't come back before that, so I'd say we're a few days off yet. If I don't want to leave her when she's out, we'll come and take Cora back with us."

"Well, that's fine."

"It isn't fine. Cora will have forgotten us."

I laugh. "Don't be silly. Of course she won't."

"Is she okay? What's she doing? Tell me everything."

"She's fine. She's just gone down for a nap." I pause. "She's a baby. She doesn't do much of anything, so how much more can I tell you?"

"Everything," he says fervently, and I laugh.

Conversation detours into work and for the next ten minutes while I add pasta to the soup and move around the kitchen, we discuss the house and the arrangements for the film crew.

Finally satisfied that we're on track and not in imminent danger of an imploding business, he moves on. "So, what are you doing tonight?"

I smile. "Not much. I'm making soup."

"Oh my God. Your minestrone?"

"That's the one."

"I love that." He pauses and when he speaks next his voice is arch. "So, you're making Niall his dinner for when he gets back to the house you're living in together?"

"I'm making myself some dinner," I say patiently. "And sharing it with him. Yes. In the house he's been kind enough to let me stay in because living in my own home currently would be like residing in the freezer section of Farmfoods."

"Hmm."

"Oh, and afterward I'm teaching him yoga. Bye."

I set the phone down neatly on the counter and laugh when it immediately rings again. "What?"

"You're teaching him yoga?"

"Yep."

"Oh my God, why am I not there? This is pure torture."

"I'm sure it won't be very eventful."

"Have you seen the man? He's tall and big and most definitely not bendy at all. It'll be hilarious. Oh, make him do that chair pose. And film it and send it to me. There's nothing funny on the television at the moment. Plus, if he falls over we could totally send it to *You've Been Framed* and get two hundred and fifty quid."

"I will not be filming anything."

"We'll share it with him," he says earnestly and pauses. "Well, we'll give him a tenner for his troubles. That's more than enough."

I hear the front door slam and the familiar warmth and fizzle of anticipation curls in my stomach at the thought of seeing Niall. I quash it. "I'm going now," I say quickly. "He's here."

"Okay, but remember Downward Dog is not a sex pose or an invitation to fuck in a car park in front of complete strangers."

"You think you're funny, but you are truly not," I say firmly and put the phone down.

I look up when Niall saunters into the kitchen. He's filthy dirty with a streak of dirt running down his face that makes him look a bit like an extra from *Braveheart*. He also has scratches running down his arms, presumably from where he's been wrestling branches. I smile because Niall is genetically incapable of standing back and issuing orders, which would be what most people would do in his position. Instead, he has to get involved in whatever his men are doing and consequently is usually scratched or bruised or both. He'd broken his arm once trying to help the roofer and that period of inactivity had been hellish, not just for him but for everyone else he came in contact with.

However, one of the scratches looks really deep and before I know it, I've crossed the kitchen and taken his arm. He looks startled and for a second I think he's going to step back, but he stays still and lets me hold it up to the light. "That's a really deep one, Niall," I murmur, running my finger gently down the side of it. It's oozing blood and looks nasty. He jerks hard like I've electrically shocked him, and I look up in surprise.

"It hurt," he says hoarsely.

"Oh, sorry," I say quickly. His arm is so strong and the skin so warm that I let it drop reluctantly and look up at him. "Why don't you go for a shower and clean up? Then I'll patch that up and we can do some yoga and you can eat afterward." I pause. "That's if you still want to do yoga?"

"I do," he says quickly. He sniffs, and a longing expression comes over his face. "Oh my God, is that your minestrone soup?" I nod and he smiles happily. "I love that." He looks around at the warmly lit kitchen with music playing in the background. "This is nice," he says slowly.

"What is?"

"Coming home and finding you …" He seems to stumble over his words for a second. "I mean it's nice finding food cooking and the house lit up." He looks almost bashful. "Usually the house is dark. I don't mind that, of course," he says quickly. "I like living on my own."

I step back and smile. "Of course you do." When he hesitates, I make shooing gestures. "Go and shower. We haven't got unlimited time for yoga because Cora will be awake soon."

He stares at me, something running over his face, and then he smiles awkwardly and is gone. When I hear the shower start, I turn the heat low on the soup and move into the lounge. I went up to the main house earlier to get my yoga mat and the spare. Now, I lay them out on the carpet and dim the lights.

I consider putting music on and lighting candles, which is what I do sometimes if I'm feeling stressed, but I dismiss it immediately. Niall will think I'm trying to seduce him and run a mile. A brief image of a Niall-sized hole in the door and dust at his heels comes into my head, and I smile a little sadly before I make myself cheer up.

It's strange, but these last few days I've almost felt like we're becoming real friends and I like it. I've always in the past felt that I'm a faceless element to him. A remnant from his past. Someone he feels obliged to look after because of Gideon. Now, I feel like he sees me, and it's nice because we actually get on very well. I rarely feel awkward around him with my words because I know if I stammer he won't mind or look at me funny. He has, after all, seen me at my worst.

So instead, over the last few days, we've talked a lot about anything and everything while we've been eating dinner. He's funny and sarcastic and surprisingly sentimental at times. He's so sure and confident and almost hard that it's been a revelation to know that music moves him and that he can't bear to watch animal programmes on television in case they're hurt or die. I'd had to switch off *Super Vet* the other day before he cried.

Footsteps on the stairs bring me out of my thoughts and I look up and swallow hard as he appears in the door towelling his hair. He's shirtless and wearing a pair of black running leggings that cling to his long legs. The low light gilds the long length of his torso and dances over the drum-tight grooves of his pelvis. For all his height he's actually very lean with a runner's body that shows itself in his tight abdominals and the muscled length of his legs.

I swallow again and manage to clear the expression on my face so by the time he lowers the towel I'm facing him with a hopefully peaceful expression. That falters slightly when he comes towards me and I catch a whiff of sugary scented shampoo from the damp tangles of his blond hair. He smooths his hair down so it falls into a neat side parting that I know in a few minutes will be lost as his hair reverts to its natural messy state. However, the deep red mark on his arm recalls me to my task.

"Let me have a look at that," I murmur, taking his arm.

"Oh, I don't need anything," he says airily, trying to pull his arm away.

I glare at him. "Yes, you do," I say firmly. "With the work you do, this could get infected very quickly. You won't be able to do much if your arm has to be amputated due to septicaemia."

"I can't help feeling that you're a glass half empty sort of man, Lo," he says, humour running through his voice.

"Well, you're definitely a fully empty one then because you'd have drunk the contents."

He laughs loudly and watches as I move to Cora's changing bag and retrieve the small first aid kit. I open it and take out the plasters and he groans.

"No fucking way."

"Yes, fucking way," I say, tossing the Mr. Bump plasters onto the table and grabbing his arm again. "You don't have a first aid kit," I scold. "What were you thinking?"

"That I'm not two years old," he says, wriggling as I uncap the Savlon and start to smooth it gently over the cut.

"Don't be a baby." My lip quirks. "Anyway, all the other boys will be really jealous of your Mr. Bump plaster. You watch, they'll all want one," I say mockingly as I put the plaster over the cut and press down gently.

Even so, he flinches and I stroke his arm comfortingly. He shudders, and the movement makes me realise how close we're standing. Close enough that I can smell the sweet woody scent of his aftershave and feel the heat of his long, slim body.

I look up to find him watching me, his eyes dark and mysterious, and I jump back as if stung.

"Yoga," I squeak and stop to clear my throat. He watches me silently and I rally and point to the mat. "Lie on your back with your knees raised and your feet on the floor."

It's much too abrupt and I immediately flush as he blinks. "I must say I've had that said to me before, but not normally in a manner that makes me want to salute first."

"You haven't lived then," I say tartly.

He smirks but lowers himself gracefully to the mat. I try to ignore the sight of him lying in the lamplight at my feet and lower myself to the mat next to him where I sit cross-legged. "This is a good way to relax the muscles before you start. You need to lie still and focus on your breathing and feel the weight of your pelvis as it sinks to the floor." He bites his lips with a smile in his eyes and I shake my head repressively. "Close your eyes if it helps."

He closes his eyes, which certainly helps me because now I can ogle him to my heart's content. "Okay," I say, adjusting myself in my shorts and wishing my voice didn't sound so low. "Now, you need to bring your right knee into your chest and at the same time stretch your left leg out on the mat. Imagine that you're in a box and the wall is against your foot, so tilt it and push against that wall."

He opens one eye. "I'm actually slightly claustrophobic. That is not the relaxing sort of image I'd expect from yoga. I'd imagined plinky-plonky music and candles and chanting."

I'm instantly diverted. "You're claustrophobic? Why do you think that is?" He opens his mouth to answer but I shake my head. "No, forget it. I don't normally have this much chatter during my sessions. Just be quiet and breathe."

"That has definitely been said to me before."

"I can well believe it," I say tartly. I direct him to do the same movement using his other side and then make him relax back into his starting position.

Dotty pads in and looks at us curiously before deciding that Niall's position on the floor obviously makes him hers.

"Ugh, Dotty," he protests. "Stop licking me."

"I think that might be the first time in your life you've ever asked anyone to stop," I say, watching as he shoos the cat away only for her to come back and try to pounce on him while he chuckles. Finally, she grows bored and leaves the room, twitching her tail and offering me a cold killer glance as she goes.

Niall resumes his position and I smile at him. "Okay, next you're going to cross your right ankle over your left knee and bring the left knee up and hug it against your chest."

"This is like fucking Twister," he says testily. "How is this supposed to relax you?"

"It's stretching you," I say patiently. "It's better than the rack. Although, that might at least have kept you quiet for a bit." I look down at him where he's lying with his face full of humour. "I'm sure you thought you'd leap straight into lotus position but that can't happen because you're a complete novice and you know absolutely nothing."

"Don't think I didn't notice how much you enjoyed saying that," he says darkly, and I grin.

"A little bit. Okay, let your spine lengthen with your breath and focus on your breathing."

"Oh, am I supposed to be breathing? How is that possible when my knee is crushing my ribcage?"

"And yet you're still managing to talk."

He snorts. "Good point."

I grin and look longingly at the way his trousers have stretched tight showing his magnificent arse. I jump when he coughs.

"When can we stop this?"

"Sorry," I say, flustered. "Come gently out of that position and then get on your hands and knees."

He smiles wickedly. "Now you're talking. Yoga is fun."

I shake my head. "This is yoga, not an audience with Julian Clary. No more innuendos."

He obediently gets onto his hands and knees and I feel saliva pool in my mouth. I walk around him, trying to think of awful things to stop my dick hardening. "Spread your fingers out," I direct, watching his long, strong hands with the blunt fingers spread on the mat. "Now, you're going to lift through your forearms and tuck your toes underneath. Then you're going to rise up, lifting through the knees and keeping your head dropped down. This is Downward Dog."

"Have you ever considered a career as a drill sergeant?" he mutters, doing as I ask.

"Not if they're all as chatty as you. Mind you, the British Army might be a bit more easy to train. Breathe through five breath cycles."

I watch as he does that, noticing that his right hip is slightly over. Without thinking, I move behind him and grab his hips to steady and correct his posture. I only realise that this is a bad move when I lean forwards and his arse nestles into my groin, settling into my cock as if it's found a home and making my dick stiffen immediately. For a second I completely forget myself, lost in the heat and pressure against my cock, and I rock slightly, making my eyes cross. He goes completely still and doesn't even appear to be breathing, which wakes me up.

"Shit. I'm so sorry," I babble as I back away. He comes out of the position abruptly and turns to face me, half crouched on the mat. His face is half in shadow and his eyes a dark navy, and I blush. "That w-w-was really bad of me. I'm so sorry," I say, feeling the stutter come out slightly to my further embarrassment.

I swallow hard and he jumps to his feet immediately, coming to me and grabbing my arms. "I'm not sorry," he says hoarsely. "Why are you?"

"I j-j-just–" I stop and cover my face.

"Rubbed against my arse?"

I nod and he raises his hands, knocking my fingers away from my face. He cups my face, staring into my eyes, his own dark and hot. "I'm not sorry," he says clearly. "Milo, I–" he stops and shakes his head and I'm held immobile as his head lowers towards me.

"Niall," I whisper, raising my face and feeling my blood run hot through my veins. "Niall."

The next second we jump apart as if we've been hit with a stun gun when the doorbell rings.

"What the *fuck*?" Niall breathes. I stare at him. He has red flags of colour along his cheekbones and he's breathing as if he's run a race. Then we both jerk into action as the high and reedy cry of a baby sounds out.

"Shit," I say and Niall nods. The heat dies out of his face and he scrubs his hands over his eyes.

I breathe in slowly, trying to conceal the tremors that are running through my body and still the thoughts that are running madly in my brain. *Did he just nearly kiss me* is followed quickly by *I'm going to fucking murder who's at the door.*

Niall steps back. He looks cross and rumpled. "You get the door. I'll get Cora."

I nod and walk towards the front door, hearing his footsteps pounding up the stairs followed by his voice saying softly, "Hey, Cora Bora. It's alright, baby girl."

I look down at my cock, which is still plumped up, and pull my t-shirt down. Then I fling open the door and gape in surprise. "Mr. Frith."

"Now, Milo, I thought you were going to call me Simeon."

He stands there on the drive looking sophisticated and cool and I'm very aware that my clothes are crumpled and my hair is falling out of its bun. I hear footsteps behind me and I watch as Simeon's eyes drift past me and widen.

"Am I interrupting something?" he asks.

I hear a sharp intake of breath from behind me and rush into speech. "N-Not at all," I stammer. "You're not interrupting anything."

CHAPTER 5

That's naughty, Lionel. We don't do that to guests. Especially paying ones who fancy me.

Milo

I stare at Simeon on Niall's doorstep. Dressed in charcoal-grey trousers, a black jumper, and a black pea coat, his dark hair is messy and shot through with grey and his expression warm. He's a very good-looking man but what had drawn me more than anything when I first met him was how soft-spoken and gentle he seemed. Not at all what I'd thought a very wealthy art collector would be.

I realise I'm staring when he shifts awkwardly. "I'm so sorry for calling on you uninvited. It's just that I stopped at the main house and a gardener told me you were staying here."

I jerk. "Oh, please don't apologise. The heating's off at the main house and we're looking after our friends' little girl."

He looks past me and his mouth quirks. "So I see."

I turn to find Niall standing behind me. I swallow hard. He's still dressed in those tight leggings, but he's slung a t-shirt on and is clutching Cora to his wide chest and looking at Simeon with a slightly dark look on his face. I bug my eyes at him and he jerks and comes forward.

"Please come in," he says deeply.

Simeon looks hesitant. "Oh, I couldn't."

"Okay," Niall says peacefully and goes to shut the door.

"*Niall!*" I jerk out.

"What?"

I gesture at the half-open door and the man standing on the step. "Don't be rude," I hiss.

He rolls his eyes. "He said he couldn't come in."

"He was being polite."

He sighs in exasperation. "I don't get that. I don't know why people–"

Forestalling his lecture on openness and people saying what they think, which I could practically recite word for word by now, I fling the door open. "Please come in," I say. "I've made some soup. Stay and have some with us."

He looks slightly awkward but allows me to pull him over the threshold and motion him in the direction of the kitchen.

"You're giving him my soup?" Niall hisses and Cora gurgles happily.

"I am," I say defiantly. "To make up for your rudeness."

Sailing past him, I head to the kitchen in time to help Simeon take his coat off. He looks around curiously. "This is a lovely house."

"Thank you," Niall says shortly, coming past him and into the room.

Dotty sits up in her basket, which I'd been amused to see was very expensive, and stares at Simeon. She looks sweet and cuddly, her green eyes glowing. He bends to her. "Oh, what a lovely–" He draws back, startled as she hisses at him and makes a swipe at his hand.

"Sorry," I say quickly. "Don't bother with affection. It only ends in pain. I'm sure she's psychopathic. She'd make Jack the Ripper look cuddly."

He turns to me. "It's so lovely to see you, Milo. I've been looking forward to it."

"Me too," I say and then stare open-mouthed as he goes to hug me only to have to step back because Niall has thrust Cora into my arms.

"Hold her," Niall says happily. "I'll just get her bottle warmed." I look down at the baby lying in my arms then up at Niall who has a satisfied look on his face and then at Simeon who just looks slightly taken aback.

"Sorry," I say as Niall moves to the kettle. "He's barely house trained."

"I heard that," Niall mutters.

"You were meant to."

Simeon's mouth quirks and I gesture quickly at the table. "Take a seat. Once Niall's done Cora's bottle I'll dish the food up."

He sits down. "She's a beautiful little girl."

I smile. "She is that." I sit down opposite him, shifting Cora as she starts to mither. I look at him and search for words and he smiles.

"I'm sure you're wondering why I've turned up on the doorstep like this."

My 'oh no, not at all' is slightly spoilt by Niall's soft snort from the corner.

He shakes his head. "I'm staying with a friend nearby and I thought why not kill two birds with one stone. I have the paintings in the back of the car, so I thought I'd drop them off with you."

I'm flabbergasted. "You've just got them in the back of the car?"

"Yes, why?"

"Well, people don't normally do that. They're usually delivered by a courier service with lots of paperwork."

"Well, I had to strike while the iron was hot. I understand that you don't take on much outside work."

I shift awkwardly, and I can practically feel Niall tense. "No. I have a lot of work here and I owe the earl my loyalty."

"No need to explain," he says kindly. "Besides, these aren't valuable paintings. They're part of a job lot I bought at auction. I thought you could clean them up and see what's under the dirt."

For some reason, it stings that he wouldn't give me valuable art to work on. As if he senses it, Niall walks over and stands next to me.

"Milo is capable of dealing with anything you give him, no matter how much it's worth. The art is the point for him," he says evenly, uncapping the bottle and testing the milk on my forearm. I nod, taking the bottle from him and giving him a grateful look. For a second he stares down at me, his eyes dark. Then he turns to Simeon. "He has more talent in his little finger than most people you know."

"*Niall*," I protest but he shakes his head.

"You have, Lo. Seems he should know that if he's going to be using you."

Simeon holds his hand up. "I meant no disrespect." He looks at Niall for a long second and then turns to me. "He's right. You are very talented. I've seen some of the restoration work you did for the Pinchton estate."

"It's conservation as much as anything," Niall says proudly. "He's keeping it around for the generations after us to see."

I blink. That had been part of a debate I'd had with Oz one morning. At the time I hadn't thought Niall was listening as he sat hungover to the eyeballs wearing sunglasses and drinking a vat of coffee. "I never knew you heard that."

He smiles slightly, the lines at the sides of his eyes lengthening. "I always listen to you."

We stare at each other for a second until Simeon clears his throat. I hand Cora to Niall and stand up. "Let me dish up supper."

Supper is surprisingly relaxing after the slight stand-off. Cora sits gurgling in her bouncy chair as she kicks energetically, setting the chair bouncing vigorously while Dotty watches her curiously, her tiger eyes gleaming as if she can't quite work out who this tiny interloper is. Niall unbends slightly towards Simeon and after he opens a nice bottle of red wine, they sit discussing the prospects for the Scottish Premiership. Niall went to uni in Edinburgh and has never relinquished his fondness for Scottish football. It turns out Simeon is the same, so they have a very spirited discussion.

When supper is finished, as Niall clears away the plates, I turn to Simeon. "Shall we look at these pictures? We'll take them up to the main house, if I can get a lift?"

He nods enthusiastically and while he goes to get his coat, I come up next to Niall. "You okay?" I ask tentatively. He looks up at me from where he's loading the dishwasher and just like that, the near kiss roars back into my mind where I'd hopefully pushed it.

He straightens up so quickly I step back in surprise. "I'm fine. Why, Milo?"

I swallow hard. "Just ..." I falter, searching for words, and he watches me patiently. "About the yoga session ..."

I fade out and his eyes darken. "The yoga session or what happened afterward?"

The front door slams. "Oh my God, no," I say loudly and he laughs. "Just the yoga," I say quickly. "I can't talk about this in front of Simeon. It was just yoga, after all."

I hesitate, waiting for him to say something. Anything. I look anxiously at the door where I can hear Simeon's footsteps. When I look back, Niall has an unreadable expression on his face.

"Just yoga. Nothing to talk about," he says evenly, no expression in his voice at all.

Something in the way he's looking at me makes me take a second glance, but he stares back at me placidly, the only movement about him a tic in his jaw. I focus on that display of agitation and raise my eyes back to him. "Niall," I start to say, but Simeon sticks his head around the door.

"You ready, Milo?"

I hold Niall's eyes for a second, wishing for I don't know what, but when he looks away and I don't get it, I sag slightly.

This is for the best, I tell myself. He's not for me. He's too forceful, too bossy, too everything. I need someone like Simeon who is looking at me admiringly. Someone quieter, someone who won't push.

Feeling resolved, I gesture him to the front door. "I'll be right with you," I say. I look behind me as Niall retrieves Cora from her chair and straightens up.

"I'll leave you to it," he says evenly, and murmuring a goodnight he mounts the stairs. I stare after him for a long second, looking at the empty stairs with my mind buzzing, but then I make myself put it away.

This is just the remnants of my childhood crush, I tell myself sternly. I have a life to get on with. I have a feeling that while I may have been on hold for a few years I'm coming out of it now, and life's too short and precious to waste. I push away the feeling that I'm doing something wrong, because it's ridiculous, and follow Simeon out to the car.

The drive up to the main house is filled with the sort of light chit-chat that I'm usually terrible at, but somehow he relaxes me so I play my own part. However, I'm still relieved to see the golden bulk of the house appear in the headlights.

"It's even more gorgeous than I remember," he says.

I smile, unclicking my belt. "It's a lovely looking place to be sure, but it's more than that. It has its own atmosphere."

"Really?"

I nod as we leave the car and the wind hits us. "It feels like home," I say, and he smiles kindly, if a little mystified.

While he goes to the boot, I climb the steps and open the front door, darting in to switch off the burglar alarm. The house is cool and still with a faint scent of beeswax lingering on the air. I move back outside and pause on the steps while he fiddles with something in the boot. While I'm waiting, I sweep my gaze across the front of the house looking for my studio window. To my surprise there's a light on in the window, and as I watch, a shadow moves across the glass. I narrow my eyes. *Who's in there when the house should be empty?* I wonder if Niall has someone working upstairs. Maybe it's the plumber. I feel a sinking in my spirits at the thought that my time staying with Niall might be drawing to a close.

"Everything okay?" Simeon shouts.

I look back at him. "Someone's in the house," I say. "Which is odd because the alarm was switched on."

"Where?"

"There," I gesture and stop dead because there's no light at the window now and *Chi an Mor* appears cold and dark again as if it's hibernating for the winter. I shake my head at my fanciful thoughts. "Never mind. I'm obviously seeing things."

He pulls out two large packages wrapped in brown paper and when I grab one, I feel the copious layers of bubble wrap squeak under my fingers. We cart them up the steps and through the Great Hall with me pausing every so often to switch the overhead lights on so we don't bang into a stray suit of armour. I've done that once and never again. The bloody things are impossible to put back together. It had been like dismantling the LEGO Millennium Falcon and reassembling it, only for it to end up looking more like something the Wright Brothers had made as a first try.

Finally, after many stops and starts to get our breaths, we end up outside my studio.

"Wait here," I say, opening the door. "I'll clear the table."

Actually, I just want a quick look at the room first because I know I saw something before. However, there's nothing. I look in puzzlement around the well-lit room. Everything is in its place. The easel stands under the light like normal, the massive table hasn't moved, and the racks and shelves with their bottles and small jars of jewel-coloured paint are all neat and tidy.

Then I inhale the scent of pipe tobacco and leather on the air, and when I look properly at the table I spy a few pictures on the far side. I walk over and see three of the small nude paintings I've been working on which have been placed carefully as though someone has been examining them.

"Lionel," I breathe. "You dirty old bugger."

"Everything okay, Milo?" Simeon calls with a note of concern in his voice.

I look over at him affectionately. *He's such a nice man*, I think. *So good-looking and concerned.* At that moment the leather and tobacco smell intensifies and with a whoosh, the door slams shut in Simeon's face.

"What the hell?" I mutter. "That's naughty, Lionel. We don't do that to guests. Especially paying ones who fancy me," I whisper. The smell intensifies along with a sense of what feels very strongly like disapproval. Then the door opens again slowly.

"What the hell?" Simeon says, blinking.

"I'm so sorry," I call. "It's just Lionel."

"Where is he?" he asks wildly, looking around.

"Sort of everywhere," I mutter. "Especially if there's a chance of him seeing something he shouldn't." I smile apologetically when he looks confused. "He's one of the ghosts here."

He looks at me as if trying to work out if I'm taking the piss. "*One of the ghosts?*"

I heft my painting up and take it over to the wide table. "Oh yes. There are a few. Lionel was an earl, so he mainly haunts this floor and the earl's apartment. Other than that, we've got a maid who does the main staircase. Poor soul. When the visitors come, she gets quite upset if there's any mess and bangs on the balustrade. And then there's the old butler. He mainly haunts the wine cellars, which from what I hear is just death imitating life."

"And you believe in them?" he asks carefully.

I roll my eyes, secure in the knowledge that he can't see me with my back turned to him. "Of course. So would you if you lived here. It's okay. They're like part of the family, really. Apart from the butler. He seems perpetually bad-tempered, so you can have things thrown across the cellar at you if he's in a mood."

"*Okay.*" He says it slowly as if at any second I'm going to stick straws in my hair and start capering about the room. Careful, I tell myself. Keep it professional.

I turn to him and gesture for his picture. "Okay, let's see what you've got." Between the two of us, we rip off the paper and tape and unfold the bubble wrap to reveal two very discoloured portraits. In one a lady sits in a chair with a vase of flowers next to her. That part of the painting is very dark so it's impossible to tell what sort of flowers they are, but the delicacy of the painting is still charming. In the other, a man in Georgian dress stands next to a huge globe. Again this is yellowed and nasty-looking.

"What do you think?" Simeon asks as I run a gentle finger down the old gilt frame.

"I can't tell you yet." I bend to peer at the surface. "I'll need to take it out of the frame and look at it under the microscope and also make sure the panel support isn't cracked. Then I'll do some tests."

"What sort of tests?"

"I need to know the composition of the varnish first, so I'll send a sample to the labs. Once I know that, I'll test the solubility of the varnish in various solvents."

"Will that damage the painting?"

I can't help feeling that he already knows the answer to these questions, but I answer anyway. "No, of course not. I'll test at the edge of the painting under the frame. Once I get the tests back, I can start to remove the varnish." I smile at him. "That's the exciting bit but it's also the most perilous because you run the risk of removing the paint colours."

He shrugs as if unconcerned by my warning, but why would he be? From the sound of it, these aren't personal or even very valuable portraits to him. That makes me feel a bit sad, like the lady and man in the portraits have been abandoned in some way.

"Should we remove it?" he asks, leaning against the table like he's at a party, relaxed and with one corner of his mouth tilted. I look at him in query. "Well, wouldn't people say we should leave it? That the patina of ages adds to the attraction and history of the painting and therefore its value?"

I smile at him. "I don't think you need to worry," I say bluntly. It's never wise to get a client's hopes up. "These are definitely not Vermeers." He laughs and I shake my head. "I suppose it comes down to whether you want the artist's version of the picture. I don't think many artists put varnish on their paintings with any intention other than to make it look attractive at the time. They wouldn't have given much thought to its appearance in hundreds of years." I shrug. "I've been a struggling artist. I can tell you they'd be more concerned about being able to eat that night."

He laughs again. "No long-held desire to be an artist now?"

"No." I smile down at the portraits. "I prefer this. It's a bit like being Indiana Jones but not so much running around and sweating and, thank God, no fedora. I've got far too much hair to keep that hat on for any length of time."

He chuckles and shifts close. I want to immediately back up but I don't, staying still and smelling the faint trace of lemon and bergamot of his aftershave. "So any preliminary thoughts? I know you have some."

I shake my head. "At first glance, I'd say that the artist used Dammar varnish which was a mix of dammar gum and turpentine. It was introduced in the early nineteenth century and was a common varnish for painting, and it's fairly easy to get off. The paintings don't have huge amounts of accumulated grime on them like tobacco and soot, which is good." I look down at the two portraits. "There is a lot of red and green in the man's portrait, though, so I'll take a very light hand with that as those colours are more fugitive or vulnerable than blues and white."

I look up and he's staring at me with something moving over his face. "Claudia Fenwick told me you were good."

I smile. "I am good." It feels amazing to say that and own it. I look at him. "I am surprised she had a good word to say for me, though."

He shrugs. "She said you were the best student she ever had but had terrible judgment in men."

I shoot an involuntary glance in the direction of Niall's house and then look back at him and shrug. "She's not wrong." Loyalty compels me to add, "That's in the past though. I think I'm a little better now."

He smiles and I wonder what he sees. He settles his back against the wall and stuffs his hands into his trouser pockets. "I'd like to take you out to dinner, Milo. Is that something you'd be interested in?"

I'm startled, even though I've known from the beginning that he liked me. I hesitate and his eyes sharpen.

"Of course, it's fine if you don't want to. If you're interested in someone else, like Mr. Fawcett for example?"

"Oh, I'm not interested in Niall," I say quickly. "Not like that, I mean. We're friends," I finish somewhat lamely.

He cocks his head to one side, his gaze steady and his expression warm.

Without any input from my brain, my head spins to look at the door as if Niall's going to appear to save me from the situation. That need angers me enough to tear my eyes away. There's nothing to be rescued from. It's a dinner with a nice man and I don't need rescuing or saving.

I turn back to him. "Dinner would be lovely."

∼

The next evening, I come into the lounge and stop short. "Hey, is she going to—"

Niall looks up from the floor. He's lying on his stomach with his long legs stretched out, his head resting on his hands and Dotty curled in the hollow of his back. They're watching Cora who has rolled onto her stomach and is staring back at them with a mischievous look.

"Not yet," he murmurs. "But she's close."

"She's been rolling over for ages but normally she just stays there for a bit making little noises."

He laughs and holds out his hands to her. "Come on, Cora Bora. Come to Uncle Niall and Uncle Milo. Let us be the first people to see you crawl."

I nudge his ribs with my foot. "You're the most competitive person I know."

He laughs. "Have you met the small Irishman you hang around with? If you were in the queue for heaven, he'd trip you up to get to the gate first."

I grin and crouch down. "True. Come on, baby," I urge. "Come here."

Cora just smiles, coming up on her hands and punting her tiny body back and forth like she's on a starting block but then doing nothing else.

He laughs loudly. "Milo, I always knew you had a dark side."

"You have no idea," I mutter.

"Make sure Art Boy doesn't either."

I shoot a glance at him. *"What?"*

"You heard." He rolls and comes to sit up as Dotty jumps down, shooting me a dark look as she does so as if I'm the source of all the world's evils. Niall looks me up and down. "You look nice," he says darkly.

I look down at my outfit of skinny grey trousers and a thin clingy black jumper. "Do you think?" I scuff my shiny black ankle boots along the carpet. I hate clothes that look so perfect. I'm happier in old stuff that I can just fling on. "He's very rich. I hope we don't go somewhere really posh."

"Like Wellington College? I do recall you went there." He winks. "Even if it was as a day boy."

"What do you mean?"

"Simply that whatever he is, you are his equal and I happen to think his better. You'd be that even if you didn't speak well and hadn't gone to a posh school. You're anyone's equal, Lo, and it doesn't matter whether he takes you to The Ivy or Burger King."

I swallow hard. "Thank you."

He nods his head slightly. "You're welcome." He looks at me. "Are you still on for coming to watch me do the mud run tomorrow?" he asks slightly diffidently.

"Of course," I say, surprised. "You asked me ages ago."

"I wasn't sure whether now Simeon is on the scene ..." He drifts off as I look questioningly at him.

"Whether he's on the scene or not, we have a date." It's my turn to pause. "Well, not a date but–"

"Never mind," he says quickly. He eyes me again. "Do you have to go?"

I stare at him. He's as unfamiliar to me at this moment as a complete stranger. "Niall," I begin but he shakes his head.

"Doesn't matter. I thought it'd be nice to have an evening with Cora. You go. Have a good time."

The last sounds like it's through gritted teeth and I open my mouth, filled with the urge to tell him I'll stay, that I'll get changed and be with him tonight and see where the evening takes us, because I sense a tug between us like he's finally noticed the rope that somehow binds me to him and he's pulling at it on his side.

Luckily the doorbell sounds and rescues me because who the fuck would think that was a good idea. To my astonishment Dotty comes towards me, her tiny white paws padding silently. She stares up at me and I cautiously offer her my hand, prepared to retract it and run like hell. However, she stares at it for a second before licking it delicately, her tongue rasping over my fingers.

"I don't know whether to be touched or run away," I say slowly. "It's a bit like Sweeney Todd giving his customers a nice scalp massage before he cut their throats."

He grins. "If she's anything like her human namesake I'd run like hell. My grandmother was very fond of shaving my grandfather with a cutthroat razor." He pauses. "I never knew what happened to him. I must ask my mother."

I laugh and the doorbell rings again. "I have to go," I say hesitantly, grabbing my black coat from the chair.

He nods, his eyes dark and searching. "Be good," he says, and it sounds caught between being a plea and a warning.

∼

The restaurant that Simeon takes me to is lovely and I feel stupid for worrying so much. It's dimly lit with booths tucked into corners, the ceiling lit with fairy lights and the tables with guttering candles.

"You don't mind this, do you?" he asks, removing my coat while I give him a startled look at the chivalrous gesture. "I love Italian food, and this is the best in a hundred-mile radius." He pauses. "Oh shit! Tell me you eat it and you're not on one of those no-carb diets?"

I laugh as I sit down. "No. I love carbs. I eat anything. I exercise a lot and do yoga intensely, so it evens it out."

"I saw the mats on the floor when I visited last night. Does Niall do it too?"

I smile. "Bloody hell, no. He's not very bendy." My smile fades slightly as I remember rubbing on him. My cheeks redden. Shit, Niall must think I'm a total weirdo.

The waiter breaks my thoughts at that second, handing us each a menu and beginning to recite the specials. My phone pings from the table, and when I check it there's a text from Niall.

Niall: Cora is making a noise like a little tugboat but still not crawling. I'm beginning to think she's taunting us.

I smile and tap a reply.

Me: Be patient. If that's at all possible. Try and

REMEMBER HOW OLD YOU ARE AND ACT LIKE THE SAGE ELDER YOU SHOULD BE.

I grin at the thought of his face when he reads that. Almost instantly the phone buzzes.

NIALL: I'M THIRTY-NINE. EVEN SIMON COWELL IS OLDER THAN ME. ANYWAY, THERE'S MANY A GOOD TUNE PLAYED ON AN OLD FIDDLE.

I shake my head.

ME: I'M NOT SURE WHY ANYONE HAD TO GO TO THE TROUBLE OF MAKING THAT HOMILY UP. LOOK AT ALL THE STRADIVARIUSES AROUND. IT SHOULD BE FAIRLY OBVIOUS THAT OLD THINGS PLAY WELL.

NIALL: THERE ARE SO MANY REPLIES TO THAT STATEMENT. JUST KNOW THAT I HAVE MANFULLY SUPPRESSED MY INCLINATION TO TYPE ALL OF THEM. ALSO, KNOW THAT YOU WILL NEVER BE CALLING ME DADDY.

I laugh.

ME: EVEN IF I'VE BEEN BAD.

There's a long pause before the phone buzzes again.

NIALL: HAVE YOU?

I stare at the screen for a long second with my heart hammering and then reluctantly type.

ME: NO.

The next text comes through quickly and I stare at the words, feeling heat rush through me.

Niall: Good boy.

"Milo?" Simeon's voice interrupts me, and I jump and look up to find him and the waiter staring at me.

"Oh, I'm so sorry," I say anxiously. "What did I miss?"

"The specials. Would you like the waiter to repeat them?"

I shake my head. "No, I'm fine. I'll have the vegetarian lasagne, please. It sounds lovely."

Simeon gives his order and the waiter smiles and leaves us. Silence settles at the table for a second until he stirs.

"You're an extraordinarily attractive man, Milo."

I immediately feel awkward. "Thank you."

He smiles. "And you hate compliments too."

"Not all compliments."

"Ah, no. You didn't mind Niall complimenting you last night."

"That was about my job," I say defensively. "And Niall is ... well, Niall is different."

"In what way?"

I bite my lip, looking around for a distraction. There isn't one. I look back to find him watching me patiently, which makes me relax for some reason.

"I've known him many years. He's known me since I was young. He's ... he's always been there for me."

His eyes are dark and almost knowing. "Ah yes, that's what I sensed."

"You sensed something?" I sound alarmed.

"Yes, a familiarity in the way you moved around each other. Whatever it was, it denoted an ease that I haven't seen in you yet."

"I'm not a terribly confident person," I say apologetically.

He smiles gently. "I think you are. You just haven't realised it."

He sips his wine. "You don't have to be a cock of the walk to be confident, Milo. Just know your own worth and value it accordingly."

"I'm not sure it's that high."

He shakes his head. "That's unfortunate, but it won't always be like that. Luckily you have Niall, who appears to know your value to the penny."

I shrug awkwardly and take a large slug of my wine. "Yes, and perfectly prepared to boss me around until I sell for a high price."

He blinks and refills my glass. "I'm not sure where that came from. Unless Cornwall is a lot wilder than I've been led to believe." I laugh. "Mr. Fawcett appears to be a very confident man." My mouth quirks and he smiles. "I'm sure that covers a multitude of sins but his regard for you seems to be … honest."

I look at him in query and he smiles sadly. "Honesty is fresh and real. Don't mistake it for disinterest because it's far from that."

I drain my glass again and look at him assessingly. There is not one iota of the lovely heat that just being near Niall runs under my skin like a mine of lava.

"This evening is not going as I intended," I mutter.

He laughs and, filling my glass again, he taps his glass against mine. "Me neither. How about we talk about me? That should make you feel relieved and me very happy."

I laugh, liking him suddenly for that wry statement. Watching him as he signals for another bottle, I search for some shred of attraction but I can't find it. I think we both know this isn't going anywhere unless it's to a friendship, which I can definitely do.

Fucking Niall is a cockblocker from twenty miles away. It's like a bloody superpower.

CHAPTER 6

I want you to call me that when we're naked and you have your cock inside me.

Milo

I crash into the house probably louder than I intended but my fingers feel twenty times bigger than they should, as does my body which keeps banging into things. Stumbling into the kitchen, I switch the kettle on and slump over the counter to wait while it boils. I lay my head down on the surface which feels lovely against my hot face. I'm just contemplating staying here for the night when I hear footsteps and the door opens.

Twisting my head sideways on the counter, I see Niall standing there with his arms folded. He's dressed in black pyjama bottoms and a thin black long-sleeved t-shirt that clings to the muscles of his chest. His white-blond hair is standing up around his face like he's stuck his finger in a socket, and he looks rumpled but still very awake.

"Why aren't you asleep?" I mutter, hearing the slur in my words. "You've got the mud run tomorrow."

"I wanted to wait for you until you got in."

"How chiv-chiv- how very nice of you," I mutter. For some reason that makes him smile, and I shoot upwards off the counter. I stagger slightly but manage to right myself, waving off his helping hand impatiently. "I'm fine," I say pettily. "I don't need any help, thank you very much."

He leans against the doorjamb. "How much have you had to drink?"

I raise my hands. "I don't know," I say indignantly. "I stopped counting after the second bottle."

"The *second* one?" A frown crosses his face. "And he just dumped you back here?" I open my mouth but he's on a roll. "Did he take you back to his place?"

"Wouldn't you like to know," I say in a sing-song voice.

"I would, actually."

He sounds grim. I lean back against the counter, running my fingers gently over the wood, tracing the grain that glows in the soft light. He clears his throat and I look up and remember that we were in the middle of a conversation. "I like drinking," I say dreamily.

"Why?" He looks concerned as if he thinks I've suddenly developed alcoholism.

"Because I speak better when I'm drunk." The kettle boils and I go towards it, but he pushes me gently back. I look down at that big, calloused hand on my chest and swallow hard.

"I'll make tea," he says. "I don't think it's wise for you and boiling water to be on anything other than sipping terms."

I settle back against the counter and try to fold my arms across my chest. It takes longer than it should but finally I manage it. "You're not the boss of me," I say peevishly, and he grins suddenly.

"No one is the boss of you, Milo. You're gloriously intractable."

I blink, my muddled brain trying to make sense of that. "I'm not," I argue. "I'm very tract-tract … Whatever that fucking word is, I'm not it. I'm shy and a pushover."

He pours water over the tea and the faint smell of peppermint reaches my nostrils. "You might be a bit shy. There's nothing wrong with that, and a pushover you are certainly not."

"Thomas pushed me over." I laugh. "In more ways than one."

He grips the side of the counter and closes his eyes. He appears to be trying to breathe deeply, and I poke his cheek carefully. Well, I mean to do it carefully, but I miss and get his eye.

"Motherfucker," he hisses. "What was that for?"

"I didn't want you to be sad."

"So you decided to take my mind off it by gouging out one of my eyeballs?"

I shake my head and promptly wish I hadn't done it when the room spins. "Don't be such a baby. Although your eyeball felt horribly squashy." I wipe my finger carefully on my trousers. "Ugh!" I laugh. "Something about you that is actually ugly. Yay!"

"What?"

I look up to find him watching me very closely. "Don't be cross," I say.

He shakes his head. "I'm not cross, sweetheart. Not at you, anyway."

"Who are you cross at?" I sit up. "Is it at Sid the gardener because of the incident with the gazebo?"

"No," he says slowly. His eyes sharpen. "But we should definitely discuss that further."

I lean forward slightly, and some excess of gravity makes me keep going until my head thumps down onto my forearms. Cushioned, I look up at him. "Are you cross at Thomas?"

"Yes, still," he says through gritted teeth. "I'd like to find him and shove his teeth down his throat."

"He's in Oxford," I say idly and pop my head back up when he swears.

"How the fuck do you know that?"

"He tells me."

"How?"

I frown, racking my fuzzy brain and trying to think. "Letters. He used to message and email but I blocked his number, so now he writes to me because I can't change where I live." I pause. "Unless I move," I say slowly and give up the fight against gravity by lowering myself to the ground where I prop myself up against the cabinet.

"*No,*" he says explosively, and I jerk in surprise. "Sorry," he says, and before I can reply he comes swiftly over and crouches at my feet. I blink slightly because his eyes look very blue in this light. The creases at the side of them are so attractive and it's only his eyes widening in surprise that makes me realise that I'm stroking his face. "Shit! Sorry," I say, pulling back. "Bloody wine. I'm never drinking again."

"No, don't," he says in a low voice, taking my hand and putting it back. "Touch me. I like it."

"You like everything," I say softly, stroking the hard cheekbones and feeling the roughness of his stubble under my fingertips skittering and catching on my skin and making me feel hot inside. "Men *and* women, they all love you."

He seems to stop breathing. "And does that bother you?"

I shrug and smile happily at him. "Why would it bother me? It's got nothing to do with me."

"But if it did?"

I frown, trying to work out what this conversation is about, but I'm getting tired and I like talking to him like this. "Why would it have anything to do with me?" I laugh. "Look at you and then look at me." I bop him on the nose, making his eyes briefly cross.

Then a frown crosses them. "And your point is?"

I run my fingertip dreamily over his full mouth. It's dry, and I dip my finger briefly into the wetness of his mouth and anoint his lips so they shine.

"Milo." His voice is low and harsh, and he shifts position slightly as if he's uncomfortable. I can feel his heat against me. He's always wonderfully warm while I'm permanently cold.

"Hmm?"

He clears his throat and sits back slightly, and my fingers fall reluctantly away. "You seem to be saying that you're lacking in some way?"

"I'm lacking in a lot of ways," I say wryly. "All of which you're aware of." I pause. "Apart from one thing."

"Milo, you are gorgeous," he says firmly, his eyes intent and warm on mine in the quietness of the kitchen. "I don't think you see it, but you are." He reaches up and tucks an errant strand behind my ear, a funny expression on his face. "You're quirky and funny and loyal and loving. How are you lacking in any way?"

I lean forwards slightly. He smells wonderful, with his sweet woody scent that always smells so warm, and I push my nose into the side of his neck and inhale deeply. "Well, I might be all that," I say dreamily. "But I'm also shit in bed, so why would anyone want this anyway?"

"Milo." He wriggles as I stick my tongue out and lick the side of his neck.

"Mmm. You taste lovely."

"Ungh." It's a low, sexy sound and I smile when I hear it.

"Nope," I say playfully. "No point in getting hard. It'd be wasted on me."

"What the fuck?" he breathes, his face dark. "Who the hell told you that rubbish?" He stops and inhales deeply, his hands fisting where they rest on his thighs. "Fucking Thomas," he spits. "I'm going to get one of his letters off you and then he and I are going to have a long and very painful talk."

I push his forehead away playfully. "No, you're not," I chide. "You're just like him."

"*What?*" He sounds taken aback and almost hurt.

I sneak a look at him and wince. "You're just both so forceful," I say slowly, feeling the alcohol slow my tongue and a headache starting to form at the base of my skull. "Always know everything. Always know the right thing to say and do. It's a lot," I finish lamely.

He stares at me, breathing very quickly. He looks as if someone has hit him in the face.

"I'm nothing like that wanker," he says slowly. "And the thought that you feel that is ..." He pauses. "It's *horrible*."

I'm instantly overcome with remorse and scramble over and land in his lap. Taken by surprise, he falls back into the cupboard but before I can move off him, he adjusts his position so he's sitting against the cabinet with his legs stretched out and me curled on his lap. His arms are around me and I feel warm and safe.

"I'm sorry," I say sadly. "I didn't mean to say that."

"I'm glad you did," he says slowly. "It explains a lot." His hands rub warm circles on my shoulders and I nestle into him. "I wish you could see how you say two different things simultaneously," he says, and I look at him quizzically.

"I don't do that. I can barely say one thing coherently, let alone bringing in something else."

He smiles. "Not with talk. Just the way you are." He sighs when I stare, puzzled, at him. "Never mind. It's early days yet. You'll see in the end that I'm nothing like him, and on that day, I want you to think really hard about how you feel when you're with me. Think about that and ask yourself if it's the same as Thomas." He shakes his head. "I don't think it is, but you've spent that long with the wanker you can't see the wood for the trees."

"I can feel your wood," I chuckle, giving up on the serious conversation and wriggling on his lap.

He groans. "Milo, stop."

I hug him. "I might as well. It would be false aggravation on my part."

"I think you mean false advertisement," he says slowly. "And that's just not true." He smiles at me. "You think you're bad in bed because one wanker told you that. Was he your first?"

I nod. "And only."

He sighs and hugs me. "Baby, I'm so sorry for that. I wish ..." He trails off and I snuggle in closer, loving the feel of him against me.

"What do you wish?"

I feel him move as he shakes his head. "Silly things."

"Is it that I'll like sex because that's never going to happen." I shudder. "I hate it. It's messy and painful and cold. Not like anything anyone else says. I think I might be a monk." I nod firmly and wish I hadn't when my stomach roils. I press back to my thoughts. "I'm going to be a monk. I'm going to get fat and wear a really long brown cassock and laugh really loudly all the time."

His face is warm when he turns it to me. "I think there's more to being a monk than obesity, wearing a cassock, and laughing loudly." He cups my face, forcing me to look blearily at him. "Baby, sex is wonderful. It's hot and sweaty and fucking transcendental sometimes. If you think it's cold, then he wasn't doing it properly."

"What?"

He nods firmly. "Sweetheart, he was your first. That first time with him should have been tender and warm and you should have come so hard you almost blacked out. If I'd been ..." He trails off and I touch his mouth curiously.

"If you'd been, what? You mean if you'd been my first, you'd have made it like that?" My voice sounds full of wonder and I wish passionately that this had happened. Then the world dims a little and I remember that it didn't and won't and that I'm just pale, thin, boring Milo who's useless in bed.

I stare at him. His eyes are dark and his lips full and he's so pretty he makes my heart hurt, and for the first time a speak of rebellion stirs in my belly. *Why do I have to be like this?* How is it fair that everyone else goes shagging left, right, and centre enjoying themselves and showing off their confidence and I'm inhibited and boring?

"Then maybe you should show me now," I say slowly, and before I can think I lean forwards and press my mouth to his.

He freezes under me and I pause, wondering what to do. I open my mouth to say sorry but as I do, he grabs my head and pushes his tongue into my mouth and *oh God*, the feeling. His mouth is warm and wet and he tastes like toothpaste, and when his tongue rubs against mine it sends sparks into my balls and my hips move and twist against him.

For a second I'm lost in a very strange land full of a hot darkness and heated sighs and it's so good, but then he stiffens underneath me, and before I can lick him again he sets me back on his thighs.

I look curiously at him. He's pink in the face and his hair looks wild as if I've been running my fingers through it. I look down at my hands. Maybe I was.

"Sweetheart, no," he says in a hoarse voice.

I smile at him, feeling suddenly bold. "I like it when you call me that," I say happily.

"You do?" He sounds bemused.

I nod. "I want you to call me that when we're naked and you have your cock inside me."

He swallows hard and loudly. "You *do?*"

I nod and my stomach lurches again. "Yes," I say faintly. "But can we do that after I've been sick in the sink?"

"Shit!"

Niall

I look down at the sleeping figure of Milo and smile. He's lying in bed, his hair wet from the shower I'd thrust him into after he threw up in the sink. I grimace. That had been lovely, as had been clearing it up. And showering him afterwards had been like washing one of the walking dead. Very unsexy.

Dotty is curled into the crook of his legs, looking very comfortable. "I know you like him really, but not as much as I do," I whisper and she purrs, her eyes green and enigmatic.

I smile and stroke one of the long waves of Milo's hair back from that heart-shaped face with the pointed chin. The vomit hadn't been sexy, but I had still enjoyed taking care of him more than I like to acknowledge because even drunk, he'd been so Milo. Quirky and funny and blisteringly honest. I stroke his hair again and he nestles into my palm, and something stirs inside me in the soft place that I don't show to anyone.

Even as a small boy, he made me smile with his awkwardness and his pithy retorts to his brother. There had been something unquenchable about him then. Even with the speech impediment and shyness he'd seemed almost dauntless, like he was a Weeble and no matter how the world knocked him over, he'd still get up with that shy smile of his.

My own smile fades. Until Thomas, that is. That wanker had managed to dim Milo's spark so thoroughly that even now, a few years on, he still bears the scars. How could someone take all that lovely stumbling warmth and shy eagerness and turn it to ashes? How could he have had that in his bed and not made him feel like a king?

I think of that moment when he'd straddled me, his face full of a sudden purpose, and how he'd kissed me. Awkward but so full of life and a heat underneath that I can sense would be in danger of burning me to death if it was let loose.

I feel the heat run under my skin and wonder if I should have another cold shower. I've slept with many men and women, some separately, some together. I've done most things, ruling out a few that make me shudder at the thought, and I've enjoyed every minute. Threesomes, foursomes, I've had them all and come every time.

I thought that was enough, but tonight Milo circumvented my impressions the way only he can, taking me by surprise with the passion that had swept through me at his touch.

The men and women I sleep with are all, without exception, assured and confident lovers experienced in having a good time with no regrets. I've always kept away from inexperience, thinking it would bore me and take too much of my time to overcome when easy pleasure beckoned within quick reaching distance.

Well, the joke's on me because I've never felt this before. This swinging of emotions all the time. The horrible jealousy that had settled in my stomach like a rock while he was out with Simeon. The way I kept texting him during dinner was out of order, but I wanted to keep me in his thoughts front and centre and not focused on the perfectly nice and handsome man who I dislike with a passion because he was with someone who is mine.

I still at the thought. *Mine.* I test it, washing it around in my mouth and swallowing the word. It feels right somehow. Milo is mine. Maybe he's always been that, in some funny way. The only man I've ever felt protective of. The only man who can walk into a room and have my whole attention no matter what I'm doing. I just don't know what that means at the moment. It used to be that it was because I thought of him as family. Now, he's something much more.

I look down at his sleeping face. He wouldn't believe any of this anyway because he thinks I'm like Thomas. Bile rises in my throat. I am nothing like him. I know it. I've always treated my partners fairly and honestly, preferring to leave them with a smile on their faces and no tears.

I know I'm confident, but I never realised that Milo would see that as a threat. My heart hurts at the thought. I don't know what to do with that. I don't know how to make him see me behind the picture of Thomas that stands between us. How to make him know that I would never treat him like that, ever.

I'm suddenly reminded of Dotty when she came to me. Dirty, unkempt, and half-starved, she'd turned up on my doorstep but refused to come into the house. It had taken weeks of leaving food and milk for her before she'd even venture inside, and even then she'd watched me carefully as if waiting for me to hit her at any moment.

I trod carefully around her at first, careful to always give her space so that even when she finally let me pet her it was with the tacit understanding between us that there was room for her to escape if she needed to. This had gone on for months until one night she jumped onto my lap, and as I stroked her I'd heard her purr for the first time. It sometimes seems as if she's never left my lap and her purr is louder now than it's ever been.

I smile slightly and stroke Milo's hair, feeling the warm, damp strands curl around my finger and inhaling the scent of my shower gel on him. I like that he smells of me far too much. My hand pauses. Dotty has grown to love me more than anyone, so I'll take that as a good sign. She's also bitten me more than a few times and has a tendency to shit in my shoes if she's cross with me. I laugh softly. I'm hoping Milo won't do the latter, but I think without knowing it he could hurt me.

I straighten my spine. But I'm not a quitter. I want him, I realise with finality. I want his insecurities and his quiet strength. His warm laugh and his sometimes hesitant speech. I want the long, lithe, and graceful body. And I'm going to have him at some point. All of him, quirks and everything. But first he's got to trust me. I wonder sadly how long that will take.

At this point he moves in his sleep and nuzzles into the palm I have cupping his head. "Niall," he whispers.

I smile widely. Now, I have hope. That's usually all I need to go forward with anything. I just wish I knew what that was.

CHAPTER 7

Oh my God, did you fuck me?

Milo

I come awake slowly the next morning as if my brain knows the scale of the imminent pain awaiting me and has decided to try and shield me. It doesn't work because as I shift position, my head throbs sickeningly. I groan pitifully, and I realise belatedly that I'm incredibly warm at the same time as there's a low chuckle from beside me.

I crack open one eye, slam it shut and wait a few seconds until the glaring light stops trying to incinerate my eyeballs. Eventually, after several false starts, I manage to crack open both eyes to a sort of slitted half-stare. And stare I do because lying next to me is Niall.

His tanned skin looks golden against the pale blue of the sheets and his hair is a tangled mess on the pillow. I move slightly, and a woody smell mingled with a faint hint of lemon and rosemary drifts up from the tangled bedlinens. Both of our scents have combined and it's strangely erotic. I bunch the sheets up over my body's reaction. The force is strong with my cock, despite my brain's opposition.

I look up and choke slightly when I find him watching me. His eyes are slumberous and sexy and way, way too amused.

"What are you doing here?" I ask hoarsely to forestall the piss taking. I can't exactly remember the precise reason why he'd do that, but I know with a deep certainty that it exists.

He stretches, giving out a low, satisfied grunt which makes me swallow hard. He moves his head on the pillow and smiles at me. It's a warm, intimate smile that hits me like a brick between the eyes because he's never looked at me like this before. My eyes narrow.

"Oh my God, did you fuck me?"

He snorts and stretches his arms behind his head. "Milo, I have done and enjoyed many things in my sexual peak, but necrophilia has never been one of them." He pauses as if considering something and then shakes his head. "No, I'm certain I've never done it."

I glare at him. "Then why are you in bed with me?"

"Well, dearest." My eyes narrow at the endearment and he snorts and bops me on the nose. "After you rather charmingly threw up in the sink, I showered you and put you to bed. I decided to sleep in with you because Cora is here and also because I wanted to make sure you didn't choke on your own vomit." He pauses. "That would have really set me back on my mud run schedule."

I groan and fall back on the pillows, putting my hand over my eyes. "Oh my *God*, I can't believe I was sick in your sink. I'm so sorry."

A warm hand pulls my fingers away from my eyes and I squint at him as he gives me a soft look. "Why be sorry? Better the sink than my crotch."

"You should put that on a t-shirt," I say sourly, and he laughs loudly. There's a rustle and a soft coo from the Moses basket and he vaults up and paces over to it. Bending over Cora, he grins.

"Hello, baby girl. Ready for a nice day out?"

I blanch. "Oh my *God*, have I still got to go?"

"Yes. Death would not be an excuse for missing the mud run." He straightens up with Cora cradled in his arms. He lays her next to me. "Here. Watch her while I get her bottle."

He exits the room and I listen to his footsteps thundering down the stairs. I look down at Cora lying next to me in her little Babygro decorated in pink flamingos. She gives me a gummy smile and windmills her arms and legs about, stretching after her long sleep.

I lean down and kiss her head, inhaling the scent of baby shampoo and sleep that clings to her. "I'm going to miss you when your daddies come back," I say softly and she coos, reaching one tiny hand and clutching a hank of my hair in a grip that's fucking tighter than The Rock could manage. It makes my eyes water.

When I've untangled her hand, I lie peacefully in the bed. It's still dark out there and I can hear the wind blowing in the trees outside. It makes me feel safe and warm in our little nest.

I shake my head and wince at the pain that catapults across my forehead. I'm trying to recall the evening but I'm coming up blank. It's a bit of a hazy mess from the point that Simeon had ordered a third bottle of wine. I scrunch up my face in concentration.

"I remember putting the kettle on," I say slowly to Cora who's watching me intently with her bright button eyes. "And I remember Niall making tea."

Realisation flashes across my brain with the speed of a comet. A comet that's intent on destroying a planet.

"Oh my *God*," I gasp to Cora. "I kissed him." I pause. "And then told him I was crap in bed and threw up on him."

"It's a charming story, but even if you put 'once upon a time' in front of it, I'm not sure you could market it as a fairy tale." Niall's voice makes me jump, and I look up to find him staring at me from the doorway. He paces into the room, unscrewing the lid. I hold my arm out automatically for him to test the bottle and nod as Cora works herself up into a frenzy. He passes me the bottle and plops himself down next to me.

I eye him nervously as I give the bottle to Cora. She grabs it quickly and possessively, her eyes sliding shut in total contentment as she sucks. The room is full of the sounds of her surprisingly loud gulps for a long minute.

He rummages in his pocket and produces a packet of painkillers. "Open up," he demands and pops two of the tablets on my tongue, handing me a bottle of water to wash them down and taking control of the bottle while I do it.

Silence falls again until eventually I stir. "I'm so sorry," I mutter. "I'm m-m-mortified."

"Milo, no," he says immediately, his hand coming down on my leg. "Relax."

"No, I said you were like Thomas. You're *nothing* like Thomas."

"Baby, I know you say that, but there's a tiny part of you that thinks it."

"I really don't." I hesitate. "It's just that you're so competent and confident that it's daunting to someone like me."

"Someone like you?" He pauses. "Ah, let me think. What did you say last night? Plain and boring?"

I feel myself flush. "I think we should try and forget last night's conversation." I nod determinedly. "Yes, that should be one of our yearly goals. We can put it as number one, just outranking world peace and working out what exactly Kanye West is talking about."

He smiles. "I don't want to forget last night's revelations."

I groan. "Oh God."

He shakes his head. "We haven't got time to discuss this, but we are going to."

"I vote no." I shrug. "It's embarrassing, Niall, but it's the truth."

"No, it's not. It's someone else's words, but the truth has nothing to do with that."

"How do you know that?"

"Because I know you," he says sharply. "Sweetheart, you're warm and full of life. You're quirky and earthy. No fucking way you'd be bad in bed. You just need someone to show you how."

"Oh my God, who would do that?"

"Anyone," he says firmly, his eyes dark with some feeling I can't work out. "Some lucky bastard can teach you and think himself the luckiest man on earth."

"I could never tell anyone what I've just told you. It would be far too embarrassing. I'm practically a virgin. Ugh!"

He hesitates for some reason before saying abruptly and rather gruffly, "Then maybe don't look too far afield. I'm always here for you."

"What?"

He shakes his head. "Nothing. I'm going to get ready. Get up and get dressed when Cora's finished."

He moves out of the room and I stare after him. "Did he just offer to teach me how to have sex?" My brow furrows. "I'm not sure whether that's embarrassing or hot." I consider it for a second but I'm too hungover to make sense of it, so I shrug. "A bit of both."

An hour later we're ready to go. Or Niall and Cora are ready to go. I, however, am hungover to the eyeballs and feel like a cast member of *The Night of the Living Dead*.

"Was that a groan?" Niall asks with an amused note in his voice.

I look sideways at him. He's sitting comfortably back in his seat, one hand on the wheel and the other resting on his thigh. I stare at the long fingers and neat nails and the veins on the back of his hands. I imagine them on my body and heat rushes through me. He clears his throat and I jump, glad that I'm wearing sunglasses and not just because the daylight will fry my retinas.

"It might have been," I say faintly. "I'm sure you don't need Cora and me for this."

"You're my cheerleaders."

"I think you need to revaluate your social life if one tiny baby and a hungover man are your cheerleading squad."

"I already did that. Now, I'm implementing changes."

"What does that even mean?" I look askance at him, but he doesn't say anything more.

My phone beeps and I look down and smile.

"What?" he asks. "Who is it?" His voice goes darker. "Is it Simeon?"

"No, it's Oz. They're on the way back now."

"Already?" Is it my imagination or does he sound slightly disappointed? Or is it me projecting my feelings onto him because I'm not ready for our little sojourn to be over? With Cora gone there will be no reason for me to stay at Niall's house anymore. I'll have to move back to the main house and my attic suite.

My mouth turns down. I won't be able to sit with him, eating and talking. I won't smell his aftershave in the air and hear his voice in the other room, knowing I'll see him in a second. I'll go back to nodding at him over dinner and watching as he leaves for the evening to meet whichever man or woman is waiting for him.

The sound of the indicator rouses me from my thoughts and I look up as he pulls into the McDonalds drive through. He orders a coffee and a sausage and egg McMuffin and I look curiously at him as we wait. "Won't you feel sick if you run after eating that?"

"It's not for me," he says, smiling at the woman who hands him his food. "It's for you."

I look down at the bag that he hands me and then back up at him. "I can't eat this. I'll be sick."

"No, you won't," he says bracingly. "Bit of grease is just what you need and then a strong coffee. You'll feel fine afterwards."

I'm not convinced, but I have to grudgingly admit that by the time we pull up to the field where the run is happening that I feel something close to human again. I climb out of the car and look around as Niall unclips Cora from her car seat. It's a cold day, but the air is crisp and the sun is shining although it's watery and thin. A wind gusts and dances around me and leaves flutter down from the trees in a flurry of reds and golds. All around us people are getting out of cars chattering and stretching, and there's a palpable air of excitement.

I look up and take the baby sling that Niall offers me. Fixing it, I take Cora and settle her in. She peeps over the top, her eyes bright and curious, looking at everything. I stroke her soft cheek and adjust her bobble hat so it's covering her ears. Then with one hand under her rump to support her, I look at Niall.

He's dressed in another pair of those gorgeous form-fitting black running tights and a black running shirt under a long-sleeved orange t-shirt advertising the run. The material clings to the bulging muscles on his arms and he glows with the last vestiges of his tan from summer. He spends so long outdoors that his colour never really goes, although he insists it's windburn most of the time. His white-blond hair shines palely in the watery sunlight and although he brushed it down firmly before we left, strands are already drifting around his face like the gold that Rumpelstiltskin wanted spun.

He's stretching his legs and doing runner things that I have no idea about, because the only time I'd run anywhere was if a lion was chasing me and I'd still hope the lion had a defibrillator after I'd gone a few steps. However, I don't have to know what he's doing to appreciate it, and I lean against the car, glad for my sunglasses and hoping they cover up my covert observation of his long, lean body.

"You okay?" he asks, a smile playing around his full lips. "You look a little flushed, and is that a bit of drool?"

Okay, they didn't cover it up and it obviously wasn't covert.

I flush harder. "I'm fine," I say in a hopefully nonchalant manner. "Just waiting to feel human. And don't be so big headed," I chide. "People dribble for many reasons."

"Babies and old people, mainly."

"And for good food."

"Hmm. So, what food am I?"

Steak, I think. "Soggy toast," I say.

He throws his head back and starts to laugh, and I smile because his laughter is so him. Big and bold and full of life.

When he stops laughing, he starts to walk towards the tent where people are registering, and I fall into step beside him.

"It's so cold," I say. "I hope she'll be okay."

He looks down at Cora. "She's a snug little bug. She's fine. She'll get body heat from you as well." He looks out over the fields. "I won't be that long, maybe an hour or so, and you've got the keys. Get back in the car if you feel too cold."

I shake my head. "We're your cheerleaders. We don't leave a man behind."

A smile tugs at his lips. "I think that might be the army." He offers me a half wave as he wanders to join the queue. Within seconds he's started a conversation with the people in front and within a minute they're laughing. I shrug. It's so him.

"What a gorgeous baby."

I turn around to see a stout old woman standing in front of me. She's dressed in a brown coat and wearing green wellies that look well-worn, unlike my navy ones that Niall gave me this morning. She has a round red face, grey wispy hair plaited and wound around her head, and a small mouth which is pulled very tight. She looks mean and cross.

"Thank you." I smile tentatively but she doesn't return the gesture. "She is gorgeous, but I'm probably biased."

"Ah, is she your first?"

"Oh, she's not mine. She's my goddaughter. We're looking after her while her parents are away."

"How lovely." She reaches out an old wrinkled hand and prods Cora's cheek. Cora looks startled and I resist the urge to move her away because the old lady is just being friendly, even if she does have the same expression on her face as the child snatcher in *Chitty Chitty Bang Bang*. "And you're carrying her around yourself. Why isn't your wife doing that, or is she running?"

I blink. "I don't have a wife."

"Ah, I'm sure you will." She gives me a thin-lipped smile that doesn't reach her eyes. "Wives are a gift from God to a young man. Stops men from being too wild. You should look for one."

I blink because that sounded way too evangelical for my taste.

And also very rude. She goes to touch Cora again, but I step back under the pretext of banging mud from my boots.

She shoots me a glance but bends and coos at Cora again. "And when are your mummy and daddy coming back?"

"Not mummy," I say steadily. "She has two daddies instead."

She freezes and slowly looks up at me with a deeper red starting to mottle her cheeks. "This child has two men for fathers?" I nod. For a long minute there's silence and then she grimaces as if she's going to be sick. "That's absolutely disgusting," she hisses. I'm so taken aback that I can't speak. Instead I cradle Cora protectively and step back, but it doesn't stop her. "I cannot stand that. *Two men* having a child. It's against nature and God. Social services should be called in at once."

Her voice is rising and people are beginning to stare. Cora startles and I soothe her, feeling anger run through me. How dare this bigoted old lady say such things?

"Last I heard, social services don't use the Bible as a handbook." She opens and shuts her mouth, looking like a fat, grey fish. "And I really think that G-God has a lot more things to be bothered about, like your terrible dress sense and the fact that you d-don't appear to have changed your hairstyle since 1975."

I come to a stop, the flurried, stuttering words dying away to a stunned silence. Taking advantage of it, I turn around and stop dead. Niall is standing there, his arms folded across his chest and a fierce, proud look in his eyes.

"How long have you been there?"

"Enough time to wonder if Oswald Mosley's mother needs to take her medication," he says in a loud voice. I hear a huff, and when I look around, the woman is marching away. I turn back to Niall.

"You didn't feel like you should jump in?" I ask incredulously.

He shrugs. "Why should I? You were handling it fine. Will you pin my number on my shirt?"

The abrupt change of subject makes me blink, but I hasten to do it. But as I'm pinning and smoothing my mind is teeming. I may have stuttered, but I stood up for Cora and Oz and Silas, and for the first time in a long while I feel a tiny part of the pre-Thomas Milo start to unfurl. It's quiet and sleepy but it's still there, and I feel a soft thrumming in my blood, like I'm waking up from a long sleep.

After we've accompanied Niall to the starting line, Cora and I stand back, watching as a very energetic woman in tight running gear leads the runners in a pre-run warm-up. I look around curiously.

The run is taking place across several fields, so I can't see all of the jumps. Apparently spectators can follow alongside the runners, but I've seen Niall in action before and the only way I'm keeping pace with him is if I attach motorised skates to my feet. What I can see are hay bales set up as obstacles and some sort of massive climbing wall which has ropes attached. I shudder slightly. It's like some sort of fucked-up sports day.

I turn when I hear the very peppy lady starting the countdown as the runners jog on the spot. There's a palpable air of excitement in the air and it makes me smile. I search for Niall in the crowd and jerk when I see him. Instead of jumping around, he's an oasis of stillness standing staring at me. For a second, it's like I have tunnel vision and there's just him in this busy field. Then the starting pistol goes off and the crowd surges forward. My mouth tilts up in a tentative smile and he grins back, touching his fingers to his forehead in a salute before turning gracefully and merging into the crowd.

I stride past some spectators to the edge marked out by yellow waist-high rope. The runners pass me in flashes of colour and noise and suddenly he's there, jogging easily, his body moving smoothly. His face has a huge smile on it, full of life and enjoyment, and it makes me laugh. He looks up and his grin widens and then he's gone.

I stand for a long minute while the line of runners surges past me and then I'm alone with Cora, her warmth solid against my stomach and chest. I smile down at her. "Well, there he goes. Uncle Niall's running again. The silly man. Like Forrest Gump with very nice hair and sarcasm."

She gives me a wide, gummy grin, her brown eyes warm and alert under the shadow of her hat. One tiny fist in a pink mitten gets out of the sling and she bats me happily. I catch her hand and kiss it. "I'm going to get a drink and then we'll have a walk, baby girl."

There's a clearing next to the run which is full of brightly coloured trailers selling everything from prosecco to artisan pastries. The air is filled with the smell of savoury things cooking, and I inhale appreciatively. I'm hungry again despite the muffin earlier. I queue, acknowledging compliments about Cora which she accepts with the ease of a small ruler of a kingdom. Finally, with a cup of hot chocolate and an iced cinnamon bun that's as big as my head, I amble along the spectator's path.

I actually like this sort of thing. I've been to some of Niall's runs before. He's been doing them since he was a teenager. However, they're usually very focused and all about finishing times. This is much more fun with an air of jollity about it. Groups run together with the faster people stopping and waiting for their friends. People of all sizes and ages run along happily. There seems to be more of an emphasis on completing the course rather than competing.

Eventually I settle at the water jump. A stand is set up alongside a large pond and a very loud man is hailing the runners as they hover, waiting to jump. I look at the water and wince. It looks bloody freezing and it must be, as one of the announcers at the beginning was adamant that anyone who wanted to do the course twice wasn't allowed to do the water bits again or they could get hypothermia.

I finish my bun and juggle Cora, cupping my hands over her cheeks to warm her as I watch people encouraging the reluctant jumpers. I'd be reluctant too, I think, watching them gasp as they pop to the surface like corks in a bath. In fact, they'd need a cattle prod to get me off that platform.

I join in with the crowd around as we count down and cheer the hesitant people, watching as they pull themselves out and stop to hug their watching families and chat as if they're at a garden party.

It takes me a second to see Niall but suddenly he's there, standing next to an older woman, and he's all I can see. He's filthy dirty, his hair is wet, and mud streaks his face and arms and legs, but he has a grin similar to what I imagine a marauding pirate would have and he radiates happiness.

The woman hesitates despite everyone's shouted encouragement, but Niall moves near and speaks to her. She listens and nods and finally they turn, and we all shout as hand in hand they jump. They bob up gasping, and in Niall's case laughing, and the woman blows him a kiss. He grins and swims for the shore and pulls himself up in one powerful movement.

Once out, he hesitates, looking around the crowd. I see the exact moment that he spots me because he jerks and stands staring at me.

"Good work," I say heartily and he grins, saying nothing but pacing towards me. I gulp as he gets to us and, holding my shoulders tight, he bends his head to drop a kiss on Cora's face. She laughs and holds her arms out to him, but I swallow hard. His scent is made up of grass, wet earth, and light sweat, and I inhale, trying to draw it into me to keep.

He straightens with his hands still holding me close, and before I can say anything, he drops his head and kisses me. It's a chaste kiss, with a nod to our surroundings, but his lips are warm and I catch the faint taste of peppermint. I gasp and he kisses me again, and everything fades away for a second apart from the realization that this is Niall kissing *me*.

We're brought back to reality when a wry voice with a strong Irish brogue says next to me, "You two had better not be crushing my baby."

We break apart, and Silas and Oz are standing there grinning. They rush forward, intent on getting to Cora who wriggles energetically when she sees their faces, but I stand still watching Niall who's looking at me with a slightly sheepish look. I can't help noticing, however, that it's mixed with a lot of determination, and I swallow hard.

CHAPTER 8

Are you a *cuddler*?

Milo

After a few hugs Niall jogs off to finish the run. Silas, carrying Cora, walks beside Oz and me, all of us carrying the fresh coffee they'd brought with them.

"So?" Oz begins.

I immediately shake my head. "No. Not a chance."

"Milo," he says in a pseudo-shocked voice. "We've been friends for most of our lives, and this is how you repay my care and devotion?"

"We've been friends for two years," I say levelly. "And in that short time, you've given me snark and tough love."

He links his arm with mine companionably. "You say potato. I say potarto."

"No, you don't."

"Stop being so literal." He shakes his head. "You have to tell me."

"Nope."

"But ... but I'll never sleep tonight if I don't know. Silas, tell him."

Silas smiles at me, his handsome face warm and familiar. "Leave him alone, Oz. He'll tell you when he's ready."

Oz shakes his head again. "So bloody reasonable."

I laugh but it stops when I see the old lady from before marching towards us and dragging a very reluctant-looking woman behind her.

"That's the one I told you about," I mutter.

His eyes sharpen. "Is it really?"

The old lady comes abreast of us and opens her mouth. "Can I just say ...?"

"No, not today," he says in a lordly fashion, waving his hand in a very dismissive manner.

We stroll past her, leaving her opening and shutting her mouth like a very ugly landed fish.

Oz tuts. "I don't know why people are so interested in other people's lives. It's so petty." Silas clears his throat and Oz glares at him. "Do you have something to say, Silas, or have you got a cold?"

He grins. "It's just that I think it might be you who buys *Heat* magazine and had a very involved conversation with Mrs. Granger a few weeks ago over whether Brad and Angelina would ever get back together."

"Was it really?" Oz say airily. "They don't count. They're not real."

"Are they made of plastic then?" Silas asks with a thread of laughter running through his voice.

"Have you seen his performance in *Interview with the Vampire?*" he says darkly. "There's your answer right there."

Silas blinks and then looks down at Cora and smiles warmly. "We're just going to find Niall," he says, kissing her on her tiny nose.

We watch him go with Oz smiling in a besotted way. I eye him and when he turns around and catches me, he flushes. "What?"

I grin. "Love looks very good on you."

"Yuck!" he mutters, and I grin wider and then flap my hands about.

"Ugh! It feels weird without Cora attached to me." I look over at him. "Are you going straight back to London?"

He nods. "Tomorrow. Another week will do it, I think. Mum's perilously close to murdering me for mithering her so I think that might be best for all of us."

I laugh. His mum is a spitfire. I look across the field at Silas who has found Niall. He's draped in a silver blanket which makes him look rather like a superhero with a cape. He's grinning at Silas, and the warmth and long years of friendship are very visible between them.

I look back and it's my turn to flush as I find Oz staring at me. I open my mouth and he shakes his head. "I'm not asking." I relax and he grins. "But that doesn't stop me from *telling*. Silas never mentioned *that*."

I have to laugh at the triumphant expression on his face. Finally, I sigh and raise my face to the sky. "Okay, get it over with."

"I'm not sure what's happening between the two of you, but I for one am very happy about it."

"What?"

"You look surprised."

"That about sums it up."

"Why?"

"Because I thought you'd say he was out of my league. That we're very different and don't suit."

"Pshaw, who wants the same? I can never understand that. I don't need to share interests with Silas to want to fuck him sideways."

There's a horrified gasp behind us and he turns to see the apoplectic face of the old lady.

"Oh yes," he says airily. "You heard right. Now, move along, Brunhild."

I shake my head as I watch the two women give him a wide berth and merge back into the crowd.

"Now, where was I?"

I tsk. "That it doesn't matter if we're very different."

"It doesn't. Both of you having the same interests is boring. Although you would get a lot of picture restoring done. The world might run out of dirty portraits." He pauses as if considering that idea but then shrugs. "It'd mean doing the same things every day. Like dating grey knitting wool when you should have rainbow colours."

"That's a very mixed metaphor."

"Okay, posh boy. You know what I mean." He pauses and looks over at Niall. "I think you'd be very good for each other."

"Erm, I don't think so. I dated someone who was like him. It didn't end well."

For the first time he looks disappointed in me. He shakes his head. "I'm sad if you think that, Milo, because it means you're judging him while still wearing your Thomas glasses. He's not the same at all." He looks over at Niall. "Sure, he's bossy, opinionated, and totally convinced that he's right in every way, and I'd kill him within approximately twenty seconds if I was with him." I laugh and he smiles but then turns serious. "But that's me and he's different with you."

"How?"

"Softer. You knock his hard edges off. Sometimes when I'm really cross with him, I just have to remember how he looks at you and I forgive him everything."

"How does he look at me?" I whisper.

He shakes his head. "I really can't tell you that." He holds his hand up when I go to protest. "I genuinely *can't*, not won't tell you. You have to see with your own eyes and when you do, I'll know you're seeing clearly. Just think on this. Niall may fuss over you and mollycoddle you, but has he ever flat out forbidden you to do anything? Has he ever said anything derogatory to you?"

I shake my head. "But that's just because we're not together. In my experience that comes after, when the charm falls away."

"Niall isn't *charming*," he scoffs. "He's funny and sometimes ruthlessly honest but he has no artifice or superficial charm." He pauses. "Niall is charismatic. It's not the same thing and it's genuine." He looks imploringly at me. "Please don't tell him I said that, will you?"

"I promise," I say, raising my hand as if we're in court.

We turn and walk back to Niall and Silas and talk turns to other things, but a tiny portion of my brain lags behind the conversation, analysing and turning over what Oz said. I haven't come to any conclusions, but I feel a softening inside me as if soon I will.

∽

That night in bed I can't sleep. The wind is blowing a gale outside. It howls around the house, tossing rain at the windowpane and filling the air with the sound of the trees blowing. Normally, I love this sort of night. I love lying in bed warm while the storm rages. Tonight, I just feel restless.

When we'd come back to the house, Oz and Silas had gathered Cora's things together and left in a whirlwind of thanks and kisses. When they'd gone it had seemed strange. I'd made a move to get my things together but Niall had insisted that I stay, saying that although the plumber had got the heating on in Oz and Silas's apartment, he was going to have to come back tomorrow to do the rest of the house.

I turn on my back again. I sort of wish that he'd let me go because with how turned on I currently feel, the cold in the main house would have acted like a cold shower.

I push the sheets down, feeling the cooler air strike my chest. There's a film of sweat on me and my cock throbs like it's got a toothache, pressing against the sheets like it's got a mind of its own. I run my hands over my chest, finding my nipples that are standing up in the cool night air. I twist them in my fingers and heat runs like a ribbon of fire to my cock. I cup my balls, squeezing gently, and then fist my cock, starting a slow slide through my clenched fist, letting the head pop through my fingers and enjoying the friction.

I work myself steadily, but although it feels good and is something I've done to myself so many times, it's not enough tonight. I feel a little like I've woken up from a deep sleep and the numbness has given way to pins and needles and a feeling of being vitally alive.

I pull my hand away and scrub my palms down my face, smelling the pre-come on my fingers. I stare up at the ceiling. I'm twenty-seven and I've only had one sexual partner in my life. I feel anger suddenly rush through my body. Why the fuck should I be alone and as chaste as a bloody nun?

Restlessness fills me, making me want to kick my feet about like a horse in a field. I want to fuck and be fucked. I want to feel alive and not like I've been left on the scrapheap without a chance of anything different.

I think back to last thing when Niall had gone up to bed. He'd looked at me steadily for a long minute before smiling and leaving me. He hadn't said anything, but that look had been a challenge and I know my dick would be very happy to take him up on it.

I look at the closed bedroom door. In twenty steps I could be at his bedroom door. A few more and I'll be standing by his bed. Will he send me away?

I shake my head. I don't know much, but I know with a bone-deep certainty that he won't send me away. I don't know how it's happened, but he wants me and it's obvious. It must be for me to have spotted it. I hesitate. Do I want to do this? He is, after all, my older brother's best friend and casual fuck buddy. They've been screwing for years. Should I even try anything, knowing it has the potential to blow up in my face badly?

I think of pulling the covers back up over me and for a wild, mad moment it seems like it would be like pulling the winding sheet around my corpse. It would be so easy to sink back into my old life, but I don't want that anymore. It's served as my comfort and ease for so long, but I know I'm ready to move on, to stretch my legs and run free.

Resolution fills me, and I throw the covers back and bound from the bed. That resolution carries me across the hallway and stays with me right up until I'm standing over his sleeping body.

He's lying crossways over the huge bed, his body lax in sleep. He has one leg out of the covers as though seeking the cool air coming in from the open window that is bringing the scent of wet earth and pine into the room. The rest of him is huddled under the covers with just the silky strands of his hair showing. It's as if he has a faulty temperature control switch.

I hover there, trying to breathe quietly through my nose and hoping that I don't look like a total creeper. He must sense something because he stirs, stretching his legs out and giving a contented grunt. Then he goes still before exploding upwards in a flurry of movement that makes me step back in surprise.

He grabs my hand in his to stop the backward movement but doesn't let go. "Milo," he says hoarsely. "Is everything okay?" He pauses. "Is Cora alright?"

I swallow at the feel of the calluses on his hard hands. "She's fine, or at least I presume she is, seeing as she's up at the main house with her parents."

Still keeping hold of my hand, he reaches over and switches the lamp on. It fills the bedroom with its warm white light and we blink like little moles coming up from underground. "Then what is it?" he asks, looking at me searchingly yet seeming content to wait patiently.

I falter. "Erm, I just thought …" I pause. "I m-mean …" I stop in frustration and huff a cross sigh. I can't even ask someone to fuck me without bloody stammering.

However, Niall waits patiently the way he always does. He's never displayed any sign of irritation with me, and somehow it allows me to gather my words.

"Were you serious about teaching me about s-sex?" He stares at me and I launch into more words. *Why are there so many of them when I don't want them? They're like fucking buses.* "It would be just sex, of course. I know neither of us want a relationship." I falter, coming to a stop. "So, were you serious?"

I expect him to feign surprise or shock. Instead he stares at me, his eyes dark as something like caution flashes across his face before being replaced by – I swallow – heat.

"I was totally serious," he says deeply, the hoarseness in his voice catching me in my nuts and making my cock hard enough to pound stone. He looks into my eyes and throws back the covers. He's completely naked, his cock already hard against his tight stomach muscles. I gulp at the sight of his body, all that tanned skin glowing gold in the lamplight. "But make sure you lose those pyjamas," he says hoarsely. "I don't want anything between us in this bed."

It's surreal and part of me feels as if I'm standing to one side watching myself wrench my pyjama shorts down, baring myself to him while he looks on with avid eyes. But the other half is fully here and I wait, letting him look and trying to overcome the urge to cover my body from him. Thomas's words echo in my head of how ugly I am. Too thin, too scrawny, and pre-pubescent are just some of the nicer things he said. I shiver at the thought of him, but Niall misinterprets it.

"You're cold," he says hoarsely. "Get in here." He reaches a hand out and grabs my arm gently, pulling me into the bed and immediately swaddling me in sheets and blankets. For a second I lie there, stunned and inhaling the sweet woody scent that clings to the sheets. They're warm from his body and I snuggle further into them.

He lies at my side, his head on his hand, staring at me. Resisting the urge to put my hands over my eyes and pretend I haven't just got naked in front of him, I summon up my most haughty expression.

"Well?" I say, and watch fascinated as his lip twitches and his long nose wrinkles.

"Well what?"

"I think I said sex. Shouldn't you get to it? You're supposed to be teaching me."

He smiles. "Well, Lord Milo, we may have a problem. You see, in my classroom I don't lecture."

"You don't?" My voice is thready.

He shakes his head. "Nuh-uh. No. In my classes I prefer practical experiments."

I bite my lip, suddenly hesitant. "Is this role play?" I whisper. "Because I'm awkward enough, Niall. That would just about catapult me into the stratosphere of awkwardness." I watch as he throws his head back and breaks into fits of laughter. "Well, I'm glad I'm amusing you," I say sourly. "Shall I tell a few jokes? Maybe do a pratfall."

He sobers. "You're bothered by me laughing?"

"Of course," I huff. "It's not funny."

He reaches out and strokes my hair back with an intent and almost tender look on his face. "Then that's the first lesson for you, Lo. Sex can be funny. It's raunchy and smelly and noisy and it can make you come so hard you black out, but there is always room for laughter there too." He traces one long finger across my eyebrow. "Do you know that laughter is tied to the production of the same positive chemicals in our body that sex produces?" I shake my head and he grins. "If you think about it, they're both physical activities that are marked by a build-up in tension, a striving for something, and then the utter joy when we reach it." He shrugs. "Coming and laughter, they're the same thing."

"I worry for you if you ever go to a comedy show, Niall," I say dryly. "You'll probably be arrested on the spot." He collapses into the covers laughing heartily, and I repress a smile and fold my arms. "Well, I have to say you're a big disappointment so far. I come to you for instruction, knowing your sexual history, and instead I get inappropriate laughter and psychobabble. I'll have to go elsewhere."

He stops laughing and I gasp as in one lithe and sudden movement he levers up and over until he's lying on me. My arms come around him and my legs automatically part so he can lie between them, and I gulp as I feel the length of his cock rubbing against mine.

Suddenly all the laughter dies away to be replaced by a breathless tension.

He rests there for a long second, his weight resting on his bent arms while those incredible blue eyes stare into me assessingly. I don't know what he's looking for, but he must find it because he nods and bends and takes my mouth.

I'd be embarrassed by the strangled groan I give if I had any part of my brain left that wasn't concentrating on the feel of Niall Fawcett's tongue in my mouth, the sweet woody scent in my nostrils, and that long body that once fuelled all my dreams which is now lying between my legs.

We kiss for what seems like a millennium and when he pulls back, I lick my lips, tasting him on them and feeling their swollenness.

"Jesus," he mutters, his breathing fast and his body still moving almost unconsciously against mine in small, unhurried thrusts that threaten to make my eyes cross. "I'm not going to ask you if you're sure," he mutters. "I know you hate that, and I know you know your own mind."

"Good," I manage to get out before groaning as his thrusts get that little bit harder, making his cock rub against mine with the perfect amount of pressure that makes me feel like my head is going to explode. I can feel the wetness of my pre-come mixing with his and greasing the slide, and I want to both stop him because he'll make me come too soon, but at the same time let him do it and send me over the edge.

"Motherfucker," he hisses and manoeuvres back so quickly that I give a cry of surprise.

"What's the matter?" I moan, holding my arms out to him in a beseeching way that I know is going to make me want to punch myself in the head tomorrow. "Come back."

He rests back on his heels, his face reddened and his chest rising and falling quickly as he pants. I wonder for a wild second if I did something wrong, but then I look at his cock which is huge and hard and almost visibly throbbing against his belly button.

"What?" he says, and he almost sounds tender. "What do you see?"

"You have the prettiest cock," I say and then throw my hand over my eyes. "*Fuck*, I'm impossible."

"Take your hand away," he says, and the deep softness of his voice makes me do it without even thinking. "That's better." His lips are swollen and his hair a wreck. "Why is it pretty?"

"This is rather embarrassing."

"Power your way through it," he suggests, and I glare at him.

"It's long and hard. I can see the pre-come sliding down it." His cock jerks a tiny bit, thudding against the flat, hard stomach, and my mouth goes dry. "I want to suck it. I want to suck kisses over all those veins." He inhales sharply, and I look at his body. "I want to lick all of you."

He's still for a second and then he moves with that graceful economy that powers all his movements, levering off me and lying by my side. He looks at me. "Okay, then do it."

"Do what?" I ask, coming up on one elbow and trying really hard not to eye-fuck him.

"Kiss me, suck me, do what you want. I'm all yours, Lo."

I blink at my nickname. It sounds wrong in this bed but at the same time utterly right, like we were always destined to end up here. But then I blink again and throw the thought away. Niall Fawcett is naked in front of me asking me to lick him. It can't get any better than this. Then my happiness falls away and I realise that it could get worse, and before I can censure my words, I'm letting them spill out.

"I want to, but what if I do something wrong? Thomas used to say how terrible I was in bed, fumbling and awkward and just shit. What if he's right?"

He lets me speak, which surprises me given the flare in his eyes when I mention Thomas. When I come to a fumbling stop, he amazes me by shrugging. "So what?"

"What do you mean?" I go to draw back and he grabs my hand gently, bringing me back next to him.

"Lo, every single person in this world has been bad in bed at some point." He smiles and there's a wry, wicked curl to his smile. "My nanny always used to say that if at first you don't succeed you should try, try, and try again."

"Oh my God." I can't stop my smile. "That's outrageous. She probably meant when you embarked on a career in the city, not initiating an awkward man in bed."

He shrugs, caressing my palm with one long finger, watching me shudder as if I'm fascinating. "Life lessons should always be about something other than money. They should be about things that you're going to do for the rest of your life, which I profoundly hope you're going to do with sex rather than hide away." He pulls me close so I'm hovering over his chest, my fingers digging into the hard, ropy muscle over his torso to keep my balance. "Lo, it's you and me. You asked me to teach you sex. Well, the only way to teach something is to do it. Use me. Experiment on me. See what you like. See what I like. Lo, listen to me." My head shoots up from my study of the sparse hair that shadows his chest. His eyes are more serious than I've ever seen. "I will never laugh at you or mock you or demean you. You're free here in this bedroom and in this bed to do what you want, and I never want you to *ever* be ashamed of what we do here."

I nod, and he smiles before lying back and putting his hands behind his head. He nods down his body. "Explore, Lo."

Almost tentatively I send my hand out, looking at the paleness of it against his chest. Niall practically glows against the sheets as he has a golden tint to his skin that looks delicious against the white of the linen. I run my fingers down his chest, following the lines of his ribs and pausing when he jerks.

"Ticklish?" I ask, looking up and stilling at the darkness in his eyes. I swallow hard and his eyes track the motion of my throat.

"Very, and not just there," he says huskily and I grin at him, feeling suddenly freer than I ever have.

"I'll find it."

"I hope you do." He gives an indrawn breath and his body jerks as I send my fingers back up and brush over the bud of his nipple. The pale brown circle hardens under my eyes and I look up.

"Not ticklish but sensitive here?" He nods and gives a choked cry as I lean forward and run my tongue over it. Then before I can second-guess myself, I pull it into my mouth and start to suckle on it like a baby at the breast, my tongue flitting around the crinkled edge.

He groans and arches his body, forcing his chest against my mouth, and for a second I hesitate. Sudden movements in bed worry me, but his head is thrown back against the pillow and his eyes are watching me with a slumberous glow to them, and I relax suddenly. I did that. I put that look on his face, and suddenly I want to do it again and again and hear his pleasure. My doubts fly away, replaced by a lovely heat which I can feel in the base of my belly. My own cock throbs heavily, but I ignore it in favour of my new playground.

"I like this," I say hoarsely, and I can hear the need and joy in my voice. "I *love* it." Then I fall on him and, wrapping one arm around his muscular torso, I fasten my lips to his other nipple, sucking and pinching while he moves underneath me like the waves, thrusting his hips up, his cock wet and slick-looking.

I look at his dick and then back up at him. The memory of a time when I'd tried to blow Thomas is very vivid as he'd choked me, forcing his cock down my throat and holding my head against him. He'd laughed when I'd struggled because I couldn't breathe but he'd stopped laughing when I threw up on him. I breathe deeply to dispel the image.

"I don't want to suck you off. There's never been anything enjoyable about that to me," I say haltingly.

He opens his eyes. "What you want," he says. "No one else. This is about what *you* want." He shrugs. "Maybe you'll do it, maybe you never will. Doesn't matter to me. There are plenty of other things we can do."

"Like what?"

"You can fuck me, for a start."

"You'd do that?" The incredulity is clear in my voice.

"Of course I would. Lo, taking it up the arse doesn't mean you're weak the way that wankhole obviously told you." I jerk, and he smiles tenderly at me. "Sex is between the people concerned, their wants and needs, and I want you to fuck me. I need your cock inside me and I want to see you come." He shudders. "I want to feel it."

I sit up, squeezing my cock at the base to stop myself going off at just his words. His eyes follow my gesture and darken with need. "I want that," I say breathlessly. "I want that too."

He lies back and spreads his legs deliberately, giving me a clear view of his balls drawn tight to his body, and below, the dark line of his taint and the small hole. "Supplies are in the bedside table," he says.

I rush to get them, almost fumbling them, and look back expecting him to be smiling, but he isn't. Instead he's watching me, or more particularly he's looking at my bare arse high in the air while I look through the drawer, and he's jerking himself slowly.

"Like what you see?" I ask, breathlessly falling back onto the bed next to him, and he grins ferally.

"I love it," he says. "I want you, Lo."

"Okay, bear with me. I know the logistics," I say, squeezing the lube out in a glistening trail over my fingers and rubbing them together to warm it. "But I might need to ask questions."

"You can ask anything," he says hoarsely, his eyes on my hand as I lower it between his legs. "As long as you get one of those fingers in … ah!"

He arches up off the bed as I send one lubed finger sliding around his hole. For a split second I tense as if I've hurt him, but my body knows what to do and ignoring my mind I move, rubbing the finger gently over the small, tight opening before pushing the tip of it gently inside him.

"Oh fuck," he chokes out as I slide it into him, feeling the heat of his passage and the tight, snug fit of him. I imagine that around my dick and have to count to five not to come. I listen to the pants of his breaths and then watch in amazement as I rub across the harder spot inside him and he arches up with a shout coming from him that could wake the dead.

I rub it again. It's like a magic button, I think wonderingly as he sinks back to the bed, and wonder how I spent two years with Thomas and he never found it.

His voice thankfully drags me away from my ex. "Please, Lo," he groans. "Another finger, please."

Unexpectedly a surge of power fills me. I did this to him. Me. Boring old Milo Ramsay is making Niall writhe on the bed like he's had an electric shock. Boring old Milo Ramsay has his fingers inside Niall's body and pretty soon he'll have his cock in there too.

The thought galvanises me and I add another digit, stretching my fingers and scissoring them and feeling his passage open. "I won't rush this," I tell him, hearing the breathlessness. "I know how much it bloody hurts when it's not done properly." I think of the tearing and wince. I won't do that to Niall.

I still as his hand comes down over my hand at his passage, and when I look up, he's staring at me tenderly. "Thank you," he says gently.

I nod awkwardly, giving him a harried smile before pumping more lube over my fingers and adding a third digit. He tenses for a second and I rub my free hand down his long flank, feeling the hardness of the muscle and almost petting him.

He raises his head, his lips wet and his eyes dark. "Now. Fuck me now."

I stare at him, unable to believe that the time has come, but then break into action. The next few seconds are full of frantic fumbling as I manage to get the condom on and I only come back to myself when I'm kneeling and have my cock at the opening of his body.

I hesitate, and he looks at me. "Do it."

So I do. Notching my cock into the opening I push, fumbling for a second as I come up against the tight muscle that guards his passage, but I remember to wait until it relaxes and then it's a long, slow slide into tight, damp heaven as his passage sits snugly round my cock, gripping it tightly and making my eyes cross. I bottom out with a deep moan and rest for a second, the two of us panting until his legs come up round me and I feel his feet at my arse.

"Move, Milo," he says through gritted teeth. "Move and fuck me. I need it."

Now all thoughts go, and the only thing left is the instinct to please him. For the next few embarrassingly short minutes my only thoughts are snapshot impressions. The heat around my cock, the feel of his hard body against mine, the sweat from his hair landing on my hot skin and seeming to sizzle there like water in a frying pan. I can hear his pants and groans in my ear and the accompaniment of my own moans and sighs over the slap of flesh meeting flesh and the meaty thwap as my balls bang into his arse, making pain and pleasure sizzle together.

It takes only a few minutes before I despairingly feel the tingle in my balls as they pull tight. "Oh shit, I'm close," I say.

"Fuck me hard," he groans, reaching down and fisting his cock.

I dig my heels into the mattress and force myself into him harder than I'd ever imagined me doing, but he shouts out, tunnelling his head into the pillow behind him with his eyes screwed shut.

"Lo," he shouts out, and I knock his hand away from his cock, taking it in my grip and trying to coordinate my thrusts with jerking him off. It's hard to coordinate, like rubbing your head and your belly at the same time, but it has the effect on Niall of almost cattle-prodding him.

"Oh shit!" he shouts out and pumps his cock into my fist. "Milo!" Then he arches and goes rigid and I watch in awed amazement as creamy ropes of come spurt out from the slit, flooding my fingers and dribbling out onto his hard stomach.

His release catapults mine and I give two more battering thrusts, savouring the almost painful grip of his passage on my cock, and then cry out. "Oh fuck. Oh fuck, Niall." I jerk and come and jerk and come hard enough I have a second to worry that I'll overflow the condom, but eventually I come to a stop and fold into him, feeling the wet hardness of his body and the tight grip of his arms around me.

"Oh God," I say slowly, feeling like my tongue has swollen.

"Hmm," he says in a contented voice, his arms tightening to stop me moving. "Not for a second," he chides.

"Are you a *cuddler?*" I ask in an amazed voice.

"No shame in this bed," he says darkly and pauses. "Don't tell anyone, though."

I sink into his embrace, inhaling the acrid scent of sex and sweat happily. *I did that*, I think, feeling one hundred feet tall. *I made us come*. Then I stiffen. "Sorry it didn't take long," I whisper, feeling heat on my cheekbones.

"It was just right," he mumbles. "Not tortoise slow and not hare fast." I laugh and his grip tightens. "It was perfect," he says slowly. "Absolutely perfect."

There's a weight to his voice I can't work out. "*Really?*"

I feel his nod against the side of my face. "Absolutely perfect."

I take his words in and let them settle inside me and ease the sting of a cut I didn't know was still there.

"Perfect," I echo and snuggle closer.

CHAPTER 9

Your pertness is quite frankly over the top nowadays.

One Week Later

Niall

I lean against the fence that surrounds the bottom field, watching the tractor plough the ground. Neat lines draw back from it, like the tracks on a railway, and it's oddly fascinating. I hear the crunching of leaves and even before Boris, the golden retriever, bounces up next to me, I know it's Silas.

"Took you long enough," I say wryly. "I was expecting you a few days ago."

"Blame getting settled back into work and home life again or I'd have been out here within half an hour," he says, standing next to me and leaning against the fence. For a few minutes there's a companionable silence that's as familiar to me as the image of my childhood home.

I've known Silas for nearly all my life. We met at boarding school at the age of seven when we were set to room together. Within minutes of meeting the gentle dark-haired boy I'd known we were going to be friends, and it's a conviction that's never waned. We've lasted through schooldays, university, different partners on his part and hook-ups on mine. With both of us being bisexual it's amazing we've never hooked up, but I think there's always been this tacit understanding that it might wreck us, and that *us* was far more important than a singular.

He's my closest friend in the world. I can and do tell him everything, knowing he won't judge because that quiet boy has grown into an honourable and warm man. It's why I'm amazed we haven't had this discussion yet. It's also why I'm hiding out at the bottom field watching Phil plough a field when even he could do that in his sleep. It's why I'm ignoring my paperwork which is at Mount Etna proportions and just as ready to explode devastation all over my office. My secretary Barb has taken to leaving waspish messages on my mobile and I know she'll force a reckoning soon.

I just don't want to talk about Milo. I want to keep it to myself. Part of that is a vague feeling that Silas will not approve of what we're doing, and despite my casualness with people, Silas's good opinion matters to me. However, the largest part is that I can find no words to describe the last week. They come to my tongue, fumbling and hesitant, but then die away instantly in the maelstrom that is Milo.

That first night with him was like nothing I've ever experienced before. He might have been a bit awkward and fumbling, but the awe with which he touched me brought moisture to my eyes, and I've never felt so wrecked by the sexual act. I don't bottom easily. I find it difficult to give someone that trust, and it wouldn't have been there with any of my hook-ups because I hardly knew them. Yet with him I did it, because a deep-seated part of me trusts him. I feel like I know him on some sort of cellular level, and that hesitant man had taken me apart so thoroughly that when I came, I had tears in my eyes.

He's no longer hesitant and he seems to have woven a spell on me. Normally the daylight hours find me at work where I can easily blot out everything and get through the jobs of four men. This week I've hardly been there because of the temptation of Milo in my home. He never went back to the main house. Instead we brought back some of his equipment from his studio and he ensconced himself in my study, his wavy hair pulled back in a bandanna and his face lost and dreamy as he worked on the portraits.

The knowledge of him there has drawn me back constantly and as soon as I walk in, I know that his dreamy expression will clear instantly and he will walk towards me, his movements sure and languid now like coloured dye moving through water. He will take my hand and we'll vanish upstairs to the bedroom.

Up there it's as if time stands still, as if I've become trapped in a magic house in the woods, locked in a room where sensual pleasure is paramount and where the air echoes to the sounds of our moans and cries.

I shake my head to try and dispel the flowery images, but they linger there where I know they will grow in intensity and I will once again find myself on the threshold of my own house, shaking like a heroin addict and blowing everything away for the sake of a few fevered hours.

Silas's voice breaks into my thoughts and I turn to him, grateful for the intervention. "So, I can't help noticing that Milo isn't in his room at the house. Do you know where he is before I contact the emergency services?"

I shake my head. "You know where he is."

"Hmm." He leans on the fence with his chin resting on his hands, looking like the teenager I knew so long ago. "Then I suppose my question is *what* is he doing?"

"I'm pretty sure you know the answer to that too. One more question and you're done."

He gives me a swift grin that quickly dies away to concern. "Then I have to ask, what are you doing?"

I turn to face the field again, my brow furrowed, unable to meet his steady eyes. "I don't know," I say quietly. "It's taken me a bit by surprise."

"Niall, I know you love to live up to the image of the Lord of Misrule, but this is going a bit far."

"Didn't the Lord of Misrule only reign over Christmas?"

"Don't distract me." He pauses. "But you are right." He shakes his head. "No. Stick to the subject, Silas." I smile but it dies with his next words. "Niall, this is serious. You were fucking his brother last month and now suddenly you're with him. Does Gideon know?"

"No," I say sharply. "It's none of his business."

"Says you. Gideon might say otherwise."

"Gideon can," I say firmly. "But we have no ties and we've never made any promises."

"Niall, I'm pretty sure that covenant didn't include fucking his brother. I know Gideon is relaxed but that's ridiculous." He stares at me. "And what about Milo? What's he going to do when this collapses around you like a paper card house?"

"Perhaps you'd be better off being more concerned about me," I say curtly. "Milo is just experimenting and getting his feet wet." I look at Silas. "You know what Thomas did to him." His face clouds with anger and I nod. "Well, those scars go deep, and Milo hasn't got the experience to know that what he had with that wanker is very far from a healthy sexual relationship." He winces, and I nod. Anything else is Milo's secret, not mine. I shrug and turn back to the field. "He's just trying things out with someone familiar. Someone he trusts enough not to belittle or hurt him."

"Why does he trust you?"

The question is gentle, but it stings me like he's taken a blade to my flesh. "I may be carefree, Silas, but I'm not fucking cruel. I would do anything for him. *Anything*," I repeat fervently.

There's a short – and I just know that it's shocked – silence. Then he taps me on the arm until I turn to him. He has a wondering expression on his face. "Oh my God," he says quietly. "You care for him."

"Of course I do. He's my oldest friend's brother and he's my friend too." The latter is said a little too hard to be convincing. He shakes his head. He'll allow me to get away with this now, but I know we'll return to it later. Silas is big on friendship and taking care of people.

"Even so, please be careful, Niall. I'm even more worried now."

"Why?"

"Because Milo, despite being shy, has an ability to bounce back from things. He's not aware of it but it's always there. It's like he's made of a very quiet and unassuming India rubber. But *you*."

He pauses, and I turn. "What?"

"You are very different," he says softly. "For all your flippancy, you're still the boy I first met who was loyal and honest and believed in true love. Wasn't it you who told me that it would come?"

I feel a flush on my cheeks. "Silas, we were ten. I still thought Father Christmas was real, albeit rather creepy with all that letting himself into strangers' houses and helping himself to food. Obviously, I didn't know a lot."

"Or maybe you were the one who really did."

I shake my head. "Silas, I hate to tell you this, but he doesn't live in the North Pole and elves did not organise your Christmas presents."

"That certainly accounts for the year I got a bottle of gin for Christmas. I always thought Santa had been having a bad day. My mother obviously forgot to go to the shops."

I laugh but sober quickly. "I don't believe in true love and that's patently obvious. I've had too many partners to count, unless we're using your fingers and mine and the villagers after that."

"You haven't had partners. You've had hook-ups," he says sternly. "A partner is someone you trust and someone who trusts you. Someone to make you laugh and someone who can make you so mad you want to leave, but at the same time so happy that you know you'll never go. A partner is someone who is there for you in good and bad times and all the in-between stuff."

"Well, that's lovely. Excuse me for not wanting to sign up for all that. It sounds positively exhausting."

"You've never signed up for it because you've never met anyone worth doing that for." He pauses. "Or maybe you've just been waiting for Milo. Waiting for him to get well and for your time to come."

"Ugh! You should give up veterinary medicine and take up writing romance. You've got appallingly and embarrassingly Mills and Boon since you met that small Irishman."

He shakes his head, an arrested expression on his face. "That's it, isn't it. I've always thought you were almost in suspended animation, and the way you hovered over him and got him better, he couldn't have had a better or more caring nurse." I grimace at him and he bites his lip. "Don't get me wrong. I don't think for a second that you did it with any forethought. That would be like Scooby Doo writing a criminology handbook." He laughs, and I glare at him until he coughs and returns to his ridiculous subject matter. "I just think you were waiting for him and you didn't know it. You've been biding your time, waiting for him to see you properly."

"I'm sure you've taken that plot from a book that probably had the words billionaire and love-child in it," I say sourly.

He laughs. "Hmm, I think that's probably one of your old ones. Didn't I catch you reading your mother's Mills and Boon once?"

"I was twelve and I told you at the time that it was for the sex scenes," I say crossly. "And may I remind you that we swore an oath never to mention it again."

He mimes zipping his mouth but breaks the solemnity when he bursts into peals of laughter. Eventually he straightens up. "I'm sorry. Let's go back to the fact that you and Milo are obviously destined to be together."

"Good luck with spinning that. He thinks I'm as bad as Thomas,"

I say morosely, that idea still having the power to stun me with how much it hurts.

His laughter dies immediately. "What? *Really?*" I nod and he shakes his head. "Rubbish," he says stoutly. I sneak a look at him. He's gazing at the field, but I can almost feel all his attention on me now like it's an invisible shield deflecting blows and protecting me.

"You don't think I am?" The question is hesitant and comes from the quiet times this week when I've lain with Lo's sleeping form curled against me, his head resting on my shoulder and my nostrils full of the scent of lemon and rosemary, that sharp, sweet aroma which is so him. From those quiet times that worry has grown and flourished. "I mean, I'm loud and confident and I do ride roughshod over people sometimes."

"Shut up," he says fiercely, and I subside. I need him to tell me because Silas always tells the truth. "Yes, you're loud and of course you're confident. That's not a sin. You just have a lot to be confident about. But you're also kind and generous, blisteringly honest and eminently trustworthy. I would trust my heart to you." He smiles. "I did, and she came back safe and sound."

"In the spirit of honesty, that was probably more Milo than me. He has an affinity for babies."

He turns and grabs my arms. "Listen carefully, Niall, and really hear me. You care about people deeply, but you offset that with flippancy, so people don't spot it immediately. And I know that if you were to upset someone it would wound you terribly. You could no more do that to Milo than you could cut off your own arm."

I swallow hard, feeling those impassioned words drift over the sore part of me like a soothing ointment mending a crack that was bigger than I thought. But the biggest doubt remains.

"You see that because you know me. He can't see it, and what if he never does?"

"Then you'll be hurt," he says quietly. "Badly. And that worries me, Niall, because I love you and I don't want to see you hurt. But then again, I'll rejoice because you're finally experiencing true feelings and that's good." He pauses and cocks his head to one side. "But I don't think I need to be worried."

"Why?"

"Because Milo can't see you properly for who you are at the moment but deep inside, he knows you. He understands that he can trust you."

"How do you know that?"

"Because he's trusted you with this. He's given you a side of him that only one other person knows, and he's done it with the innate knowledge that you'll treat that gently and you won't harm him." He smiles. "So, have a little hope, Niall. I have enough to spare."

He leaves me soon after that, muttering about how he's home early enough to bathe Cora for a change, and I smile as I watch him go. I couldn't be happier for him because in Oz he's found someone who loves him completely and watches out for him. Makes me feel like I can set that down now because it always used to be my job.

I settle back against the fence in my idle watching pose, and I'm so deep in thought that when his hand comes down on my arm, I give a rather high shriek and jump in the air. I whip round to find Milo looking at me. His face is split into a wide grin and his eyes are alight with amusement.

I straighten my clothes. "I did that for you," I mutter.

He snorts. "Thank you. It was quite lovely."

I shake my head, trying to conceal my grin, and settle back against the fence, gratified when he immediately leans into me. I savour the feeling of his warm body against mine and the fact that a week ago he'd have hesitated to touch my hand, and now it's as if he has part ownership of my body. Whenever I'm near him some part of him will immediately touch me, whether it's his hand on my arm or side or the way he'll swing his legs over mine when we sit watching TV. And I like it. No, I love it, and that's a huge revelation to me. I've always thought of myself as very open and I've obviously had many sexual partners, but their touches were usually the prelude or finish to a sexual act. Milo's touch comes quite simply because he wants to touch me.

We stand quietly for a while until he shivers and I turn to him. He's wearing black skinny jeans, old Vans, and a thin black jumper under some sort of oversized grey woollen hoody. I frown. "No wonder you're cold. You've got hardly any clothes on for gallivanting about in the woods."

He smirks. "You okay there? Did you enjoy your trip back to Victorian England?"

I smile and shake my head. "Your pertness is quite frankly over the top nowadays."

He laughs and settles his body further into me, and I kiss the top of his head and inhale the scent of lemon and rosemary that clings to him. He stiffens as if surprised and I immediately launch into counter manoeuvres. "Milo, your hair is extraordinary. It's expanding as I look at it."

"Shut up." He nudges me. "I can't help it. It's flyaway."

"But it isn't," I say patiently. "Because it's all still here rather than flying off somewhere." I savour his laughter about something he was so worried about at one time and drag him close. He mumbles objections, but they're so fainthearted they're laughable because the truth is that Milo is a cuddler too. In bed he's like a human octopus when he goes to sleep. All arms and happy snuffling.

I fish my thick gloves out. "Here, put these on. You're freezing."

He shakes his head but lets me help him and only raises his eyebrows when I remove my beanie from a pocket and pull it down over his mass of hair, loving the way it accentuates his winged eyebrows and sharp chin. With his eyes sparkling with mirth he looks so cute I can't stand it, so I go back to my view of the field.

"Why are you watching Phil plough?" he says after a few minutes of silence. "Are you looking for tips in case the estate managing gig falls through?"

"The only way I'm falling through anything is in a big hole and I'd still have to dig it because Phil can't do anything right," I say tartly.

"This morning I asked him to turn over the ground in the east field. It's only pure chance that I managed to stop him ploughing up the Kayling Lawn."

He shudders. "The tales Oz has told me about that place, I hope you were wearing a Hazmat suit."

"With a full face guard. You can't afford to take chances," I say solemnly, loving the way he laughs. It's open and joyous rather than the muted sounds he always used to make, which were immediately followed by a haunted glance around like he was going to be punished for the gift of laughter. I inhale deeply to quell the desire to punch Thomas, which grows stronger every day.

He looks at me curiously. "You okay?"

"Yes, of course," I say hurriedly. "Just a bit tense with all the work on here."

He stares at me for a long second and then grins, but it's a wicked smile with mischief written over every centimetre of his face.

"Oh no," I say slowly. "That look never means good things."

"It does," he says primly. "But just for you."

"You bet it's just for me," I growl and then flush as he looks at me with his mouth open in amazement. To forestall any smart remarks I fit my lips to his, kissing the full curves before sending my tongue flitting inside to tangle and rub against his. He rewards me with a deep moan and suddenly my arms are full of him as he pushes me against the fence, kissing me furiously while rubbing against me.

He breaks away for breath and I inhale, feeling woozy. "Shit," I murmur, and he nods frantically before dropping to his knees in front of me. "Oh my God," I mutter. "What are you doing?"

He pulls off my gloves and hands them to me before unbuttoning my jeans, his brow furrowed in concentration. I look behind me quickly, but Phil has crested the wave of the hill and is now out of sight, so we're the only two people around for miles.

I look back down at him and hiss as he reaches into my briefs and pulls out my cock. "Fuck, your hands are cold," I say hoarsely, and he looks up at me, his eyes sparkling with humour and life.

"I know. Your dick is now cold, and I suppose it would be quite kind of me to warm it up for you, wouldn't it?"

"You are kind," I say in a low voice and then groan in gratified surprise as he licks a strip up my very erect cock.

"Lo," I groan, knocking the hat off his head and grabbing a handful of his waves gently and pulling his face up to me. "Are you sure?" He hasn't attempted this yet and I instinctively get why not. I just try not to understand too much because even the subtext of his worries makes me so mad at Thomas that I could weep with rage. He opens his mouth with a frown on his face, but I forestall him. "I know you don't want me to ask these things because you want to be treated like everyone else."

"I do."

"But you're not everyone else," I say calmly. "You're Lo and you mean something to me, so I need to ask this just once and then we'll never speak of it again."

He kneels up and grabs my hips in his cold hands. Then, keeping my gaze, he leans forward and in a deliberate motion he takes the head of my cock into his mouth and starts to suck.

"Oh God," I groan. "Okay, you're fine. I understand that."

He hums under his breath and pulls back before taking me deeper this time. I groan at the feeling of his hot mouth and cold hands and then murmur in concern when he tries to take me too deep and chokes.

"Easy," I croon. "Take your time. There's no need to deep throat. You're not Linda Lovelace."

He obeys me instantly, backing up before taking me at a different angle, using his hand on the base and taking the rest into his mouth and sucking hard while fluttering his tongue along the frenulum.

"Oh fuck," I gasp. Feelings swirl in me as he starts to suck in earnest. Sensation upon sensation piling onto the already high heap of feelings of gratitude that he picked me along with a fierce pang in my heart to know that while he listens to me in bed, his confidence outside is growing so quickly that he's showing his true self, which is feisty and lively. I love that he feels comfortable with me enough to do that.

Then all my thoughts fly away. "Oh fuck," I choke. "God, darling, that's amazing. Keep going." I grunt as he cups my balls in his hand. "Fuck, that's good. Roll them." He obliges before sending a finger wet from his spit back to my hole where he rubs it gently and almost tenderly.

I look down at him and have to close my eyes for a second at the image of him with his mouth stuffed full of my cock and the almost transcendent pleasure on his face. "Take your cock out," I order. "Touch yourself."

He moans around my dick and sends one hand down to fumble at the opening of his jeans. Then it's my turn to moan as he withdraws the ruddy length and starts to jerk himself off.

"Oh fuck," I moan. "So hot. That's it. Suck me now." He returns to his task and within seconds I can feel that tingle in my bollocks. "Oh God, I'm close," I grunt. "Move off if you don't want a mouthful."

He gives a tiny shake of his head and carries on sucking me, one hand holding the base of my cock so I don't choke him while my hips are moving, thrusting at his mouth, chasing my pleasure. His other hand is a tight fist through which his own cock is shuttling. The sight of the red, slick head in his fist and the feel of his mouth send me over and I cry out so loudly it disturbs some birds nearby. I come, pouring myself into his mouth in a seemingly endless flow while crows wheel in the sky around us, cawing crossly.

I'm still coming when he moans, and I look down with bleary eyes to see him shooting in great spurts over the grass at his feet.

For a second we stay still, panting and wheezing, but then he shivers again and I urge him to his feet. I help him with his clothes, straightening them and pulling his huge hoody around him again before doing my own with cursory attention. Then I grab his hand full of come and suck and lick it slowly off while he watches me with fascinated eyes. By the time I've finished his cheeks are red and renewed lust is brewing there.

I sling my arm over his shoulders, feeling the slender bones underneath that old jumper and inhaling the smell of him. In these woods with his wavy hair and sharp, angular face he looks almost fey.

"Come on back to the house," I mutter. "I'm going to feed you and then we're going to fuck some more. There's so much more to learn."

That open, lusty expression crosses his face, turning him into someone earthy and warm. "Surely there isn't more?"

I grin, feeling like I should be banging my chest, and instead bend in to nuzzle his neck. He moans, and I feel my cock stiffen so fast it should give me friction burns. "So much more," I promise him.

I guide him down the path to my house, burying my face in his neck and whispering filthy thoughts until he stops dead in his tracks.

"Lo?" I say questioningly, following his gaze which is full of trepidation and fixed on the forecourt of my house where a figure is standing. The figure turns slowly and elegantly, and I know before I even see his face.

"Gideon," I gasp.

CHAPTER 10

This is where you are. So, if I want to sleep that's where I must be.

Milo

With a sinking in my stomach I feel Niall's arm drop from around me, and in three strides he reaches my brother and drags him into a tight, laughing hug. I shift on my feet, watching them anxiously. They're the same height, both big and bold, but while Niall is golden and seemingly gilded by the late afternoon sun, my brother is his dark foil. His black hair is cropped close to his head and he's grown a beard since I saw him last. It suits him, giving him a piratical intensity accentuated by his ice-blue eyes.

Only they aren't icy now. They're warm and affectionate as he hugs Niall and says something into his ear. Then they fall onto me and an indecipherable expression comes into them. I swallow. I love my brother and I know he loves me, but circumstances in our childhood meant a close relationship was never going to happen.

He's older than me, being the same age as Niall. I was a late baby and treated very differently from Gideon. While he was ferried off to boarding school when he was seven as so many children in our circle were, I was kept at home, babied by my parents because of the speech defect. I'd always thought that my mother felt guilty over Gideon and had seized the opportunity to correct her parental deficit by going in the opposite direction with me.

However, I'd adored him, dogging his footsteps when I was little, and he'd been kind and generous initially, but as time passed I think he found his family in Niall and Silas. He got more and more distant and preoccupied and with an air of almost melancholy about him. Then his star had taken off when he was in the sixth form and he abandoned his studies for the film role that launched him into the stratosphere and far away from me. Now, all that's left is a vague filial relationship and a sad yearning for more on my side.

He smiles at me and as normal, there's a sad twist to his mouth. It's always there, giving all his performances a tragic, flawed air. Critics praise it, but I know it's not acting. It's who he is, and it saddens me. He releases Niall and comes towards me.

"Little brother," he says in his deep, rich voice with the roughness in it that's led to him becoming the king of the audiobooks. He's narrated so many of them that Niall once recorded him asking for a cup of tea and used it for his ringtone.

"Gideon," I say and swallow as he brings me into a hug. It's more tentative than the one he gave Niall, but I feel his warm arms around me, and the scent of his grapefruit shampoo reminds me of when I was little and had a nightmare and he came to me. Rather than ignore my fears he'd listened intently and then appointed one of my cuddly toys as my guardian, lecturing Paddington sternly and propping him by the wardrobe. It had worked far better than my mother's dismissal of my fears and I'd slept securely after that. The memory makes affection uncurl in me, sweet and slow, and I hug him back robustly, ignoring his shocked inhale and then feeling his body soften against me.

He kisses my forehead and steps back. "You're looking well," he says, examining my face.

I shrug. "I feel well." I can't resist a quick look at Niall and find him examining me intently with a half-smile playing on those full lips.

Gideon glances between us, his brow furrowing, and he shoots Niall a strange look. "You were right to bring him here."

"I'm always right," Niall says complacently and grins lazily at me when I snort.

Gideon laughs. "I can think of many times you weren't. Do you remember the time at school when you insisted that you could put tin cans in the microwave? I honestly thought we were going to be expelled." Then they're off, laughing together over a time I can't share, and I step back, feeling stung and absurdly lonely.

And it is absurd to feel that way because I have no right. Niall and I are … My brain stutters. I don't know what Niall and I are, but it's certainly nothing compared to the relationship he had with Gideon. My stomach clenches. *Has.* The relationship he has with Gideon. It's still going on and I'd forgotten that, lost as I've been in the passion we've found this week, the connection. I'd forgotten that my brother has a much bigger claim on him.

My thoughts scatter as a woman appears from around the side of the house. Rail thin and wearing a dress that's so short it could be a pelmet, she has blonde hair and a beautiful wild face. She looks like a fairy conjured up from the woods. Her mouth opens and it immediately dispels the notion. "Fucking hell, Niall. Where have you been? I'm dying for a pee."

Her voice is impossibly posh but there's a slur to it and her eyes are bright.

"Jacinta," Niall says. He looks at me quickly and almost guiltily, and I see Gideon note the movement and his eyes sharpen. "What are you two doing here?"

"We were invited," Gideon says, and Jacinta goes to him, wrapping her long, thin body around his. "Don't you remember?" Niall's brow furrows and Gideon laughs. "We were in bed at the Dean Street Townhouse and Jacinta had to head off for a modelling job. You said to bring her down and we'd finish the night more thoroughly. Do a proper job of it." He shrugs, looking at Niall intently. "So, here we are. Entertain us."

"Stop quoting Nirvana," Niall says curtly. He looks at me again, his eyes eating my face up and an air of worry about him. "Milo," he says almost imploringly, and I stiffen. I am definitely in the way again, like always, and my stomach lurches. I feel suddenly like the child I'd once been following him around, begging him to notice me when all his attention was always and forever tied up with Gideon.

I step back again. A bigger step this time. "It's fine," I say, and I'm so proud and relieved in this moment that my voice holds up. I don't need to stutter to relegate myself to desperate hanger-on. I've always been that. I make myself smile at my brother and Jacinta. She looks bored and glazed while he still has that watchful air about him. "I've been staying here while the heating was off but I think it's back on now, so I'll get out of Niall's hair and let you all get on …" My voice falters but I stiffen my spine. "Get on with what you have planned."

I take another step and then before Niall can stop me, which he definitely is going to do judging by the aborted move that he makes towards me, I half walk and half run back down the path. It's not the most graceful exit I've ever made, and my face flames in embarrassment.

After five minutes I come to a stop, leaning against a tree and fumbling for my inhaler in my coat pocket. After a quick puff, I feel the tight grip of my lungs ease a little, but I stay still for a second. The woods are silent around me, apart from the wind rustling the leaves and the soft slither as they fall gracefully to the ground.

He hasn't followed me. The fact is stark in my head, no matter how I try to bolster myself. All week I've looked on this as some daring experiment on my behalf, a chance to exorcise my childhood crush and move on with life. It had been so stupid because it's not freed me from my infatuation. Instead, it's entangled me further in its clutches.

I look up at the darkening sky, the sun sinking into the horizon and leaving behind a cold navy sky shot through with red, and I shiver as a chill seizes me. This week has been so amazing. I never knew sex could be like that. Before it had been painful and awkward and filled with a half-formed permanent fear that Thomas would really let go and hurt me. Being with Niall has been as different as night and day. Or maybe a deep, warm twilight when the whole world seems touched with purple and gold and hovering on the brink of beauty.

I've explored every inch of his warm body, inhaling the scent of him into my body, twisting him and turning him, all that power at my command. I've watched him shudder and come, looking more naked and vulnerable at that moment than I'd ever dreamed he could.

But he's done the same to me, and I see now that while I revelled in my power to make him groan and cry out, he's been exerting his own power over me and not just in the ability to make me come harder than I ever thought possible.

Instead, he's talked to me. Lying side by side, sharing the same pillow with the sweat drying on our bodies, he's shared things. Favourite things, childhood memories. He's fed me, bringing plates of cheese and fruit to bed and licking the sticky juices from my lips. I'd seen it as just refuelling for the next bout. A sort of foreplay, but it wasn't that. It was so much more.

I shake my head. If I'm not careful I'll be right back where I started. Wanting him more than anything I've ever desired and somehow weak in that wanting. I square my shoulders. I'm not going back to that, begging for scraps of attention and becoming less in the begging.

Nevertheless, I look back once more before starting up the path to *Chi an Mor*.

He didn't follow me.

. . .

Niall

I watch the lithe and graceful figure of Milo disappear down the path. "Shit!" I say forcefully. "Shit!"

I go to step after him, but I'm brought up short by Gideon's restraining hand on my arm. "Gideon," I say warningly, but he shakes his head.

"I don't think so. You and I should have a little talk first."

"Talk," Jacinta pouts, inserting herself between us, her slim body pale against the tan and brawn of our bodies. "Why are we talking? Let's fuck."

I look down at her, feeling as removed from this display as if I'm bricked off by an invisible wall. There isn't even a stir from my cock and I know in that second that I'm fucking doomed. "Not tonight," I say smoothly, detaching myself from her arms and stepping back. "I need to go after Milo."

"I don't think so," Gideon says, and the coolness of his voice is roughened by either anger or concern. I can't tell which, but for the first time in years, his calm demeanour is looking slightly ruffled. "First we talk about my brother. What the fuck is going on between the two of you?"

"You're fucking Milo?" Jacinta purrs, sniffing slightly and wiping her nose. "That's so hot. Do you think he'd join us?"

"No," Gideon and I shout in stereo and she shrugs sulkily.

"I can already tell this weekend is going to be fucking boring. The two of you are getting staid." Then she brightens and roots around in her pocket before retrieving a small plastic packet with a triumphant air. "This will sort you both out. Just what you need. Have a bit of blow. It's amazing shit."

I push her hand gently back. "No thanks, and you won't be doing that in my house either, Jacinta." She pouts at me, but I shake my head sternly. "Not even once. I catch you piling that shit up your nose in a house where a baby visits and you and I are going to fall out in a big way."

She shrugs crossly and turns to Gideon, winding her way around him. "Such a party pooper," she slurs. "Niall's no fun anymore. He's got so boring and suburban lately. Fix him with your magic cock, darling."

He stands still, his face set and chilly in the darkening light. "I don't think that's going to work anymore."

I feel a pang of something like sorrow and loss in my belly and chest. It's always been Gideon for me. The two of us bonded and have never let go since the early days at school. Silas has always been my best friend, but Gideon and I were something more. We were each other's family and my loyalty to him was unswerving.

I've fucked him and Jacinta in so many different variations. It was hot and fierce but over the last few years, it's been the only way that I could be with Gideon because he wields Jacinta and other women between us like a sword cutting off his real desires as if they'll die and go away. I know it tortures him, but I can't be part of that. I know it with a sudden deep certainty, and looking at him, I can tell he realises it too.

Jacinta huffs and wanders towards the house, calling for her cases to be brought in, but he and I stand still staring at each other. For a few minutes there's silence except for the distant hooting of an owl, but then he stirs and turning, he starts to walk to the house. I notice the fucker has left his bags as well, like I'm their butler as well as their co-fucker.

He looks back and inclines his head at me. "Come on," he commands. "You and I need to have a chat."

I look back longingly at the way Milo went but he shakes his head. "Now, Niall. You owe it to me to tell me what the fuck is going on with you and my baby brother." The anger vibrates through his voice as well as something that sounds very much like pain. It's that last note that makes my feet move reluctantly after him like he's wielding the dark magic of my loyalty to him to make me obey. I look back once more at the now dark lane before shaking my head.

I have to make this right because otherwise there will be no going forward with Milo, and the desire to do that is becoming stronger every second I'm away from him.

Milo

I manage to get halfway up the first set of stairs to the attic without seeing anyone, but as soon as I hear footsteps behind me, I sigh resignedly.

"Well hello, Milo. I thought you'd moved out," an amused voice calls out.

I turn and face him on the stairs. "You know very well that I haven't."

Oz shrugs, his face alight with mischief. "How would I know? You never call. You never write. You use this place like a hotel."

"I'm sure this lecture is being recycled from your mum."

He laughs. "If it was it would be minus a lot of expletives. You try not calling her for a week and see what you get."

I turn and walk up the stairs, the sound of my feet on the wood as familiar as the skin on the back of my hands. I clear the stairs and look around the attic rooms that are mine. I claimed this area when I moved out of Niall's rooms as soon as I felt better. Silas had offered me a lovely room with a view over the lavender garden, but somehow this place at the top of the house seemed more me.

I came up here and fell in love with the beamed ceilings and the sloping wooden floorboards that were scuffed and worn to a soft, dusty sheen by generations of Ashworth servants. I remember clearing away the cobwebs from the windows and seeing all the way down the majestic gravelled driveway until it curved away into the distance. Another window gave a panoramic view of the sea and I placed my bed directly opposite that, so now I can curl up at night watching the moonlight sparkle on the waves.

Despite the uncomprehending objections of Niall and Silas, I spent a few weeks up here clearing out the attics of all the broken furniture and old boxes. I then sanded the floorboards and varnished them. Niall had insisted on helping, and I'm sure if we've left any remnant of ourselves here for future generations, it will be Niall's curses that will echo down time. One day *Most Haunted* will visit and all their machinery will pick up is an endless repetition of the word *motherfucker*.

Once that was done, I set about painting the walls. Niall had taken one look at my colour choices and blanched, refusing to do any more and saying it looked like a brothel. I look around and hum contemplatively because actually, it looks like a lovely, warm boudoir.

One wall is painted a deep purple. In front of it is the golden-coloured sofa that I'd found in the corner of the attic and cleaned up because it was insanely comfortable. Now, it's stuffed with cushions and soft throws and it's my favourite place to read, like a warm jewelled nest.

The other walls are painted a deep golden colour. Against one wall is my bed, which is a huge cast iron monstrosity that generations of children have probably been born in. But it's wide and has the most comfortable mattress I've ever lain on. And when I lie with the sheets and blankets piled around me, I feel warm and safe.

Through one door is a small bathroom with a cast iron bath and a shower that's inserted neatly into the slope of the ceiling. It's painted a bright peacock blue, and when candles are lit it's like sitting inside a sapphire.

There's also a small kitchen, which Silas insisted on putting in. I still remember him looking around with a half-sad smile on his face, saying that he hoped I would feel free up here and safe from everyone. At the time I didn't understood his sadness because safety and solitude were things I yearned desperately for. Now, I think I get it because this place has been my sanctuary for too long and I recognise that fact now that I don't want to retreat here anymore like a tortoise into its shell. It's like I've been asleep for a long while, but now I'm coming awake slowly and at times painfully.

I look around and have a sudden yearning to be back in Niall's bed with the curtains billowing in the wind while I snuggle under covers that smell of a mix of our sex and nestle into the heat of his body as he grabs me tighter. I remind myself that he's probably wrapped around Gideon and Jacinta's bodies at the moment and feel the dip of my stomach like I might throw up.

The clattering of footsteps is a welcome interruption to my thoughts, and I turn to see Oz pushing into the room. "Fucking hell," he gasps. "You must be part mountain fucking goat, Milo. Only that could explain why you aren't purple in the face after climbing those stairs."

"The stairs aren't that steep," I say, smiling. "You just need to work on your fitness."

"I'd have to have the fitness of Tom Daley to cope with those stairs."

He throws himself onto the sofa, disappearing into the cushions for a second. Wriggling around, he reappears and pats the seat next to him invitingly. "Come to Oz, Milo. Let's have a look at you."

"Please don't say that. Our old nanny used to use the phrase shortly before she made us clean our ears out."

"Well, I'm sure you're perfectly capable of cleaning your own small appendages." He pauses. "At least I hope so." I chuckle, and he grins. "Come and sit down. I need to talk to you."

I grimace. "Is it something to do with Niall?"

"Nooo," he says somewhat unconvincingly. "I just want to know why you've come home."

"So, it is about Niall."

"Ah, but you mentioned his name, not me," he says somewhat triumphantly. "Please remember that if Silas questions you." He turns suddenly serious, giving me that far-reaching look that always makes you think that he really knows you. I look at the smile in his eyes. Knows and likes you.

I shake my head defeatedly and slink over to the sofa. "Okay," I sigh. "Let's get it over with."

He makes a moue of distaste. "*Please,* Milo. You're making this so much more painful than it should be."

"How is that even possible? Okay, I'm home because it was time for me to come back."

Silence reigns for a second. "And that's it?" His disgust is my undoing and I snort. "No, seriously, is that it? No drama, no throwing of pots, no cutting up of clothes?"

"You've been watching one of the *Real Housewives* programmes again, haven't you?"

"It's either that or *In the Night Garden,* which is a lot less exciting than the name makes it sound." He stares at me. "No argument at all?"

I give him a look of incomprehension. "Oz, this is me. When would I ever use loud words and shout?"

He shakes his head. "All the time around Niall. He brings it out in you."

I sigh and lie back against the sofa, grabbing a throw and winding it around my shoulders. "That's not very good, is it?"

"Yes, it is," he says simply, moving in next to me so he can share the throw.

I look around in an attempt to distract. "I need to turn the heater on up here." He doesn't take the bait, so I give in with a sigh and look back at him. "Why is it good?"

"Because it shows you're alive." He shudders and twists the throw closer. "Although I'm beginning to doubt that if you're staying in this temperature. Milo, it's like a meat freezer up here."

"I never notice it."

"That's because for the last week you've been wrapped around the handsome estate manager." He pauses before saying with a tone of delighted revelation, "Oh my God, it's like *Lady Chatterley's Lover.* Oh, please make Niall develop an accent like Sean Bean. It'd make him so attractive."

"Well, if he wants tips on doing accents, he could ask for them from my brother who is staying with him at the moment."

"What?"

I nod and close my eyes. "Yep. Gideon is down there. I'd say he hasn't wasted any time replacing me but that would be ridiculous because I was always in Gideon's place. Keeping it warm for the real owner."

"What utter bollocks."

My eyes fly open. "What?"

"You heard. That's such a load of crap."

"You do know that they've been sleeping together since they were at secondary school?"

"I do now," he says primly. "Silas had to spill the beans."

"How did you get him to tell you that?"

He twists his lips. "I have my ways."

I shake my head. "I'm sure you have. Don't tell me because you might scar me for life."

Amusement flares in his eyes but it vanishes quickly and he twists to face me. "I knew Niall had a good mate that he was fucking for years. I didn't know it was your brother and I had no idea he also happened to be a very well-known actor famed for his voice and acting ability."

I sigh. "I know. Now can you see why I was just a bed warmer."

"No."

I stare at him and the abrupt way he said it. "What?"

He grimaces. "Niall's been fucking him for years, but I'll tell you right now he has never been emotionally attached to him. Silas says he never fell for him."

"He's closer to Gideon than anyone other than Silas."

"He might be. Doesn't mean that he fell for him. I tell you now, I know how Niall looks when he's interested. I wonder that you can't tell the difference."

"Why would I be able to?"

"Because the person he looks at like that is you."

"It is not," I scoff, feeling my heart begin to beat fast. "You've been reading too many Catherine Cooksons."

"While it's true that Mrs. Cookson does prepare you for any eventuality to do with badly behaved men, I don't need her to see the truth about Niall. I just need a workable pair of eyes. Even Silas has noticed."

Hope twists in my heart. "Has he?" Then I slump. "No, I think you're seeing things. We're just fucking at the moment. It doesn't mean anything. If there's softness there it's because of who I am in relation to Gideon, not for myself. Niall has never seen me as anything other than a little brother."

"I think that's more of a plot for *Hollyoaks*," he says primly, then sighs. "You're wrong. Out of everyone, Niall has always seen you clearer than anyone. It's like he has X-ray specs just for someone called Milo Ramsay."

"Well, I hope he's taken them off while he fucks my brother and Jacinta tonight, or it might make things uncomfortable," I say sourly.

He gets off the sofa and bends over to kiss my head. "While that sounds like a Jackie Collins novel, we both know that won't be happening tonight."

"How?" I mutter but he just shakes his head.

"I'm off. We'll discuss this tomorrow."

"Oh, will we?" I shout after him. "Maybe that won't happen."

"It will," his voice floats up the stairs before there's a click and the door shuts at the bottom of the stairs.

It takes me a long while to go to sleep that night. I twist and turn on the mattress as if it's made of stone while my mind races and twists down labyrinthine paths. That's probably why it takes me a second to realise that the lamp switching on in my room isn't part of my dreams.

I sit up, blinking and pushing the covers away before scraping my hair back from my face. Then I gape at the figure at the bottom of the bed. "What are you doing here?"

Niall pauses where he's taking off his jeans. He's already

managed his jumper and the light dances over his hard, muscled chest. "You're here, aren't you?" he says somewhat crossly.

"I don't understand," I say blearily, watching as he flings his jeans over the sofa and slides into bed next to me.

He looks around. "This bloody place," he mutters. "It's like Helena Bonham Carter decided to take up interior decorating for *The Swiss Family Robinson*."

"And yet here you are, rather than in your white and grey bedroom in the white and grey house."

He eases next to me and raises one eyebrow. "That sounds like a subtle hint?"

"If a subtle hint means saying that you have the decorating ability of a Travelodge decorator, then yes, it's subtle."

"Ouch!" His mouth quirks and he nestles closer, pushing me gently onto my side and snuggling up behind me. I can feel all his long, warm body against mine and his arm is a heavy weight across my hips. I feel my body unravel the tension in it as if I've got into a hot bath.

"Mmm," he says hoarsely. "That's more like it."

"Why are you not in your own bed?" I pause. "Is it too full for you?"

"That's very catty." His voice is sleepy and curiously pleased, but his arm tightens so I can't turn and see his face. "Settle down," he grunts. "I need to sleep."

"In here?"

"Yes. This is where you are. So, if I want to sleep that's where I must be." He settles into the mattress and me with a soft grunt of pleasure. "I can't seem to sleep without you at the moment."

The darkness makes me brave. "I know," I whisper. "I'm the same. What does it mean?"

His body goes tight against mine as if I've taken him by surprise, and his voice when he speaks is cautious. "Why don't we just take it as a fact. Don't overanalyse, Milo. You'll only see problems that way."

I know there are tons of things wrong with that statement but because it echoes my own need to hide my head in the sand, I adopt his suggestion. "Where's Gideon?" I whisper.

His arm tightens almost painfully, and I murmur a complaint. He relaxes immediately and kisses my shoulder in a sweet gesture that's so very him despite his sardonic exterior. He's actually one of the sweetest men I've ever met.

"He's back at my house in the guest bedroom."

"Did you?"

His indrawn breath stops my words. "That you could think that."

I grab his arm and squeeze it. "I'm sorry," I say immediately. "I know you wouldn't." And I do. It's not him. No matter what Niall is, he's honest. It can be brutal, but he always tells the truth.

"So, why didn't you come after me sooner?" I whisper and feel my cheeks immediately heat when the words come out without my permission.

He stiffens as if surprised and then croons something under his breath and kisses my neck, nestling his long nose under the fall of my hair. I shudder at the touch of his warm, soft lips and the tickle as he breathes in deeply.

"He wanted to talk to me," he finally says. "And I couldn't stop my arrangement with him without speaking first. I owe him that."

I breathe in. "You're stopping it?"

"Of course, sweetheart. You know I am."

Silence falls as I digest his words but despite my best efforts, I'm sleepy. The warmth of his body, the way my body has relaxed its tenseness, and the late hour conspire to make my blinks longer until my eyes drift shut. Nevertheless, I stir myself with one last question. "So, how did it go?"

He chuckles sleepily. "It didn't. We got in the house and he started talking about other things. No matter how I tried I couldn't get round to the subject. You Ramsay men are determined."

That should bother me, I think sleepily. But I'm so tired and when he whispers 'Sleep, darling,' I let the sweet words push me into sleep.

CHAPTER 11

Is it because I'm fucking Niall? I have to have a holiday because of that?

Milo

He's gone when I wake up the next morning, and when I slide my hand across the bed it's as cold as if I dreamt him being here. However, when I move in the sheets, I can smell his woody scent and it makes me smile a little. I wonder what time he left.

Shaking my head, I slide out of bed and hiss when my feet hit the cold floor. Servants' quarters in old houses are notoriously cold and this is no exception. It's a miracle no one died of hypothermia. I bolt into the bathroom and turn the shower on. It heats up quickly, which is a blessing, and I sigh with pleasure when I climb under the spray and feel the hot water sliding down my body.

I twist and turn under the spray, letting my mind wander. I can see marks on my body that are subtle mementos of the last week. Tiny fingerprint bruises on my hips where he grabbed me, impatient in his need to come. Red marks over my nipples where he licked and sucked and bit. My cock stirs and I groan, reaching down to fist it.

I reach up and squirt some soap into my palm and then, making a tunnel of my fist, I start to shuttle my cock through it, twisting my hand as I get to the top.

A montage of memories, explicit snapshots flit through my head and I marvel that the wild-looking man in them is me. It's been a revelation to me, having sex with him. I come away from it sated but with an undercurrent of needing more underneath. More kissing, more sucking, more coming. It's like I have a previously unknown engine inside me and it's constantly idling. Even when I'm spent, I'm inventing reasons to get there again. I've never been less than half hard all week.

I reach back and feel between my arse cheeks. I trace a finger delicately over my hole, shuddering at the silvery pleasure that runs through me. He hasn't fucked me yet. I've held out against that because my only memories of this are pain and tearing and as such, I've tensed every time his hand even goes near my backside. However, he's kept at it, tracing a fingertip there when I'm fucking him, tracking my taint while he blows me, and slowly he's getting me used to having his fingers there and even wanting them.

I wonder what it would feel like to have him fuck me. To have him over me, all that big body bearing down on me. The image is so vivid I groan and shout out, coming in long creamy ropes against the shower wall.

I rest my hands against the tiles as I pant for breath. I wonder whether that means I'm ready to try anal sex again. I frown. Maybe I won't get the chance. I remember his words as I slid away from him and into sleep. My brother hasn't spoken to him yet and I know where Niall's loyalty lies. He may be enjoying this with me but it's temporary, no claiming words uttered, no declarations of fidelity. The only thing stopping him would be me, and I've never expressed a wish for a relationship with him beyond what we're doing. Do I want that after all? The thought stops me dead, but I shake my head crossly and stop the shower. No more thinking.

Finally, dressed in jeans and an oversized scarlet jumper which I'm sure used to belong to Gideon, I clatter down the stairs and towards the dining room. When I enter it's to find Oz trying to feed Cora while Silas gathers his vet's bag and coat together.

"Morning," I mutter, crossing to Cora and dropping a soft kiss on her forehead. She crows happily at the sight of me and offers me the spoon she's been banging on her highchair.

"No, thank you," I say. "You have it back. You make far more noise than I ever could."

"That's a fact," Silas says, wincing as the banging recommences. He crosses over to Oz and kisses him goodbye. I avert my eyes and focus on getting my breakfast from the side table. When I turn back, he's standing back up and Oz's mouth is swollen.

I shake my head. "Have a good day, Silas."

He smiles, no doubt because for the first few years here I'd struggled to call him anything except Lord Ashworth. It had seemed at the time that my security lay in being polite and keeping him happy. I'd learned that he was actually made happy by being treated normally, and now he exists in some way as my older brother.

"I'll be back late," he says, patting my shoulder and looking back at Oz.

"I'll wait up," he says steadily, and Silas gives him a warm, loving look before ducking out of the room, rapidly followed by Boris the dog. I set my plate down on the table and sit, looking at Oz.

"You okay? You look like you've got something to say." I pause. "Not that you don't always look like that. You have so much to say."

He raises his middle finger at me. "I actually have something very important to announce." He pauses as if listening for an invisible drum roll before shrugging when it doesn't come. "Silas and I think you should have a holiday."

"What?"

He nods happily. "You did us such a favour with Cora and it's been so hectic lately and you've worked so hard."

"Why now?"

"Milo, I think you've got about three years of holidays stored up. You never stop." He looks at me. "We just think that maybe you should slow down for a week and it'll refresh your brain."

"Is it because I'm fucking Niall? I have to have a holiday because of that?"

"I personally would recommend a stay in a lunatic asylum, but that's just me," he says pertly, and my lips twitch. Taking that for the sign of encouragement it will undoubtedly turn out to be, he presses on. "We've actually given the two of you the same week off. What a coincidence. I can't *imagine* how that happened. Maybe the two of you could go away together."

"Oh my God," I sigh, resting my head in my hands. I look up at him through my hair. "You're giving us both a week off and expect us to go away together. How does that even work? Are you forcing him to take me away for romance and drinks by the sea?" I pause. "How would you even do that?"

He blinks. "It's a week's holiday, not *The Love Boat*." He smirks. "We're giving you a week off at the same time. Whether you go away together is nothing to do with us." He looks around as if making sure Silas has gone. "*Nothing*," he whispers fervently and spoils it by winking at me.

"You look like you've got a squint," I say gloomily. "It'll never work out anyway. He won't take a week off. He loves ploughing those fields too much."

"Maybe he can plough your field. Maybe he'll find out that he prefers seeding your crop if you actually go away for a week together."

My mouth drops open. "I don't think I've heard a sentence like that since my grandmother made me watch *Dale's Supermarket Sweep*." I throw my napkin down. "I'm going to get back to my restoration. Because long-dead people in pictures are a lot less problematic than the living ones around here."

I'm just heading out of the back door and dragging my coat on when I hear my name being called. I turn to find Mrs. Granger approaching with the figure of her five-year-old granddaughter, Molly, dancing around her.

"You okay?" I ask as she nears me. Her hair is dishevelled and her face is redder than when she bends over the ovens in the tea rooms.

"Oh, Milo, can I ask a huge favour?"

I smile at her. "Of course. What's up?"

She looks down at my coat. "Are you going out?"

I wind a big red and black striped scarf around my neck. "Only over to Niall's." For some reason, I redden, and her eyes linger on my flushed cheeks but she doesn't say anything. Seizing the reprieve I rush on, and I mean rush on. I actually babble. "Not because I want to see him. No, *definitely* not. Ha! Because that would be ridiculous. No, it's because of the pictures. I've got some pictures to restore. They're over in his house because that's where I'm working on them. Not because his house is so cosy. And not because I live with him. Good grief, as if I'd live with him." Her eyebrow rises slowly and I come to a stop, sweating profusely. "Phew!" I mutter and her lip twitches.

"Well, that's lovely," she says bracingly. "Would it be possible for you to watch Molly for a bit?" I open my mouth and she rushes into speech before I can say no. "It would only be for an hour. She stayed with me last night and her mum's car broken down and it'll be an hour before she can get here. I'd keep her with me but the man's coming to repair the big oven today and I've got to grab him while he's around. He's so difficult to get hold of." She looks down at Molly who is doing a headstand against the wall. "She won't be any trouble," she adds rather doubtfully.

I smile. "Of course, it's fine. I'll keep her down there with me. She can colour or something."

"Oh, thank you, Milo. You're such a good boy."

She thrusts a small purple rucksack at me before I can change my mind and backs away. Calling to Molly to follow me, I wave goodbye. We're a few steps away when Mrs. Granger calls me. I turn back.

"Niall eh, Milo? I must say I approve. Big handsome lad you've got there." She winks and laughs, rushing off and leaving me open-mouthed.

I look down at Molly, who is trying to let go of my hand subtly, then I look over at the field of sheep she's eyeing. "Nope," I say cheerfully. "You can run free in the woods, not amongst the poor old sheep."

She comes along with me happily, chattering about school and friends. She's a lovely little girl, smart and happy, and I let her chatter fill my head so I don't have to think about where Niall had gone this morning. My first thought is work, but he's never raced off like that before. He loves morning sex, so it's a fact that he's always slow to leave the bed.

Molly dances off to tunnel her way through the fallen leaves. Her boots make a crackly noise in the red and gold carpet and I smile at her as she throws handfuls into the air. The morning is crisp and cold with a watery pale gold sun trying valiantly to hold the frosty chill back a bit longer. My breaths make clouds in the air and I inhale the scent of the woods –earth and leaves and a cold autumn smell.

It improves my mood so that I'm smiling when I emerge out of the wood ahead of Molly and stand on the drive in front of Niall's house. I'm acutely aware of that smile dropping from my face as I stand and look up at the figures of Niall and Gideon on the balcony that runs off Niall's bedroom.

Gideon is barefoot and in pyjama pants and a black t-shirt and Niall is in just a pair of shorts with wet hair. They're holding cups of coffee and standing very close to each other laughing. I stare up at them, feeling like I've been punched in the throat. Then I turn and wheel back the way I came.

. . .

Niall

I stand on the balcony of the house, sipping coffee and watching the leaves flutter down from the trees and onto the gravelled drive. It's a very cold morning with the mist still clinging to the branches of the trees, but I feel a smile on my face that has nothing to do with the weather and everything to do with the man I left this morning burrowed under the covers like a very small mole seeking shelter.

I hear a step behind me and when I turn, Gideon is standing there. His eyes are still hazy with sleep but the coffee he's sipping is rapidly clearing away the cobwebs. My smile falters slightly and I immediately bolster it, but the quirk to his lips tells me I didn't cover it enough. However, staying true to his enigmatic personality, he just smiles and comes to stand next to me.

He looks over at my wet hair. "Is it safe to stand so close?"

"Fuck off," I say companionably and nudge him with my shoulder. "I slipped. It's not my fault a fucking fox had decided to shit in the place I chose to land."

He laughs. "It was rather rancid."

"No more than that twink you picked up a few months ago. His aftershave smelt like someone had died and they'd bottled the body odour."

He shakes his head. "And yet you still managed to fuck him."

"My nasal cavities might have died but my bodily urges still worked."

He looks at me searchingly. "Unlike now. What a difference a few months make."

I stare back. "So, we're going to talk about the elephant in the room, then?"

He takes a sip of his coffee, his face calm and pensive. "Not sure Milo could ever be described as an elephant, although he was a very rowdy toddler, if I remember rightly."

"He was a noisy bugger," I say, smiling at the thought of him rampaging through the house when I'd visited, holding my hand and always talking, talking. My smile dies as I remember the fact that this had vanished after his head injury and I'm actually fucking the adult version of that boy.

Gideon shoots me a look as if he knows exactly what I'm thinking, which wouldn't surprise me at all. At one point we were so close we could echo each other's thoughts. I frown because at one point I'd thought myself in love with him, and that delusion had allowed us to fuck each other and other people through many hedonistic years. Now, I know it was never love, although I shy immediately away from why I'm so sure.

His voice interrupts my thoughts. "How long?"

"A week." I look at him but he just nods. Then his mouth pulls tight.

"Is this just fucking?"

"No," I say hurriedly and forcefully. "No, of course it's fucking not."

He sighs. "Part of me is happy about that because he's my brother but the other half..."

His voice falls away and I look at him. "The other half, what?"

He shakes his head and I know he won't tell me. Finally, he sighs. "It seems strange and yet somehow inevitable."

I'm startled. "*Inevitable*. Why?"

"Because you've always been so protective of him when you're not like that with anyone else." He hesitates. "You weren't like that with me."

"Because we never let our relationship develop like that." I shrug. "Maybe it would have if we'd fed and watered it, but we didn't and it died."

He winces. "And Milo is different?"

"Milo has always been different."

He shrugs and then suddenly laughs. "You can say that again. Do you remember his habit of stripping his clothes off when he was five? He used to walk everywhere naked, apart from a little plastic builder's hat."

"He's always made odd sartorial choices," I say, and he laughs again. It's only a slight turn of my head that lets me see the flash of Milo's red jumper on the drive before he whirls around and vanishes back into the woods. I look at Gideon and myself and wince. "Fuck!"

"Was that Milo?"

I nod.

He looks almost amused and it makes me want to punch him. "So, he must think that we …?" I nod and he laughs. "Well, we still could."

I pull away, stung. "I spill my heart out and you joke."

His arm shoots out and he grabs me. "Your heart." He sounds almost winded. "Your heart, Niall?"

I look at him. "I think I'm falling for him," I say steadily. "I know that might worry you, but I can't help it." I pause. "You don't look surprised."

He looks thoughtful. "Some part of me isn't. Maybe I've always known that the wind would blow this way."

"Are you worried?"

He shakes his head slowly. "No. I think you've kept him safe all these years. That's why I sent you to him when the Thomas situation got out of control. I knew you'd protect him and watch over him. I just didn't know it would be until he was ready for you." He shakes his head and raises his hand to cup my cheek. "I knew someone would take you away from me because you wouldn't be happy with what I offered for forever."

I jerk my head back. It feels wrong for him to touch me.

An almost cruel look crosses his face. "Yes, it's awkward to know how each brother fucks, isn't it? It's some men's dream, but it won't be Milo's."

"I'm sorry," I say slowly. "I'm sorry I hurt you."

He draws back. "You haven't hurt me. You've just finally seen that all those times you looked at me you should have been looking beyond me at who was waiting for you to notice him."

"Is this going to cause a problem between you and Milo?"

He shakes his head thoughtfully. "No." He shoots me a suddenly spiteful glance. "It's got to last a while for it to maybe become a problem. You'll grow bored in the end of pedestrian sex with the same person and when you're finished with it, come and look for me. I'll be waiting."

"You and Jacinta?"

He shrugs. "Who cares. It will always be me, anyway. That's the way it's always been with us."

I catch an edge of desperation in his voice and it stops the angry words from flowing out about how the sex with Milo is beyond anything I've ever done. Transcending the tawdry with shine and soft beauty and feelings that run through to the depths of me like I've tapped a previously unknown lake. I can't say that to him, no matter how he behaves, because a part of me will always care for him. It's just not the rest of me, which yearns for Milo.

"I have to go," I say abruptly. "Don't play games, Gideon. It doesn't become you and if you hurt him, you'll have to come through me first."

"Threats before breakfast," he muses casually. "How very *Dynasty*."

I break away, desperate to get to Milo and explain, shoving Gideon's last expression away to examine later. The banked anger in his face which had glowed clearly for a second.

Milo

I hear him before I see him. Pounding footsteps echoing along the path.

Molly looks up. "Ooh, is it a monster?" She seems more happy than bothered.

I shake my head. "Not recognisably."

She opens her mouth with a question on her lips but at that point, a now fully dressed Niall crashes through a bush and lands in front of us.

"Niall!" Molly squeals with delight, displaying no consternation that he's just barged through some shrubbery.

"Molly." He smiles at her but it dies as he looks between the two of us.

"I'm watching her for an hour for Mrs. Granger," I say curtly. "I thought I'd work on the pictures until I realised that the revolving door on your bedroom might make that slightly awkward."

"Does your door turn around?" Molly asks, immediately interested. "I wish mine did that, Niall."

"No, I erm," Niall falters and Molly loses interest, preferring to stride over to grab a loose branch so she can knock seven barrels out of a pile of leaves. I watch her while trying not to look at Niall. I know it's childish, but I can't escape the thought of him and Gideon standing so close together and laughing when he'd left my bed to go to him.

"Milo," Niall says in a low voice. "Nothing happened."

I force myself to look at him. "Well, you w-would say that, w-wouldn't you."

I close my eyes at the stammer and the stricken look on his face when he hears it as if I've punched him.

"Sweetheart, look at me." His voice is firm, and my eyes fly open and I take an automatic step back when I find him directly in front of me. It's nothing but an instinctive gesture born of my time with Thomas, but he flinches as if I've hit him. "*Milo*," he says beseechingly.

I immediately shake my head and step into him. "That wasn't you," I say, breathing in between the words when it feels like they might get twisted. "Never you. You were just so close and it was automatic to move back."

He shuts his eyes and breathes out slowly. "Okay. That's good, right?" My lip twitches and he shakes his head. "Ignore me. I'm babbling. Come back to the house with me," he says suddenly and passionately. "You didn't interrupt anything."

"So why were you gone so early?" I wince at the note of whiny complaint.

"Baby, you were fast asleep. I woke you and told you I had to be out by the lake today and you actually spoke to me." He shrugs. "It was a bit like I'd imagine it would be to talk to Jason Voorhees if he too were a cover stealer, but I was sure you were listening. I'll learn, I suppose." He smiles tentatively at me. "I slipped while I was down there and fell in some fox shit, so I came back to shower and change. Gideon had only just come out when you saw us. He was barely more awake than you." He pauses. "Do you believe me?" he asks in a low voice.

"Why is that important?"

"Do you believe me?" he repeats stubbornly.

I consider him and then nod slowly. "I do."

He sags slightly and grabs my arm. "So, come back to the house, have some breakfast with me." He pauses. "And maybe have a conversation with your brother because I'm getting tired of being the registered talker around here at the moment."

I smile, feeling sunshine wash across my heart despite the fact that I have an awkward conversation looming over me. "Okay. We'll follow you there."

"Thank you," he says, grabbing my hand.

Molly comes up to us. "Are you Milo's boyfriend then, Niall?"

He looks at me and smiles. "I think maybe I could be," he says almost challengingly. My hand jerks in his in complete shock but he holds tight.

Molly shrugs. "I don't think I'd like a boyfriend. Ginny at school has one. He's called Simon and he smells. I think I might like a girlfriend instead."

"Would you?" Niall asks.

"Yes. They smell better, and my mum says girls should cook and clean. I don't like doing that but surely another girl will. Then she can cook and clean for me while I go out and fight monsters."

"I'm not sure that's a very modern take on relationships," I say doubtfully, but she looks at me almost pityingly.

"Milo, you're very old. I don't think you know about things like this."

Niall's laughter rings around the wood.

CHAPTER 12

Maybe stop having sex long enough to get to know him, Milo.

Milo

Molly and I follow Niall into his kitchen. I look around but I can't see any sign of Dotty. She's obviously heard the sound of the little girl's voice and done the sensible thing and hurled herself out through the cat flap.

Molly looks around with eager curiosity. "Do you live here, Niall? It's like a fairy-tale cottage. I like fairy tales. I like *The Gingerbread Man* and I like *Hansel and Gretel* where the witch lived in a house made of sweets and *Goldilocks and the Three Bears* with the porridge."

I grin at Niall. "You sound hungry, Molly. Would you like some breakfast?"

She nods eagerly and Niall laughs. "I'll make tea if you do food."

He looks at me hopefully. "I could eat breakfast too." He pauses. "But probably bacon and eggs are better for someone who's been hard at work since dawn."

I shake my head. "You were rolling around in fox poo, not resolving Brexit negotiations."

He laughs, and Molly sidles up. "Granddad was on about Brexit yesterday. He said Boris Johnson couldn't find his bottom with a map, but I couldn't work out why he needed a map. I can find mine easily. It's always in the same place." She shakes her head in a very bemused fashion as Niall laughs loudly and smacks a kiss on her head.

I get the bacon and sausages out of the fridge and stick them on the grill before grabbing the porridge and starting to slice fruit. "Molly, get the golden syrup out, lovey. It's in that cupboard by the big window." Humming tunelessly, she skips across to the cupboard next to the French doors.

She stands there for a second, looking out at the garden in a contemplative manner. "There's a lady running around the garden in her bra and knickers," she finally says in a very matter-of-fact voice.

"What?" I look up, startled, in time to see Niall pace over to the doors.

"*Shit!*" he shouts loudly and books it out of the room, banging into the doorframe as he goes.

"Niall said a bad word," Molly says happily.

Silence descends for a split second and then I dart over to the window in time to see Jacinta clad in very fetching lilac underwear, dancing around the garden and laughing uproariously while my brother claps and cheers.

For a long second, I'm held immobile as Molly and I watch while she dances around to an invisible tune. She's obviously either spectacularly drunk or stoned or both, but she still manages to avoid the clutches of Niall as my brother laughs loudly at both of them.

Finally, I realise that I'm probably scarring Molly's delicate mind for life and usher her away from the window. "Come on," I say heartily. "Help me make breakfast for everyone."

"I think porridge is the right choice, especially for the lady. She's going to be very cold when she comes in," Molly says sagely, letting me tie an apron around her and accepting a spoon to stir the oats into the cold milk.

I look up in time to see Niall corner her and whip his shirt off to cover her. I roll my eyes and try to ignore both Niall's bare chest and the fact that my brother is also ogling it.

"She needs a proper bra," Molly intones in a slightly scandalized voice. "Her boobies are flopping about all over the place."

"She needs a sense of decency," I say with a sniff and then halt. "What do you know about bras?"

She shrugs. "Granny has a proper bra. It's big and white and I can stick my head in one of the pouches."

I blink and try to rid my mind of the image of Mrs. Granger in her underwear. The back door opens and Niall comes in, followed by my brother who is leading a sulky Jacinta.

Niall ushers her to a seat and reaches for the coffeepot while my brother slings himself into a chair, looking disgruntled.

"Party pooper," Jacinta sneers at Niall. "You've really changed. Time was you'd have liked to see me dance in my underwear."

"I don't think asking you not to do it in front of a five-year-old really deserves the title of party pooper," Niall says wryly.

"What five-year-old?" she sneers, accepting the coffee he pours her with a huff and getting out a cigarette from a packet on the table. "I'm sure Milo looked a lot older than that."

"He is," Niall says patiently, removing the cigarette from her pouty mouth and throwing the packet neatly into the bin. "I'm talking about the little girl making porridge over there."

Jacinta squints for a few seconds. Her pupils are huge. She then obviously gives up. "I left my cigarettes around here," she says querulously. "Where are they?"

"I don't know," Niall says quickly and my brother snorts.

He's wearing old jeans and a black jumper and looks handsome. Although he's not saying much, he has a way of filling a room. He's always been like that. There's just something about him that draws the eye. He looks over at me where I stand with Molly and something dark flashes across his face. Then it clears so quickly I wonder whether it was even there. Still, I'm a little unnerved and for some reason, my eyes instantly look for Niall.

He's pulling on a crumpled t-shirt from the ironing basket and watching me carefully. When I catch his eyes, he immediately smiles reassuringly, so I relax. When I turn back, Gideon is examining my face carefully. Then he sits back.

"God, I'm bored. How do you stand it around here?"

"It's lovely here," I say, feeling incredibly stung. How dare he criticise the nicest place I know and my sanctuary. "Just because it's not wall-to-wall orgies and nightclubs doesn't mean it's automatically boring."

"Tsk tsk, Milo. How very unexpectedly snappy of you." He smiles. "Sometimes I forget how very young you are."

"Stop sniping," Niall orders, and I'm not sure which of us he's talking to. Maybe both of us.

I subside and start to heat the porridge, passing Molly the bowls to put on the table. She passes Niall the jug of orange juice carefully, her little tongue sticking out in concentration, and Jacinta unexpectedly revives.

"Is that vodka and orange?"

Niall blinks. "No."

"Why not?"

"Because it's nine in the morning, darling."

"How provincial you are now."

He shrugs. "It doesn't go with porridge, love. Not a good mix."

She subsides and starts to hunt through the pockets of her jacket on the chair for her cigarettes. By unspoken consent, we leave her to it. It's more peaceful that way. I dish up the bacon and eggs and Niall stands to hand the plates out. He leans into me as he stands next to me and one of his hands goes under my jumper, his long, cool fingers caressing the skin of my lower back. I shiver and smile. "Stop it," I mutter, and he looks innocently at me.

"I can't think what you mean," he says blithely, and I jump as he pats my arse before stopping and coming back to caress it. We're covered by the kitchen island, but when I look up my brother is glaring at us, so I nudge Niall to get moving with the plates.

I pour the porridge into bowls and slide them on the table. Jacinta looks at hers like I've put a pile of steaming shit in front of her but Gideon unexpectedly smiles, grabbing his spoon and digging in. He groans. "Oh my God, you've made it like Derry did."

"It's brown sugar and a bit of cinnamon," I say. "It's funny that the only thing she could cook was porridge. She'd have made an excellent addition to the three bears household, but not so much for us."

He laughs. "Do you remember the Ready Brek advert with the red outline? Well, the amount of the stuff we ate, we must have looked bloody radioactive."

I laugh and when I glance at Niall, he looks almost ecstatic, glancing between me and Gideon like he's a parent forcing two children to play nicely. I shake my head at him and dig into my breakfast.

Once we're all seated with the food in front of us, conversation ebbs and flows, helped by Molly's monologue about school and the problems she's having with someone called Michael Sanders.

We've just pushed our plates back and I'm on my second cup of tea when the doorbell rings, followed quickly by the sound of the front door opening and Mrs. Granger's voice. "Cooee, Niall, are you here?"

"In the kitchen, Mrs. Granger," Niall shouts, double-checking that Jacinta is fully covered.

She comes into the kitchen and Molly immediately dances happily over to her. "Say thank you to Milo and Niall for having you," Mrs. Granger instructs her after accepting a hug.

Molly skips over and I accept the tight grip around my neck. She moves over to Niall and shrieks happily as he tilts her upside down and pretends to drop her. Jacinta makes a moue of distaste at the noise but my brother grins lazily, watching Jacinta with slightly malicious enjoyment.

"Thank you for having me," Molly shouts once she's been righted.

"Did you have a nice time?" Mrs. Granger asks.

"I did. It was ever so good. Milo made porridge and bacon and eggs, Niall said shit, and that lady over there was dancing around in the garden in her knickers," Molly says excitedly.

There's a long silence and I almost look around for the tumbleweeds which will undoubtedly soon be rolling through the kitchen.

"Oh, erm," Niall coughs. "Oh, Mrs. Granger, it wasn't quite like that." She looks at him and he stumbles over his words. "Well okay, it might have been a little bit like that, but really I think if you just listen to my side of the story."

Mrs. Granger shakes her head and shoots me a quick wink that Niall misses in his stumbling apology. Then she shoos Molly out of the kitchen with Niall following her earnestly. When she's gone the silence falls awkwardly.

I look towards the hall where we can hear the strains of Niall's apology tour and laugh. Gideon looks surprised but then he grins at me and for a brief second it's like we're at home again. The old age divide is still there, but I feel startlingly close to him for a second with a rush of affection.

Then Niall comes in and Gideon's smile fades and I sigh silently. I look up as Niall sits next to me. "Everything okay?" I ask.

He groans. "Well, I'm reasonably sure that she's not going to murder me at the moment, so we can rest easy for a bit."

"Probably eat some more porridge quickly though. And then maybe pack a getaway bag," I advise.

He laughs. "We'll run away together. It'll be like Bonnie and Clyde."

"I really don't think a speech impediment is what you need when you're holding up a bank. They'd drift off before they even realised they had to get the money out," I say sagely. "Plus, my hair is really too wild for a beret."

He laughs and ruffles my hair affectionately, and I watch my brother's expression tighten as his eyes follow Niall's hands. Then he heaves a heavy sigh. "Fuck, I'm bored. Let's go away."

"What?" Niall jerks out. "*Now?*"

"No, next year. Of course now," my brother says somewhat petulantly. "I'll go mad if I have to stay here."

"May I point out that you're the one who chose to come here and no one has handcuffed you to the table yet," Niall says patiently.

My brother winks. "Well, not yet. Do you remember Geneva?"

Niall swallows with a click and looks at me uneasily. "Let's not go over old history," he says quickly. He looks at Gideon. "If you want to go away, why not take Jacinta?"

"I don't want Jacinta. I want you."

My head shoots up and I watch as he and Niall exchange a whole conversation with their eyes. I feel shut out and isolated, but then Niall's hand comes down on my thigh holding tight and I remind myself that he wants me here. I'm not an interloper. My brother is.

My brother changes tack with that dazzling ability to switch emotions he uses so well on the stage. "Let's go to the chalet."

"What chalet?" I ask before I can stop myself.

"Niall's chalet in Verbier."

I blink. "I didn't know you had a chalet," I say slowly. *How can I not know this?* We've seen each other every day for years, not to mention been sleeping together lately. My brother looks almost jubilant at my lack of knowledge but Niall just shrugs.

"I thought you knew. But now I think about it, it was way before you came here. Silas sold me the chalet when he inherited the estate. He couldn't afford to keep it anymore with the things that needed doing here."

"That must have cost a lot."

"I bought it with my inheritance from my grandfather and asked my brother to pay me out of my share of Dad's estate." He shrugs as if that means nothing.

"I bet you paid top whack though," I say cautiously.

He grins, looking almost embarrassed. "Of course. Silas needed the money."

"And did you even want a chalet?"

He shrugs, looking bashful. "Honestly, it had never occurred to me, but if Silas ever mentions it to you, make sure that you say how I've always wanted one desperately." I laugh and look at him affectionately only to find him staring at me, seemingly transfixed. My brother clears his throat and Niall jerks. "Anyway, I do love skiing and the place is gorgeous. It's really homely and comfortable."

"I'm surprised you've never been there," my brother says smugly, pushing his bowl away and sitting back in his chair. "Niall goes all the time."

"Not all the time," Niall says quickly, obviously hearing the note of challenge that was directed at me in that statement. "I haven't been in ages."

"Well, we should go as soon as possible," my brothers says smoothly. "Come on, Niall. We can go and ski all day. You need a holiday."

Niall looks at me. "Funnily enough, Silas has just given me a week off." My brother whoops and I feel my stomach tumble to the floor.

I swallow hard and gather my dignity. "Well, there you are. That's all sorted. I'm sure you'll have a wonderful time."

"What do you mean that I'll have a wonderful time?" Niall asks, his hand tightening on my leg to stop me getting up. "You'll be there too."

My 'what' is drowned out by my Gideon's *really* but Niall grins happily. "It's perfect. Silas said he'd given you the time off too. I was going to suggest going away together, and this is even better." He grins at me, looking flushed and happy. "I can't wait to show you the place. You'll love it, and you're a good skier from what I can remember."

"I'm not sure that's a good idea," I start to say and hesitate when I see the joy drain from his face.

"Oh please, Milo. It'll be brilliant. Please."

I waver, looking for some reason at Gideon who is gazing at me steadily, a hint of a challenge there. In all my years as his brother, I've never challenged him. I always accepted what he said and did as he told me because he knew more than me and was more forceful. I've never questioned his authority until now. Now, when he's coveting someone I'm coming to care for.

My thoughts veer away from that thought at light speed, but something makes me straighten my spine and smile at Niall. "That sounds good. Let's do it."

"Really?" he asks joyously. He hugs me and I close my eyes for a second, lost in the heat and scent of him. "It'll be amazing, Milo."

"I hope so," I whisper.

∽

Verbier is pretty in the twilight. I peer out of the windows of the minivan at the village square where shop fronts glow gold and strings of fairy lights shine, their dancing colours bright against the whiteness of the snow. People are everywhere on the main street, walking along in their colourful skiing gear. Someone opens the door of a bar and I can hear the distant sound of oompah music across the chatter of the pedestrians. And above it all are the dark mountains that loom over the tiny village like hovering parents at a children's party.

A warm hand comes down over my knee and I turn to see Niall smiling at me. "Okay?" he asks.

I grin at the look of suppressed excitement on his face. "It's so pretty."

"Have you ever been here before?'

I shake my head. "No. We went skiing in Austria when we were kids."

"How are you at skiing?"

I consider. "I'm pretty good, but I'm better at snowboarding." I nudge him, thinking of the fact that he was practically skiing before he could walk. "Don't worry, you won't have to babysit me. I know you and Gideon are good, but I'll keep up."

He frowns and shoots a look at my brother who is sitting on his other side, his face blank as he stares out at the village. Niall turns back to me. "I don't want you to have to keep up," he whispers. "I'm here with you."

I look involuntarily at the other people in the minivan – my brother, Jacinta, her friend Sam who's a fellow model, Jacinta's sister Daisy and Daisy's husband, Adam. Niall shrugs and leans in and I shudder at the feel of his breath on my ear. "If it was up to me it would be just the two of us."

I want to say that it *was* up to him because it's his house for fuck's sake, and he must read that on my face the way he does so much because he shrugs awkwardly. "I couldn't," he whispers. "I just couldn't, not after what I told him earlier about no more between me and him. And then Jacinta was sitting there so I had to ask her. Everything just snowballed."

I look into his blue eyes shining palely in the dim light and warmth fills me along with understanding. Of course he couldn't leave anyone out. He cares for my brother, and I wouldn't have wanted that last conversation between them to be the end of their friendship. I squeeze his hand in silent comradeship and inhale as he lifts my hand and drops an absentminded kiss on my fingers.

I go back to staring out of the window, his hand a warm weight on my leg. In the glass, I can see a reflection of my brother and I frown. I love him dearly and would do anything for him. Apart from share Niall. I grimace and watch it ruffle my forehead in the glass. I shouldn't be so territorial over what was supposed to be a hook-up. Niall was never going to be mine, so why does it feel like he was meant to be? Why is it so painful to imagine us parting and him moving on?

I try to remind myself that he's not what I'm looking for, and I endeavour to bring up my image of the perfect man. However, I can't see him properly anymore because Niall blots him out like he's standing in front of a quiet, peaceful man and replacing him with all that he is. Sardonic and funny, quick-minded and kind. Forceful and confident, I remind myself for the billionth time, but it doesn't seem to have the same impact anymore and I sigh.

The car slowing pulls me out of my thoughts and I look out, eager to see the chalet which Niall said was called The Little House. The car pulls up the hill and onto the drive in front of a beautiful chalet, making me smile because that name was a misnomer. It's big and three storied but almost higgledy-piggledy looking, as if there have been many additions made to it as the time has passed. Constructed of local stone and wood, it looks incredibly welcoming with lights blazing in every window and spilling their warm light onto the drive.

The others exclaim and get out, chattering madly, and I climb out at a slower pace, stretching and looking around. The air is crisp and so cold it seems to sear my throat. I shiver and drag my coat around me. Niall comes up next to me and slings his arm around my shoulder, and I lean gratefully into his side so I can feel the furnace-level heat of his body.

"What's the forecast for snow?" I ask. "Is it going to be good for skiing?"

He looks around, raising his face to the breeze and breathing in. "There's snow in those clouds and on the wind," he says decisively. "A lot of snow."

I smile and shake my head as he looks around happily. He's a force to be reckoned with at home, and the men who work for him adore him. He's always ready with a joke and a smile but he's equally prepared to muck in with anyone to help. However, seeing him here, relaxed and happy, he looks younger somehow, as if he wears a mantle of responsibility that he doesn't allow anyone to see is heavy. I nestle closer to him. I want to help him with that, make him smile and look after him, and somehow at this moment that doesn't seem like an insurmountable desire the way it used to when I was a teenager mooning over him.

He moves away to help with the luggage and I rush to help him, only to come up short when I find Gideon already at his side. They haul the bags together, chatting and laughing with Jacinta and the others, and for a second I feel a resurgence of that sense of inferiority. These are all wealthy and successful people with years of friendship. The friendship may have boiled down to how many positions they could shag in, but they all have an air of success compared to me, a failed picture restorer hiding away on an estate in Cornwall where the world can't find him.

Then I mentally kick myself in the arse. I'm more than that and Niall sees it, so I make myself smile at Niall and follow everyone into the warmth of the house, inhaling the scent of pine and cinnamon that greets me.

We're greeted by a small woman with grey hair curled neatly into the nape of her neck. She giggles as Niall sweeps her into his arms. I gape as he launches into a fast-paced conversation in German.

"Didn't you know he was multilingual?" my brother asks, bringing the final bag in and dumping it at my feet in the wood-panelled foyer with a staircase that twists out of sight. "He speaks French, German, and Swedish." I open my mouth to say that I knew he spoke Swedish because his mother is Swedish for Christ's sake, but he tuts disapprovingly before I can say anything. "Maybe stop having sex long enough to get to know him, Milo. There's more to him than a big cock."

"Well, you'd know about that," I say waspishly, stung because he's right and cross because he knows so much more about Niall than I do.

He smiles slowly. "I *do* know that, Milo. Is it going to be a problem?"

"No," I say hurriedly. We don't need to do this in the foyer of someone's home. "No, of course not."

For some reason, he looks almost disappointed in me, but the expression falls from his face too quickly for me to tell.

Niall turns to us and the old woman coos and goes to hug my brother, smiling happily with the ease of familiarity. My stomach tightens, and Niall comes over to me with a frown playing on his face. "You okay?"

"I'm fine," I say quickly.

"Okay, let me introduce Sofia to you." He calls her over and says something in scattershot German. She smiles adoringly at him, giving me the same smile and making some of my tension drop. She turns to Niall and says something with a lilt of laughter in her voice, but I don't take offense because her eyes are so warm. She turns away and Niall grins. "Sofia says how pretty you are. All hair and eyes."

"That makes me sound like Dougal from *The Magic Roundabout*," I whisper, and he laughs and hugs me close.

"Let me feel your nose just to be sure it's wet."

I swat his hand away, grinning in spite of myself. "Were you speaking German?"

"Yes. Do you speak any languages?"

I laugh. "I had enough of a job speaking English. Foreign languages were judged as something that might have been a step too far."

He looks at me searchingly. "I'll teach you."

I shake my head. "Swear words, I suppose."

He laughs. "Of course. Grab your bag and we'll take them up to the rooms. Sofia has done supper and it'll be ready in half an hour."

I grab my bag and follow him up the staircase. I catch a glimpse of a huge wood-panelled room with floor-to-ceiling windows offering a glimpse of the mountains, a fire burning in a large stone fireplace and deep comfy-looking sofas and chairs surrounding it. Then Niall climbs the stairs and I hasten to follow him. The others split off at the first floor to their rooms, but I follow him up another set of stairs and gasp when I round the final one.

I'm in a room that seems to stretch across the top of the house. Ahead of me is a floor-to-ceiling window next to French doors that let out onto a patio on which a hot tub sits with steam rising from it. The mountains are in full view, dusted in snow and framed through the first lazily tumbling flakes of snow flittering down from the lowering sky.

A long and deep plum-coloured sofa is situated in front of the window and off to one side is a grey chaise lounge that's big enough for two. It's positioned in a nook formed by a smaller window and the wooden wall, and it's packed with enough pillows and throws to earmark it as a perfect place to read. On the other wall, which is made of stone, is a massive bed big enough to sleep four. My lips tighten because it probably has in the past. It's made up with grey and white striped bedlinen and fluffy pillows and a plum-coloured eiderdown.

I wander across the room and open another door as Niall follows me like I'm the Pied Piper of the Master Suite. I'm looking at a small sauna and the scent of hot wood billows out. Another door leads to a dressing room and then finally a wood-panelled bathroom with a shower that runs along one wall and a huge clawfoot bath which is positioned in front of another window.

I turn to find Niall looking at me almost anxiously. "Do you like it?" he asks.

I smile at him. "It's so beautiful." His shoulders relax, and I nudge him. "Did you actually think I wouldn't like it?"

He laughs. "I don't know why I doubted it. It's made of wood and at the top of the house. Of course you like it. You're like bloody Heidi."

I laugh and then look around curiously. "Do you rent this out?"

He nods. "I probably couldn't afford to keep it otherwise. But I mainly rent to friends and family and leave plenty of time to come out here myself."

"But you're always working."

He smiles. "I said that I left time for me, not that I managed it." I laugh, and he looks at the room assessingly. "I'm thinking of trying to spend more time out here, actually. Make a change and try to have a life outside of work."

For a second I feel jubilation at the thought of being part of that, of coming here with him in all seasons. But then I grow cold again as I remember that this is nothing but an instructional set of hook-ups and at the end, he's anticipating being able to go back to his footloose lifestyle.

I immediately change the subject. "Where am I sleeping?"

He gapes at me. "In here, of course."

"With you?"

He frowns. "Of course. Who else would you be sleeping with? Is that okay?"

"Of course. But what about the others?"

"Milo, I may have been fond of company in my bed, but even I'm discriminating enough not to fuck six people at once."

I stare at him. "So what? You'll fuck me and then what? When we stop will you move back to my brother?"

He leans against the wall, staring at me as though I'm fascinating. "No, Milo," he says quietly. "That door is closed and locked now."

"Why?" The question sounds breathless because that's how I feel. Like he's just blown my words away.

He gives me a strange smile. "If I say just because, will you accept it?"

I cock my head to one side. "Of course," I say simply.

He nods. "That's why."

CHAPTER 13

I don't want anyone putting their hands on him.

Niall

The nightclub in Verbier is packed. Men and women twist and writhe on the dancefloor as icy-white lights flash around them. I stare at the club we've found ourselves in tonight. They've opted for an ice theme, which seems kind of redundant to me. If I'd wanted to sit in the snow I'd have done so outside where I wouldn't have had to pay these extortionate drinks prices.

I look around the table we were lucky enough to snag at the people in my party. I'm not convinced of the wisdom of any of this. When Silas had informed me that I had a week off, the first thought that had popped into my head was me and Milo by a swimming pool wearing very little.

Somehow it's not quite worked out that way because instead,

we're in sub-zero temperatures with my best friend and former lover, another fuck buddy along with her drunken friend, and her shrew of a sister and henpecked husband.

My phone chimes from the table in front of me and, lifting it up, I smile when I see Silas's name. It's like he reads my mind half the time.

SILAS: I HAVE TO SAY THAT WHEN OZ AND I SUGGESTED A MINI-BREAK FOR YOU AND MILO WE WEREN'T ANTICIPATING YOU TAKING TWO OF YOUR FUCK BUDDIES WITH YOU. IT'S LIKE THE PLOT OF A PORN FILM I WATCHED ONCE

ME: NOT QUITE. JACINTA HAS INVITED HER SISTER ALONG TOO

SILAS: DAISY? LOL! I'M LAUGHING SO HARD AT THE MOMENT

ME: I HOPE YOU DON'T STRAIN ANYTHING

SILAS: SERIOUSLY, SHE BROUGHT DAISY ON YOUR ROMANTIC GETAWAY?

ME: DO YOU REMEMBER HER?

SILAS: VIVIDLY. THAT WOMAN IS THE BIGGEST KNOW-IT-ALL I'VE EVER MET AND MORE SANCTIMONIOUS THAN KATIE HOPKINS. SHE SPENT A WEEKEND HERE ONCE AND TOLD HENRY HE SHOULD STOP SLEEPING AROUND AND PRAY MORE

I laugh, and Gideon looks at me queryingly. I shake my head at him and sit back, looking down the table at Milo. He's taken the holiday and present company in his quiet stride when to anyone else this would have had more disaster written over it than getting a ticket on the Titanic.

I've loved every second of the time I've spent with him here, but it's still not the best way I can think of to spend my time with him. That's in bed together after sex when we lie sweaty and covered with come but too satisfied to move.

My cock stirs, and I inhale and try to think of something unpleasant so I don't sit with a hard-on that I can't exactly do anything about. I look down the table and spot the something unpleasant. Daisy. She's sitting and having an irate conversation with her sister, which I have to say is about as common an occurrence as me needing a piss in the morning.

When put together with Jacinta, it's very obvious that they're sisters as they look so alike with their blonde hair and big blue eyes. But they couldn't be more different.

While Jacinta is wild and free and doesn't give a shit about anything much, Daisy is buttoned up and repressed and gives entirely too many shits about everything, particularly other people's business. She seems to have cast herself as the Virgin Mary on this trip and Jacinta as a scarlet woman, and the two of them bicker more than the members of the Tory Party over Brexit.

Daisy's husband, Adam, seems resigned and so under the thumb that he must be underground by now, and Sam is no better. A beautiful man, he's pissed most of the day and night. I look down at him where he's sleeping peacefully with his head on my shoulder and shrug him off irritably. He subsides gracefully down until he's asleep facedown on the table. When I look up Milo is grinning at me, his white teeth gleaming in the cold light of the club.

Dressed in ripped black jeans and a plain black t-shirt and with tattered old black suede Vans on his feet, he should look out of place in such a trendy club. But with the lights from the club playing on the rich brown of his long, wavy hair, he looks gorgeous and a world away from the pale, thin man I'd found a few years ago. I wonder whether there will ever be a time when I don't think about that.

I hope so because it's peculiarly painful, not just because of what he went through but also because of the fact that he'd been in love with the wanker. Something about Thomas had called to Milo, and I hate that for reasons I'm trying not to think about. In another way, those events gave him to me and I treasure that more and more each day, as I do him.

The more time I'm with him the more I see I him, to the extent that I now wonder how I ever came to miss him. It's as though for years he's worn camouflage and faded back into the woodwork so no one saw him, but now his real colours are emerging and they're so bright. He's utterly beautiful and people are starting to notice the wide shoulders and long legs, now that he's not stooping anymore. They see the pretty brown eyes and the full mouth, now that he lifts his face up and meets the world a little more head-on. I wonder if anyone realises how funny he is and how fiercely bright and big his brain is.

I shift position, feeling awkward as I stare at him, as though everyone in the club can tell how far he's gotten under my skin and how close I came to losing him the other day when he thought I'd slept with Gideon. The thought still makes me go cold, a faint vestige of the panic that had swept through me when I'd chased after him into the woods. I've never felt that before. Lovers come and then they go. Literally. For me to chase one is unheard of, but the relief I'd felt when he came back inside with me tells me that it was the right thing to do.

I become aware that his smile has slipped slightly and he's examining my face intently. I offer him a half smile before realising that Jacinta and Daisy have come to a sort of stuttered stop in their argument, which is probably a bit like the occasion in World War One when Britain and Germany left off fighting and killing each other for Christmas Day and played a game of football instead. Although looking at Jacinta's face, I wouldn't dare give her a football at the moment for fear she'd insert it somewhere in Daisy's person.

She glares out over the dancefloor, ignoring Daisy. Thwarted, Daisy looks around and finds the perfect person in Milo who's sitting next to her but, unfortunately for him, not paying close enough attention to the danger threatening. I smile evilly as she nudges him and he jerks back to very unpleasant reality.

She says something to him that's too low for me to catch, but the lecturing note is clear in her voice, and I see Milo sigh and smile at her. He's too kind to be rude, which means I'm going to have to rescue him. I don't want to think how happy that makes me. However, I don't get the chance because at that moment Jacinta stands up and, grabbing his hand, she pulls him after her onto the dancefloor while Daisy stares after them with her mouth open.

"You'll catch flies," I shout to her over the music. "Maybe a whole colony, given the way your mouth is constantly open and telling people your opinions."

"I beg your pardon."

"I said how time flies."

She glares at me and Gideon laughs. "She's as fucking unbearable as ever. Whose bright idea was it to bring her?"

"I think your partner for the evening." I look at the dancefloor and stiffen immediately. A man is dancing with Milo and as I watch he edges behind Milo, grabbing his hips and grinding into him. The lights pulse over them which is nothing compared to the red rage that fills me, making my head feel like it might explode all over this glittery club.

A hand comes down on mine and I realise that I've stood up. I look down at Gideon. "Let go of me," I say through clenched teeth.

"No," he says calmly. "You're about to make a massive tit of yourself and as your best friend, I'm here to save you. No, no." He waves his hand in a cavalier manner that makes me want to smack him. "Please don't say thank you. It was nothing." He exerts pressure on my arm until I sit back down. "That's better," he says serenely. "Now, watch and learn."

"I don't want anyone putting their hands on him," I growl.

"*Why?*" he asks incredulously. "You're not in a committed relationship. He's free to do what he wants and with who he chooses. How will you feel about that when it happens or when he sets you free to do your own thing? He's young. It's bound to happen." I flinch back from him and his eyes focus on the dancefloor behind me. "But you can relax because I don't think you need to worry about that tonight."

I turn around and find Milo in the act of sharply elbowing the barnacle who's attached himself to his arse. The bloke winces and steps back and Milo turns, his mouth working furiously as he shouts in the man's face. I'm not sure if he's stuttering because that happens when he's really feeling something, but the ire on his face and the hand he places on the bloke's chest and pushes him back certainly gets his message across.

I stare at him, feeling intense pride rush through me. It happens a lot with him because I know probably better than anyone the battle he faces with the stutter and his self-confidence.

"See," Gideon murmurs. "All sorted. You have to be careful, Niall," he continues. "I know you want to fight all his battles for him, but that's just fucking stupid."

I turn my head and glare at him. "Why?"

"Because, stupid, you won't leave him any of his own to fight," he says simply. "And he needs to do that. Win or lose, he needs to make his own decisions, and you're going to have to step back and let him or you'll lose him in the end because he'll think you're another Thomas."

I breathe in sharply, Gideon's dig hitting my chest and mixing with the fear I have there that maybe I'm no good for Milo. I look up and find Milo standing and watching us. His eyes are dark and he looks concerned. I smile at him, but it must be pathetic because he shakes his head. I make another attempt which he obviously finds more satisfactory because he nods happily and turns back to dancing with Jacinta, the two of them looking gorgeous amongst all those people.

I turn back to Gideon to find him watching me. "Why are you helping me? It's very weird," I say abruptly but he laughs.

"Because it's funny." He sobers up. "And I love you, Niall. You're the best person I've ever known."

I stare at him, unsure how to take this, but I'm distracted when Sam raises his head from the table. His hair is sticking up everywhere and he has a beer mat stuck to his cheek. "What day is it?" he asks blearily.

"I don't fucking know, mate," I say disconsolately. "Everything's topsy-turvy now."

Milo

A few days later I sit back in the hot tub on Niall's balcony and look at my view. The mountains rise over the village like humped figures under white blankets. It's twilight and lights are coming on all around, but out here it's private as no one overlooks this side of the house. Fat, fluffy flakes eddy down from the sky and land on my face, their cold touch giving tiny shocks.

I smile and wriggle further under the hot churning water, feeling it tug and pull at my sore muscles and inhaling the scent of chlorine. We've skied every day from early until late and I feel as if I've done an intensive workout. My arms and legs are sore and my arse is tender. However, I feel alive and buzzing.

I've adored these last few days with Niall. We've been with the others in the party, but he still managed to sneak some time for the two of us when he took me snowshoeing at dusk. That had been memorable with the swish-swish sound of the shoes through the snow, the wind howling around the trees, the feel of his hand on mine, and the sight of his face tanned from skiing and glowing in the low light.

I wriggle even further under the water and smile. The sound of the door opening and shutting and the pad of footsteps makes my grin widen, and I open my eyes to find Niall standing on the balcony. He's got rid of the grey ski trousers and red and grey checked ski jacket he was wearing earlier and is now clad only in thermal underwear, the tight dark-grey fabric hugging the long length of him and displaying the bulge of his groin. He's also carrying two big mugs with steam coming from them.

I sit up eagerly, water sloshing over the side of the tub and onto the ground. "Oh, is that hot chocolate?"

He grins, handing me both mugs and then starting to strip. I stare at him, the cups in my hand forgotten as his long, golden body comes into view, his cock hanging softly and his balls bunching as he moves to hop into the tub.

"Fuck, that's good," he groans, and the sound makes me shudder. He grins at me and holds out his hand for his mug. Taking a sip, he groans again before putting it on the table by the tub. "God, that brandy in it makes it so good."

I smirk. "You sound like you need alcohol."

"Yes, thank you so much for abandoning me. I really and truly loved being left with the Grady sisters."

I grimace at the thought of Jacinta and her sister, who take sibling rivalry to previously uncharted heights. The comparison with the twin girls from *The Shining* is very apt. "Was it bad?"

He shakes his head. "Put it this way, as I was leaving Jacinta offered to insert Daisy's skis somewhere that the manufacturers certainly weren't prepared for."

"It's hardly *Little House on the Prairie*, is it?"

He shudders. "Only if it had been set in a hell dimension."

I throw my head back and laugh loudly. When I recover it's to find him staring at me. "What?"

He shrugs. "Just looking. You're gorgeous when you laugh."

I hum awkwardly. "Well, I'll be less gorgeous when this next batch of bruises come out."

His expression instantly smooths into concern. "Yes. How's the knee?"

I shrug. "It's fine. Just a bang."

"You went down with a real clatter, Lo. I thought you'd broken something." He pauses. "Maybe we should get a doctor to have a look. Just in case." I stare at him open-mouthed and he looks instantly self-conscious. "What?"

I shake my head. "Did you just offer to get a doctor? You, the man who went two days with a broken leg because you said you were sure it was just a muscle strain."

He rubs his hand over his face, looking awkward. "Yes, well, this is different."

"How?"

"It's you."

The simple words stop me dead and I stare at him, an awful suspicion running through me. "This isn't part of you still thinking I'm ten is it, Niall, because I can assure you that I'm old enough to look after myself. I don't need a protector."

"Ugh, I'm totally aware that you're not ten." He shrugs. "I don't want to be your protector. I want ..."

He hesitates. "What?" I ask softly, almost unwilling to ask for fear of what it will reveal.

"Nothing. It doesn't matter." He shrugs and gives a wry smile, and I know he feels the same and he's not going to analyse what is growing here. I don't know whether I'm disappointed or relieved.

He settles back against the tub and, reaching one long arm out, he pulls me to him. I plaster myself against his side and sigh happily. He grins and lifts his head to let the snowflakes kiss him, and I stare at the wide cheekbones dusted with freckles and the full lips and big nose.

Without opening his eyes, he squeezes me. "When are you going to talk to him?"

I stiffen slightly but he doesn't stir, just tugs me closer. "Not yet," I mutter. "It hasn't been the right time."

"Really?"

"Yes," I say, slightly stung. "What with the homicidal twins going at each other all the time, Sam pissed from seven in the morning, and my brother doing his whole enigmatic Greta Garbo act, there hasn't exactly been time."

He groans. "I'm so sorry. I thought having others would lighten it up. I just didn't want you stuck with the three of us with that look on your face."

"What look?" I ask crossly, and he grins.

"The sort that says you're trying to work out all the sexual positions that were involved." He opens his eyes and directs a very serious expression at me. "Don't bother. What I did with them is like comparing mutton to steak."

"Oh, a lovely meat analogy. Lucky, lucky me."

He grins. "It's true. Nothing I did with them is anything more than a pale echo of the way we are. Nothing."

I stare at him, my fingers stroking down his chiselled chest. "Really?"

He nods. "I wouldn't say it if it wasn't true."

"But this thing between us is still going to get too boring for you in the end." He stares at me and I rush on, blurting out my secret thoughts. "I mean it's just sex with one person. At some point, it's going to feel too staid for you and I know you'll want to be off and filling your bed with more people." I hesitate, wishing my voice had some conviction in it when I say the next words. "I'll be fine if you want to finish whatever this is and move on. I just ask that you're honest and tell me before you do it."

He sits up, his eyes turbulent. "You'd be fine with me fucking other people?"

I nod, biting my lip, unable to hold his eyes which are burning with some emotion. "We didn't start this with any commitments beyond hooking up, so you're still free."

"Stop right now," he says sharply. He stands up, unleashing a surge of water over the sides of the tub. "Just stop fucking talking, Milo."

"Niall," I say urgently and try to grab him but he turns and storms off, banging into the door in his haste. "Niall," I shout and jump out of the tub, hissing as I land on my bad knee. I scramble up and dart into the bedroom, which is empty. For a second I think he's gone out, but then I hear movement in the bathroom and I rush to the door.

He's towelling himself off, his movements sharp and jerky, and he doesn't meet my eyes.

"Niall," I say imploringly. "I'm sorry. That came out wrong."

"Oh, so you didn't mean to say that it was fine for me to fuck other people and there's nothing between us apart from sex which is bound to get boring as there aren't multiple penises involved?"

"No," I say miserably. "P-Please, Niall. L-Let me talk." I hear the stutter and want to punch myself in the fucking throat. *Not now.*

He folds his arms. "Go ahead. " His expression is stormy.

"I d-d-don't want ..." I pause. "I don't ... I don't ..." Powerful red-tinged rage fills me suddenly from somewhere deep inside me, the place where I have to watch myself stammer and pause and deep breathe all the time. And before I know I'm going to do it, I grab a vase from a side table and throw it against the far wall. The sound of the smash of the pottery echoes through the room and everything goes still apart from the noise of our breathing. I stand and pant, unable to believe that I just threw something during a row. I never once lost control like this with Thomas. I wouldn't have dared.

"Feel better?" he says roughly.

"Oh God, Niall," I start to say but then gasp as he comes away from his standing position so quickly I don't have time to move before he grabs me, fisting my hair and kissing me furiously.

For a second I tense with old memories rising, but then the smell of him surrounds me and he gives the low groan that he always gives when he kisses me and I relax suddenly. And now that I've relaxed, I can recognise that although his grip is tight and his mouth impassioned, the hand in my hair is still gentle. I sag into him and kiss him back and for a second, all I can feel are heat and panting breaths and hot skin sliding against hot skin.

I give a groan when he pulls back as quickly as he kissed me. "Oh shit, Lo," he groans. "I'm sorry. Did I hurt you?"

"Oh no, Niall." I grab his arms as he tries to move back. "Don't you do that. Don't pull away and treat me like I'm made of china. I don't want that."

"What do you want?"

"I want you to treat me as your equal. Someone who stands on the same ground as you. I don't want you to hesitate with me and second-guess everything. I want you to talk to me honestly and tell me what you're feeling. And don't hold back."

"Really?" His breaths are more like pants on the side of my face and there's rosy colour in his cheeks. "So, if I tell you that I don't think I'll ever grow bored of having one person in my bed if that person is you, you won't freak out? When I tell you that there is no room for anyone else in my head at any time? That you fill me up all the time, in bed and out of it, so that all I can think of is you? That I can't remember a time when you didn't occupy some part of my mind, but now you're lodged in all of it?"

I swallow hard, feeling panic and joy winging equally through me, and he glares at me. This has drifted so far from what we were when I climbed into his bed a couple of weeks ago, and I don't know what to do. He must sense it because his next words echo my thoughts.

"So, you're okay with hearing that, Milo? Because it doesn't seem to fit with any of these fucking parameters that you keep banging on about."

"I'm not sure what our parameters are anymore," I say slowly, my tongue freed with him. "The only thing I know is that I want to be with you." I stare at him, looking into his turbulent eyes, and hesitate over my next words.

He immediately shakes his head. "Oh no, Lo. You wanted no barriers. What were you going to say?"

"I don't want you to sleep with anyone else," I whisper, breaking into his words and stopping him into absolute stillness.

"Milo," he says brokenly, and suddenly I'm in his arms and he's taking my mouth with a feverish determined kiss that somehow hurts my heart, and I wind my arms around him and pull him close to me.

"What else do you want?" he whispers, leaving my mouth and burying his head in my shoulder. "Tell me."

I pause, and the words flood out. "I want you to fuck me." He stiffens and I fist my hand in his hair, pulling his head up. "I want that," I say fiercely. Seeing the doubts rising on his lips, I shake my head crossly at him. "I've wanted it for a while and it's becoming a need." I twist against him, feeling his cock hard against me and hearing his groan. "I need you to fuck me. I trust you. I don't want gentle and holding back. I want all of you."

He pulls back and stares at me. His eyes are dark and his mouth swollen and he looks at me closely, his eyes intent and almost blind. "You're sure?" he asks and when I go to object, he raises his hand to stop me. "You'll get all of me, Lo, but a lot of me is this desire to protect you. It'll always be there as will the need to check you're okay. Get used to it."

I take a deep breath. "Niall, I want you to make love to me." I don't realise what I've said until he gives a stifled gasp and I redden. "Oh, I didn't mean to …"

"Shut up," he mutters, grabbing my face between his big hands and dragging me near for a deep kiss. "Shut up and get on the bed."

I swallow hard and move slowly as if I'm drifting through deepening waters towards the bed, feeling his body at my back, the heat wafting from him. I almost wish that I could pause this so I could analyse and pick apart all these conflicting emotions in me that both push me towards him and make me want to pull back at the same time. Then his hand trails down my back and I decide thinking might be overrated.

I climb onto the big bed and lie back looking at him as he stands by the side of the bed, his towel tented at the front and his eyes avid as they roam down my body, pausing at the tight nubs of my nipples and the hard length of my cock.

I lift the covers up. "Get in. It's cold away from the fire." A soft expression crosses his face and he pulls the towel away, letting it drop in a puddle at his feet as he climbs into the bed and lies down next to me.

For some reason, I feel open and exposed under that clear gaze, and he reads me easily. He always seems to find it easy. Bending to take my mouth, he kisses me for ages until my breaths are short and my mind clouded. Until my lips are swollen and my cock is hard and leaking.

Then he pulls away and tracks biting kisses that leave marks on my skin all down my body, tracing the sharp bones of my ribs and sucking on my hipbones like an animal nibbling and licking, before moving into my crotch. He nestles his face there, inhaling deeply and biting gently at the area where my thigh meets my groin.

I can hear my breathing loud in the quiet room, and I groan under my breath at the touch of his tongue to my cock. My brain has gone dark with no worries or concerns, just a drifting warm pleasure with no room for anything else because Niall is bossy in bed and that bossiness sets me free.

In the past few weeks, it's occurred to me to worry over it, to fret over the fact that once again I've handed control to another man, but then I'll look at him and know that I'm safe. He won't hurt me in bed. I know this as surely as I know my name, and it has set me free.

I cry out as he licks and suckles my cock, taking me deep down his throat with the same grace and sensual ease that he displays in bed. His mouth works on me and when he swallows, I fist my fingers in the white-blond strands of his hair.

"No," I shout out. "I'll come. Not like this."

He releases my cock with a pop and moves up to lie at my side where he grabs the tube of lube from under the pillow. Staring into my eyes, he uncaps the bottle and pours a stream onto his fingers. Still holding my gaze, he reaches down and cups my balls, tugging them gently so a low ache settles in the pit of my stomach. Then I swallow hard as he reaches lower and touches my hole.

Almost instinctively I spread my legs, trusting him, and I watch as a muscle ticks in his jaw. Impulsively, I raise up and kiss and lick at it before he takes my mouth in a heated kiss. I open my mouth to groan as he sends his fingers rubbing over my hole and seemingly waking about twenty billion nerves. He seizes the opportunity to thrust his tongue into my mouth, and the next few minutes are marked by the noise of our groans as he kisses me furiously, eating into my mouth while I gasp and arch under him as he fingers me open.

At first, it's strange and the burn scares me, but I relax as the pain that usually followed Thomas doing this never comes with Niall. Instead, he replenishes the lube frequently and takes his time until he hits my prostate and I arch up, choking on a scream as pleasure sears me. "Oh fuck," I cry out.

"Good?" he whispers.

I nod, staring at him. Sweat is coating him but his expression is calm. If it weren't for that tick in his jaw and the fact that his chest is rising and falling with fast breaths and his cock is hard and angry-looking, I'd never know he was getting desperate. But he is. I feel it.

Finally, I grab and stay his fingers. "Please, Niall. I need you."

He pulls back instantly, and I settle back in the bed as he reaches for a condom and rolls it on with expert moves, settling it with a snap. Then he reaches for a pillow and I lift up obligingly as he shoves it under my arse. With a graceful movement, he's kneeling at the entrance to my body before I know it.

He looks at me, checking I'm okay, and when I nod he closes his eyes and breathes deeply. Then I deliberately spread my legs further. "Fuck me," I gasp and he's there instantly. Notching his cock against my hole with one hand, he uses the other to rub my chest and hips soothingly as he starts to push.

I tense and he stops immediately. "You okay?"

"Just nervous," I say, hating the threadiness in my voice, but his face softens.

"It'll be okay," he says, sitting back slightly but not leaving my body. "It'll feel strange, but I swear it's not going to be like before." He holds my gaze until I nod, and then he pats my hip. "Okay, I'm in, but now you're going to take me the rest of the way in your own time."

I nod, looking down at our bodies. I can see where his cock is just in me, my hips and arse raised and my legs spread over the top of his thighs. He rests his hands on my hips and I cant my bum and pull him further in me. Slowly at first, but getting faster as my confidence builds, I grab onto his legs for traction and push down on him until finally, he bottoms out.

"Slow," I say on a gasp. He feels huge in me and strange and I take the moment gratefully, just breathing. He looks down at me and then, licking his palm, he reaches down and takes my cock in his hard, callused palm. His movements are so gentle it's like being stroked in a dream. His hand moves slowly and almost delicately and I chase it, but as I move my hips his cock presses against the knot in me and heat surges through me, and abruptly all that glorious, wild energy that I associate with being with Niall roars through me.

"Oh, God," I gasp and he looks at me. "Fuck me now. Please."

He nods and surges forward, his hips starting to piston gently at first, but as I urge him on with breathy cries and groans he gets harder until he's slamming into me and I'm urging him on, grabbing his arse to pull him in and winding my legs around him. What felt strange at first with something inside me now just feels glorious.

"Oh fuck," I cry out, and my hands slip around his arse cheeks to grab them and hold him in me. I graze his hole with my fingers by accident but he goes rigid.

"Yes. That's so fucking good. Do it."

I raise my fingers to his lips and he kisses them, sloppily mouthing and sucking them until they're wet and I can feel the pulse in my cock. Then I send them back and dance them over his opening before pushing one digit into him. His thrusts accelerate and I writhe under him, feeling my cock slip and slide along the ridged abs that are wet with sweat. I strain against him, searching for the end, and suddenly I'm there.

"Niall," I shout loudly, and he groans.

"*God,* yes. Come."

Then I'm coming, shooting between us without getting a hand on myself.

He lifts up slightly and stares down between our bodies. When he looks up, his eyes are dark and his expression frantic. "So hot," he says hoarsely. "You're so fucking good, Lo." The last is choked and he grunts as he starts to come, his face twisting almost as if he's in pain as he thrusts and thrusts, filling the condom inside me with heat.

Then he collapses onto me and we both lie there for a while as our breathing slows and we mumble soft asides and kiss. Finally, he levers off me, grabbing hold of the condom and tying a knot in it before he slings it into the bin near the bed.

I watch him, feeling a curious emptiness and already missing his body heat, but then he rolls over to me and pulls me into his arms and instantly the odd emptiness is gone, replaced with warmth and a very cautious joy.

"You are my equal," he whispers, answering my earlier words and pulling the duvet over us. "You've always been my equal. You're spiky and clear-headed and calm but to me, you're also precious and that means you can't ask me not to care and look out for you. It's what makes me the person I am."

I nestle further into him, running my fingers along his forearms, relishing the darker hair that grows there and tracing the long veins that marble the surface. "As long as you're okay with me doing it back to you," I whisper. "As long as you're okay with me caring if you're hurt or getting worried about you. Because sometimes you need me just as much as I do you."

He's still for a second as if surprised that anyone would want to take care of him. Then he hugs me closer. "I don't doubt that," he whispers, and the words echo in the sleepy silence between us.

CHAPTER 14

I have all these feelings.

Milo

I feel mellow and loose-limbed when I make my way downstairs dressed in old ripped jeans and an oversized high-necked cream jumper. The clothes feel comfortable and soft on my skin and I've left my hair loose. I follow the sound of conversation to the dining room. This is a cosy room situated at the back of the house with views of the village through its floor-to-ceiling windows. Tonight the village is lit up like one of Blackpool's illuminations.

The others are seated at the large table. A fire is crackling in the fireplace and Frank Sinatra is crooning about letting it snow. I inhale the scent of something wonderful cooking and my stomach rumbles. Almost without thought, my eyes search out Niall.

He's slumped in a loose, contented sort of way at the head of the table talking in a low voice to my brother. Barefoot and wearing a green and blue plaid shirt with threadbare Levi's, he looks gorgeous. I pause at the sight of the two of them with their heads together, but almost as if he senses my presence he looks up and grins widely at the sight of me. It's a warm and wide smile with an edge of satisfied contentment about it, and I flush because surely it's screaming at the others that yes, he got inside my arse this afternoon.

I sneak a quick look at them but luckily no one has noticed. Sam is slumped looking half pissed already while Jacinta and her sister are indulging in a conversation that has more hissing than a nest of snakes. Daisy's husband, Adam, is rubbing his wife's back somewhat anxiously.

He looks up and spies me and a rather relieved look crosses his face. "*Milo*," he exclaims as if Madonna has just walked in the room. "Look, everyone, it's Milo."

Niall snorts and Jacinta and Daisy break off their argument for a brief second to smile before immediately returning to it. Adam slumps and I pat his shoulder gingerly as I make my way over to the table.

As I near it, Niall jumps up, and I stare at him as he pulls out my chair. Conversation stops immediately and everyone stares, making him redden.

"What are you doing?" I whisper bemusedly.

"Pulling your chair out for you. I would have thought that was obvious," he hisses back.

I shake my head and sit down, wincing slightly when my tender arse protests. A smile plays across his lips and I shake my head. "Just because I took it up the arse doesn't suddenly mean I can't move furniture out for myself," I whisper.

"Babe, the way you did it I'm inclined to give you a golden chair to sit in," he says with a smirk. "And a silk cushion."

I can't help my smile. Sometimes it seems like it's been grafted on there when I'm around him. I only have to look at him and my lips want to turn upwards. Feeling slightly flustered at the thought I look determinedly around the table, flushing when I find my brother's eyes on me. He's watching me curiously, as if I'm some sort of rare animal at the zoo. He's been doing it for a few days and it's alternately worrying and annoying me. I grimace at him irritatedly and an amused smile ticks at his lips.

Daisy breaks off her hissed conversation with Jacinta and eyes me. I immediately slump slightly in the vague hope that she can't see me. It doesn't work, and Niall snorts.

"So, Milo, have you given up the idea of snowboarding since you came off again today?"

I blink. "No, of course not. If I quit something just because I fell over, I'd never have learnt to walk as a child."

She stares at me unblinkingly, like a rather judgemental owl. "You're not terribly good at it though." My brother bites his lips to keep a smile in and she continues remorselessly. "I think it's always good to know one's own limitations."

"*Do you?*" I'm startled because there's no way she recognises her own. She's so hugely pleased with herself it's not possible that she recognises her own faults, legion though they are.

She nods happily. "Of course. It's so important for one's personal development. Every morning I meditate for half an hour on my character. Adam is very keen on it."

I bet he is, I think. *It must be the only time in the day when she's quiet.*

The sudden shocked silence alerts me to potential danger which is elevated to Def Con One when Daisy glares at me. "What did you just say?" she asks in a dangerous voice.

"Oh my God, did I say that out loud?" I groan and Niall starts to laugh helplessly.

"You really did." He leans forward. "Watch this," he whispers and sits up straight, saying in a loud voice, "Daisy, you must tell me what I did wrong at skiing today." She immediately unbends after giving me a caustic glare. "Thank you, Niall," he intones to me as she launches into a whole monologue about his skiing technique.

"I don't need to thank you," I say sourly. "She'll forget all about her grievance with me the second she spots me doing something wrong. I've never known anyone so obsessed with judging other people. I'm surprised she hasn't popped up at the bottom of our bed with scorecards yet."

"They'd say ten," he says loyally and probably completely erroneously. Then he shudders. "I think you just gave me performance anxiety."

I grin and shake my head at him and turn to tune into Daisy's monologue. It's abruptly broken by Jacinta who yawns widely and loudly. Daisy falters but valiantly continues to dissect Niall's stance, then gives up when Jacinta makes snoring noises.

"I'm sorry," Daisy hisses. "Am I boring you?"

"Yes, but don't worry about it," Jacinta says blithely. "It won't stop you anyway."

"I'd like to think that I can take conversational cues as well as the next person."

"Only if the next person is Helen Keller."

I choke on my first sip of water. Daisy turns to stare at me. "Sorry," I mutter. "Wrong hole."

Niall tops up my glass. "We'll have to work on that, sweetheart. That sounds like a problem for Niall Fawcett to fix."

Daisy ignores him and turns back to Jacinta. "At least I don't think I can fuck my way through awkward silences."

"Oh, I say," Adam interjects, and the two girls turn furious faces on him. He subsides, holding his hand up in surrender, and gulps his wine down quickly before she can lecture him about his alcohol content, which has been a common theme this week.

"Well, excuse me for having a healthy sexual drive," Jacinta says and glares at Daisy when she smirks. "At least I use mine. I bet Adam would have to fight his way through cobwebs to get into your vagina."

"How dare you?" Daisy shouts, rising up from the table. I brighten up at the thought that she might be leaving but then slump as she lowers herself back to her chair.

"No, really," Jacinta says. "I'm surprised he hasn't got a fedora and a bullwhip. Didn't Indiana Jones go after ancient, dusty relics?"

"You're a fucking bitch," Daisy yells abruptly, discarding her impression of the Virgin Mary which she's been aiming at all week.

"And you're a dried up, desiccated, prissy old know-it-all."

"You have spots."

Jacinta gasps. "You bitch."

"Ladies," Niall says. "Please don't argue." They turn as one to glare at him and he holds his hands up. "Well, if needs must, then please go ahead. But make sure you go outside and let the neighbours hear. It'll reaffirm their impression that this chalet is the new outpost for Sodom and Gomorrah. You'll make them very happy."

I snort at the thought of his well-to-do neighbours who scurry away as soon as they see him, as if they wait for a second too long, he'll expose himself. Mind you, I suppose if he's been as wild as I've heard about, I can't blame them. The thought sours my mood and I automatically look at my brother, as he's been Niall's partner in crime for so many years.

I jerk as I find him looking at me. "*What?*" I say sharply. "Shall I take a picture and then you can really examine it?"

"*Milo,*" Niall says in a surprised voice.

I shake my head. "Don't start, Niall."

"What do you mean?"

"Every time I've said anything to him this week you've jumped in and defended him." I glare at him. "Pick a fucking side." I pause. "Unless you've already done that."

"Don't be fucking ridiculous," he says in a suddenly grim voice. "You know where my loyalties lie."

"Not with me," I say hotly but all of a sudden Gideon stands up, his chair scraping back.

"Stop behaving like a fucking child," he growls and stalks out of the room, slamming the door behind him.

Silence falls, apart from Sam who jerks awake with a sudden start. "When's breakfast?" he asks blearily.

Adam drains another glass of wine in a surreptitious manner. "This is like the dinner party from hell," he slurs.

Daisy turns her glacial stare on him. "Adam, how many glasses have you had? You know how I feel about your drinking. Think of your waistline."

"I'm more concerned about the damage that your voice is doing to my eardrums," he says peevishly, pouring himself another glass.

"Adam," she whispers furiously. "Remember who you're talking to."

"Yes, the Duchess of Do Nothing Right," Jacinta says tartly. Daisy hisses and turns on her and they're off again.

Niall throws his napkin on the table and goes to stand up, but my hand shoots out and stays him. "I'm sorry," I say quietly.

He has a very disappointed look on his face which makes my stomach drop. "Until the next time," he says slowly.

"What do you mean?"

"I mean that you're obsessed with the fact that I fucked him." He shrugs. "I can't take that back and honestly, I wouldn't want to."

"What?" My hurt is visible, and he shakes his head crossly.

"It's part of my past and I don't regret anything. It's what's gone towards making me who I am now. It's created the me who's with you now. I can't ever regret that because I'm happy with the place I'm in." He pauses. "Well, I would be if you'd get your head out of your arse."

"Really?"

He stares at me, his eyes wide and unblinking. "You need to sort this out. I don't think the problem is me and him. That was never anything that was going anywhere and at the heart of you, you know that. The problem is actually you and him." He sighs. "The two of you have this awkward push and pull where one pulls while the other isn't watching and then he pushes. Then before you know it, you're in a fucking tug of war. You need to stop it because I think you're missing out on a relationship with him that would do you both good. Milo, you need your brother." He smiles at me. "And he needs you."

"As if," I scoff, and he shakes his head.

"Get out of your head and away from where you think everything he does shows you up in a negative light. Like you measuring yourself against him all the time and thinking you come up short. The truth is so far from that, it's laughable. Actually see him, Lo, because at the moment he needs you more than you need him."

"He needs you."

"No, he doesn't," he says simply. "Or if he does, it's because he's clinging to familiarity."

Dinner is quiet after this, as though Gideon's disappearance has put a pall on things. I can't concentrate on anything because Niall's words echo in my head, and when everyone has gone to bed, I roam the ground floor looking for my brother. I find him outside on the patio wrapped in a blanket and sitting on the wicker sofa looking down at the lights of the village.

He looks up when he hears the door and gazes at me solemnly while he sips from a bottle of vodka. Feeling unnerved by the silence I hover, shifting from foot to foot.

"Don't you want a glass?" I ask.

The words are so innocuous that I'm not surprised he smirks. "Nope," he says calmly, popping the p. "It would interfere with the speed at which I'm intending to drink this bottle."

I drift nearer to him and shiver violently. "Jesus, it's cold out here."

He shakes his head but holds up the edge of the blanket in silent invitation. I take it, diving under gratefully and pulling the blanket around my shoulders. It smells of his Tom Ford cologne, which is his signature scent, making it at once somehow exotic and yet as familiar as our childhood home.

He offers me the bottle silently, and I take an enthusiastic gulp and immediately cough as it burns my throat. "Shit," I say morosely and he laughs unexpectedly, his eyes warm and his face open, making him look suddenly young.

"You never could drink well," he says almost affectionately. "I remember Niall giving you a sip of his whisky one Christmas and you coughed so hard you spat in his hair."

"Oh lovely," I say faintly. "I'm surprised his dick can get hard around me with those lovely memories in his head."

"I don't think you need to worry about that," he says slowly and instantly the awkwardness roars back in.

"Do you mind?" I ask suddenly, breaking the silence as surely as if I've put a brick to it.

He stares down at the village, looking meditative. "Would it make any difference?"

Alarm flares in me. *Is he going to make me choose between him and Niall?*

He shoots me a slanting glance that seems almost amused. "I can hear your brain working from over here."

"And what is my brain saying?"

"Who you'd choose if it came down to it. Would you choose your hook-up or your brother?"

"Niall is not a hook-up," I say indignantly and he turns to me, all humour gone.

"Isn't he? You might want to mention that to him, because as far as I can see you're just using him to see what sex should feel like." He settles back and smiles. "I have to say he's the best person for that. He's an amazing fuck."

Rage fizzles in my stomach at the thought of these two together. It mingles with misery because Gideon is so much more understandable with Niall. They look as if they belong to each other. Gideon is the same as him – confident, funny, and assured as opposed to shy, stuttery me who probably makes Niall look like he's babysitting me for my mum.

Gideon shrugs when I say nothing. "So, why would I be bothered? I'll wait for this whatever it is to blow itself out and then Niall will come back to me." He smiles. "He always does."

My vision seems to go dark for a second as if all that rage has short-circuited my eyeballs. "He won't come back to you," I say, breathing deeply at the start of the sentence so it comes out properly.

His eyes seem to soften at my indrawn breath, but they harden a second later. "Why do you want him, Milo? He's just a training cock for you. The two of you don't go. He doesn't read much because he can't sit still for long. That means the cinema and the theatre are out. Museums and art galleries are a no-go too. He gets this hunted look like the room's too small and he'll have to hold it up by his shoulders. What would you ever have in common with him when you get bored of his cock?"

The words spill out of me now like they're greased with coconut oil. "We *do* go together. You just can't see it. Yes, he's all of the things you mentioned but he's so much more. He's funny. So funny. He can make me laugh even when we're arguing. He's passionate and kind. He's the kindest person I've ever met. He would give anyone the shirt off his back, but he covers it up with sarcasm and flippancy. Every night he wraps the covers over me so that I don't get cold. Then he tells me that it's because otherwise my hair will escape and fill the room. He makes sure I eat while I'm working, through an unholy alliance with Maggie the cook. Then he says it's because he needs me in working order for sex. He might not read many books but he's still clever. He has a vast knowledge of politics and the world and I can talk to him for hours and never get bored. I don't want someone to share my hobbies. I just want someone who's interested enough in me to really listen, and he does that. Always."

I stop for breath and only then notice that he's smiling. "What's so bloody funny, Gideon?"

He shakes his head as if in dismay. "Listen to yourself," he says deeply, that rich voice of his weaving around me. I look at him in confusion and he sighs. "All that you just said is not someone talking about a sexual experiment. You're talking about a real man made of flesh and blood and for all his failings, a really lovable man, and you see that." He looks intensely at me. "Now, tell me you're just hooking up, Milo, because I've had many hook-ups and I've never talked to them for hours." He grins. "Fucked them, yes. Talked, not so much." He looks sad. "And I can concretely say that none of them have ever made sure I eat." He pauses. "Even Niall."

I stare at him. "Oh my God," I say slowly. "I have all these feelings, Gideon." I shake my head. "Fucking Niall. Even in this, he has to complicate things." I breathe in deeply, feeling panic rush through me. "Oh fuck. This was never part of the deal we had."

I think of Thomas and that panic accelerates. This is just how it was with him. I never understood what he saw in me at first and so I kept my distance and my heart. Then by the time I came to trust in him he'd grown disenchanted and cruel, but it was too late for me and I stayed hopelessly and blindly loyal. It's even worse with Niall. I have so many feelings for him. How much will this hurt if it goes wrong and he despises me? Will I have the strength to leave him if it goes wrong? I'd only just got away from Thomas. Leaving Niall might just kill me.

Gideon gives a loud, startled laugh and I push the teeming thoughts away. I can't help but smile at him because it reminds me so much of when he was younger and the brother I idolised. Then I have a blinding realisation that practically smacks me in my face.

"Oh my God, has this been deliberate?" I breathe. He looks at me with an innocent expression on his face and I gesture furiously. "All this. The trip away, the goading me. Has it all been for this?"

He shrugs and takes a long sip of the vodka. "I don't know what you mean."

I nudge him. "Yes, you do. All this posturing about Niall and making me jealous. It feels like you've been prodding me along this path. Why haven't you been as concerned about Niall?"

He shakes his head, a serene expression on his face. "I'm not worried about Niall's part in this. He and I know where he stands."

"Where?" He immediately shakes his head, so I know I won't get an answer on that. "Are you bothered that I'm with him? Honesty, please." I pause and hold my breath.

He looks down at the village and the lights seem to flash across his face, making it mysterious all of a sudden. Then he smiles almost sadly. "No, not now. I was at first. I was very angry and hurt when I found out. But over the last few days here I've realised that I love him because he's my best friend. *Not* because he was my lover. And that will never change."

"I wouldn't want it to," I say slowly, and he nods.

"At the end of the day, though, it was just sex. Stupendous sex," he adds, winking at me. I shake my head and he sighs. "But it could never have been more than that because I wouldn't let it." He bites his lip. "And I wasn't the right brother for him. He just had to wait around for you." He shrugs. "Once I realised the truth, I wanted you to see it too." He pauses. "I also have to say in the interests of complete fairness that the goading is completely natural and unfortunately one of my main character traits."

"Won't this be awkward?"

He scoffs. "Of course not. This is the same family where Aunt Margo has been fucking Uncle Jeff's wife for years. If they can sit down for Christmas dinner, then so can we."

I gasp. "She's fucking Diana?"

"Have you been living under a rock? It's been going on for years."

"Is that why they keep going away on spa weekends?"

"I don't think it's for the seaweed wraps and the deep-tissue massage."

I look at him. "I don't just want dinner once a year though. I want my brother in my life all the time." I pause. "Why have you told me all this about Niall?"

He turns to me, his face serious. "Because he's my oldest friend and he deserves so much more than what I gave him for years. But mostly because I want you to be happy, Lo, and you were in danger of ruining everything with him." My eyes fill at that old nickname and his smile becomes tender. "You deserve to be happy. So happy. And I'm your brother. It's my job. I haven't always been good at it, but I'd like to try harder if that's okay with you?"

I nod and hug him, resting my head against his shoulder. "I'd like that." I look up at him. "But it goes both ways, Gideon. If you can meddle then so can I."

He scoffs and kisses the top of my forehead. "What on earth do you have to meddle with in my life? It runs like clockwork. I have fame and money beyond most people's imagining, a beautiful house, good friends, and an annoying brother." I snort and he smiles. "What more could I want?"

"Someone of your own," I say softly, and he flinches. "You're lovely under all those caustic comments. I'd just like someone else to realise and value that."

"I am not lonely," he says, taking another sip of his drink. "I have people around me all the time."

"Who want something from you. What about someone who just wants something *for* you? I want you to find that someone."

He shakes his head. "I've never met anyone who was worth stopping for."

"You will." I pause. "I wonder if it will be a man."

He looks diverted. "I shouldn't think so. I'm attracted to men, but I don't know whether I'd settle down with one."

"That's because you're thinking with a bisexual penis rather than a bisexual heart. Someone's going to come along and shake that up. I can feel it."

He shudders. "Well, don't. Take some penicillin and stop it." He pauses and looks pensive. "Anyway, it couldn't be a man."

"Why?"

"Because it would finish my career."

"Would it, bollocks," I say crossly. "There are plenty of gay men in the industry."

"And you don't see many of them playing the roles I do. The leading man walks off into the sunset with a woman, not a man."

"It hasn't done Asa Jacobs any harm."

He shakes his head. "He's different."

"How?"

"He was bisexual from the beginning. He was always honest."

He pauses and takes a slug from the bottle. "I haven't been honest," he continues in a whisper. "And my fans would never forgive me. I would feel as if I'd let them down."

"They buy tickets to your films, Gideon. It doesn't give them an automatic backstage pass to your life. They'd get over it. You're still an amazing actor."

He shakes his head impatiently. "You don't understand. Frankie says–"

"Oh, Frankie," I say scornfully, thinking of his wanker of a manager. "Frankie would sell your used tissues if he felt it would make him money. You're a cash cow to him and that's all." He snorts, and I grab his arm. "You're not that for me, Gideon. You're my brother and I love you." The words fall into the silence like petals on a pond and to my amazement, his eyes fill. "Gideon," I say, and he sniffs.

"Ignore me. I'm just being disgustingly sentimental."

I nudge him. "Who knew I'd be around for that? I think the last time was 1997."

He laughs and hugs me tightly. "I love you too," he says softly. "I'd like to see more of you though, if that's possible?"

It's my turn to blink. "I'd like that very much."

He kisses my head affectionately, the way he used to before the differences in our ages and the disparate way our parents treated us pushed us away from each other like we were on diverging currents on a river. "Well, I've accepted a job in a series that's filming near you, so we can do that."

"Where?" I ask but he bops me on the nose.

"Nowhere you know," he says comfortably and passes me the bottle. "Let's finish this and reminisce about the time that Niall got drunk and mistook our neighbour's house for ours." He smiles. "I can still hear Mr. Finton's scream when Niall got into bed with him."

CHAPTER 15

Lo, there's more than a touch of the minx about you.

Niall

I find him in our room later that night. The lamps are lit, filling the room with a soft glow, and a fire crackles in the grate, making the room warm and cosy. He's lying on the chaise lounge wrapped in a blanket and watching the snow fall outside that's lit strangely by the balcony light.

When I close the door he turns and for an instant, there's a very strange expression on his face. I want to call it happiness mixed with apprehension, but it disappears so quickly I can't manage to categorize it. Nevertheless, I feel uneasy for some reason, as if something has shifted that I didn't pay attention to.

Then he smiles and I forget about it, lost in the curve of that full lip of his.

He lifts up the corner of the blanket and I kick off my shoes and climb into his nest happily. He turns on his side and I spoon up behind him. He's only wearing a pair of pyjama shorts and I can feel his soft skin against mine. Silence falls for a while as we watch the fat snowflakes twirl in a hypnotic pattern. The only sounds are his soft breathing, the delicate patter of the snowflakes on the glass, and the pop as wood shifts in the fire. It's extraordinarily peaceful and not something I've ever done with a lover before. I've always been antsy and on the move, so it's a surprise to find the contentment I do in lying with him in sleepy warmth.

I send my hands down his body, admiring the sleek skin under my calloused palms. He twists under me, languorously stretching, and words spill out. "You remind me of the willow trees in the south field."

He cocks one eyebrow, his hair falling around his face in loose waves. "Why?"

I swallow but the words come out anyway. "Because you're slender and look delicate but you twist and bow with whichever way the wind bends you. You never break because your roots are deep and sturdy."

He's silent for a second, obviously thinking my words over, and I feel a flush on my face. Then he twists to see me and a warm smile plays on his lips. "That's the nicest thing that anyone has ever said to me," he murmurs.

I shake my head, thinking grimly of Thomas. "You should listen to the right person." I pinch his hip and he jerks and laughs. "That's me, by the way. I'd recommend that you always listen and obey me."

He snorts. "That's not likely."

"I know." The satisfaction with that is clear in my voice and I see him smile. When he says nothing more, I cuddle closer and we lapse into a comfortable silence.

I'm half dozing when he stirs. "We go back tomorrow," he says.

I nestle closer and blink sleepily. "I know. Will you be sad?"

He runs his slender fingers over my forearm almost absentmindedly. "I will," he says with an air of discovery. "I've loved it here. I don't want to leave."

I hesitate. "Well, it's always here," I say, mentally holding my breath. "We'll come back in January and have a few days skiing. Then it's beautiful in the spring and summer. We could come back and hike. The air is so clear and perfect. We'll do it on our own though." I come to a stuttering stop, aware that I'm babbling, but he doesn't laugh. Instead, he turns around to face me so we're sharing a pillow and staring into each other's faces. It's extraordinarily intimate.

He smiles at me and it almost seems like tenderness hovers on it. Then he traces one long finger down my face, coming to a stop at my lower lip. I pretend to bite it and he gives that wide, unguarded smile that I'm seeing a lot of lately.

"I would like that," he says softly. "Just the two of us."

Emotion fills me all of a sudden, like I've inhaled happiness helium. It flows through my veins and from the time it takes to draw one breath to the next, I know that I'm in love with him. I become aware that I'm holding my breath and I exhale unobtrusively. I wait for the panic to fill me, but it doesn't come.

It's strange that I've lived a life full of excess, never risking my heart, and now I'm gambling everything on the whim of a beautiful man who pretty soon may unfurl his wings and fly away, and I still feel nothing but gratitude. I'm grateful that he's in my life at this moment. That I can hold him in my arms at night. That he trusts me with his inner feelings, when he doesn't do that with many people.

I know he may go, but that has no bearing on my feelings. This whole thing feels inevitable and unstoppable, like a small part of me always knew that we would end up here, lying together in a peace that I've never felt before.

I shift position, using the opportunity to shield my expression. I may have had a revelation but I'm realistic enough to know that he hasn't. I'm just a familiar figure he feels comfortable enough with to act on sexual attraction. He'll probably settle with some artistic man who shares his interests and he won't think of me again beyond a few good memories, but I still wouldn't change anything.

I pause for a second and contemplate that unexpectedly selfless thought. Then I think of that unknown man and scowl because fuck that wanker. I'm going to fight for Milo even though hopefully he won't realise it, and I'm going to win and keep him. I'll just have to be careful about it because my Lo does not like being manoeuvred into anything.

When I look up he's staring at me, his eyes dark with some emotion.

"How did it go with Gideon?" I ask quickly. I don't need him seeing inside my head the way he has a funny knack of doing.

He smiles and I relax slightly. I've hated the tension between the two brothers this week. They're both so similar underneath. They love each other and just don't know how to show it because they're essentially strangers who share the same blood. Nevertheless, if Milo and I are to stand any chance together, he has to be at peace with his brother and vice versa. If I had been made to choose between them then it's obvious that I'd have chosen Milo, but I'd hoped never to have to do that because I'll always care for Gideon.

"We talked," he says, slowly nestling into me and pushing his head into my neck. It's something he does a lot, like he feels safe there. I treasure it, so I immediately curl my arms around him, loving the soft sigh he gives. "He wants to spend more time together."

"Well, that's good then, isn't it?" I say softly, and he nods, his hair scratching at my neck and his sharp scent of lemon and rosemary rising around us.

"Yes. I feel like we could be close now. I've always wanted that."

"Good," I say quietly. "I want that too for both of you."

He hums his agreement and I relax. That's one hurdle out of the way. Now, I just have to tackle the small issue of him only seeing me as a handy cock. Piece of cake. I've never yet met a challenge I've backed down from. I kiss his head and we turn back to watch the snow, but my mind is plotting and motoring throughout the quiet peacefulness.

One Week Later

Milo

I straddle Niall, sweat pouring down my body, and give a guttural groan. His cock is a hard spike inside me and I ride it, feeling it press against my prostate which sends sparks through me and makes my vision blur.

I look down at that long, strong body. His hands are fisted in the sheets at either side of his hips and his head is thrown back, his teeth bared in a grimace.

"Niall," I gasp out and his eyes open, the pupils making them look almost black. "Fuck, I'm close," I groan and he grunts.

"Do it, sweetheart. I want you to come all over me." He reaches out and his hand which is still wet with lube circles my cock. I look down at the ruddy length of my cock shuttling between his long fingers and the visual sends me over.

"Oh fuck!" I choke out and squeeze my eyes shut as I start to come.

"Yes," he moans and levers his hips up once, twice in a series of battering thrusts and then he gives a sharp cry and I feel heat inside me where he's filled the condom. "Fuck," he mutters, his voice wrecked, and I shudder as another wave of aftershocks runs through me.

When we both quieten and have stopped gulping for air as if we're on a planet with no oxygen, he grabs the base of his dick and the condom with the ease of practice while I lever up and off him. I collapse next to him in a sated sprawl.

"I know it's customary for the person on top to rush off and get clean towels and tenderly bathe your body," I murmur.

"But?"

"But I'm knackered and I really feel that I did all the work. I'm afraid you're on your own."

He snorts with laughter and I feel him sit up, and I listen as he gives a contented groan. I open one eye and gaze at him sitting on the edge of the bed and stretching. I've never known before how much I love men's backs. I mean, how could I? I'd only ever seen Thomas's and I was usually glad of it because it meant he was walking away from me. But Niall's back is beautiful.

His shoulders are wide, tapering down to a narrow waist, and it's pleated with muscle. But my favourite parts are the tiny imperfections that only a lover would notice. The freckles on his shoulders from a holiday in Spain when he was little and burnt badly. The two-inch pink scar on his lower hip where his brother hit him with a sword when they were playing *Lord of the Rings* after reading the book. According to Niall, his brother was pretending to be Aragorn, but he looked more like Gimli. I smile because that's just not true, as his whole family is pretty. His mother is Swedish and an extremely beautiful woman, so all of her children look like they're ready to pose for a Nordic fashion magazine.

I watch as he gets up and pads to the bathroom. I can hear the sound of running water and a cupboard opening, and I must have dozed off because his hands on me startle me awake.

"What?" I ask blearily and he smiles.

"Nothing, sweetheart. I'm just cleaning you up. Go back to sleep."

Instead, I stare at him as he works, cleaning my cock and balls gently and removing the lube and sweat from my arse. His expression is soft, and I'd say it was unguarded and almost hesitant if it was anyone other than Niall, and I'm fascinated.

He's been almost gentle this week since we got back from skiing. Gone is the wild frenzy that marked our early sex. Now, it's languid and lasts a long time because Niall has edging down to a dark art. But it's not just that. He touches me more outside the bedroom. When we walk, he'll throw his arm around me or touch my hand. He's quick to brush my hair back or touch my mouth, and when he does that, his expression is always the same as the one he's wearing now. Soft and almost content.

I frown because I can't parse the emotion in him, used as I am to his lively sarcasm and cheerfulness. He seems almost meditative, as if he's come to a conclusion over something that's been bothering him and is content to stay there in that position for a bit.

He looks up, and when he catches my gaze, he stills for a second as we look at each other. His eyes are dark and mysterious and almost fierce for a second, and then he wipes them clean of expression and smiles happily before leaning forward and kissing my forehead.

"There. All done," he says tenderly and roots his nose into my hairline and inhales as if taking my scent into him.

I blink and he's gone, pacing back to the bathroom and throwing the towel in. He turns at the door. "I'm going to get a drink. What shall I bring you?"

"Tea," I say in a heartfelt voice and he grins suddenly. It's wide and white in his face and the lines elongate along his eyes.

"Of course. You're like the anti-Ernest Hemingway."

"I'd be glad of that," I shout after him. "Given his fondness for guns and whisky."

His laughter grows faint as he walks away, and I roll onto my back and look up at the ceiling before exhaling slowly. I don't know what to do with this feeling that wells inside me every time I'm near him, like a helium balloon is expanding inside me. Since Gideon made me admit that I have feelings, they seem to have kept growing until they're out of control now. I think about Niall constantly, often smiling like an idiot at something he's said. I bring his name into everything to the extent that Oz had challenged me to go five minutes without mentioning his name. The penalty had been to stand in the garden for ten minutes. It had been cold out there, but Oz had lent me his coat.

I scrub my hands down my face and groan. *What the fuck?* One fling, I wanted. One measly fling with the man of my dreams. No ties, and then I'd be off to find the real man I'd end up with. Someone quiet and steady, who would give me quiet, unassuming love and contentment and no switch-streams of emotion that would leave me fumbling like an idiot.

Instead, I've fallen for the one man I shouldn't, and I'm caught in a whirlwind of emotions every time I'm with him. I'm fascinated with him and almost bespelled because every day he shows me more of the real him. I've learnt that he has an unexpected sweet tooth and adores rose and violet creams, to the extent that he can devour a whole bag in one sitting. I know that he's too busy or too tired at night to read but he has an addiction to audiobooks and always has one on the go in his car. His feet are always cold but he can't bear to wear anything in bed. I've seen the quiet him who's content to lie with me, despite Gideon's depiction. And the part of him that's at home outside like it's his natural habitat but who still wants me alongside him as we tramp across fields out in the open air, laughing and talking.

Then there's the man who dares me to do things outside my comfort zone that I immediately do because I feel safe with him and I know he won't let me come to any harm. Like the other night when he'd dared me to fuck him in a club. I'd done it, relishing the dark thrill that anyone could walk in at any point and see me fucking this gorgeous man. But later I'd found out that he'd paid a bouncer a hundred quid to say the toilet was out of order so I'd be safe and wouldn't regret it.

I still. But surely it's my responsibility to make sure I'm safe. Not his. I frown. I've always felt like I've coasted along in life like a piece of driftwood on the tide, letting others make my decisions. I never even managed to save myself from Thomas. That was Niall. And that makes me feel weak. I don't want to rely on someone to rescue me or be responsible for my happiness. I should do all that myself.

I hear his footsteps and clear my expression. I'm no nearer knowing what to do. All I know is that I'm falling for him so fast that it scares me and exhilarates me at the same time. Like a rollercoaster that hopefully isn't going to make me chuck up my dinner on the person in front. I snort.

"What's so funny?" he asks from the doorway, and I turn to smile at him.

"Nothing," I say quickly. "Come back to bed. I'm getting my second wind."

"Milo, I swear you've got a problem. You get your wind up quicker than a kite."

I laugh as he slides into bed, pulling the covers over us and lifting one arm so I can take my now customary position curled into his side, my head tucked into his shoulder and his hand pushing my hair back because he complains that it goes up his nose.

We lie silent for a long second until he stirs, shifting his legs about. When he does it again, I look up at him curiously. "You alright?"

"I'm fine, why?"

I raise my eyebrow at the slightly defensive note in his voice. "Nothing. It's just that after sex you normally pass out quicker than Oliver Reed after a dinner party."

He huffs but doesn't dispute it, which is good because he can't.

Finally, he speaks. "I was just thinking that maybe we should go out for a meal or something rather than just have sex."

I pull away and come up on one elbow so I can see him properly. "Like on a *date*?" I ask incredulously and watch as his face flushes. I bite my lip to stop myself kissing him because I love him when he's unsure. It touches me deeply.

"Not exactly a date," he says quickly. "Maybe look on it as two people just taking a breather before someone's cock gets inserted into an orifice." He pauses. "And maybe the two people should eat dinner at a restaurant because it refuels them and they could talk while they're doing that."

He falters, and I grin at him. "That's a date, Niall," I say with a smirk. "I realise that in your legions of meaningless sexual encounters that you might not have come across this concept before, but here in this realm we think that the times when a couple come together to eat, drink, and talk are called dates."

"Fuck off," he mutters, pulling the pillow over his eyes. I'm so charmed by this, I can't say. I pull the pillow away and look down at him, loving every sulky line of his face.

"Why?" I ask.

He tosses the pillow to one side and bites his lip, looking unsure. "I just want to do something that doesn't involve come for a bit." He looks at me and adds hastily, "Not for long obviously, because that's amazing. But I just want to get to know each other."

I smile calmly down at him. If it were anyone else I'd let them off the hook for being so adorable, but it's Niall, who once rubbed gravy on the bottom of my jeans to the avid delight of the dogs, so I won't.

"I do know you," I say calmly. "I know that you take your tea so sugared that the spoon practically stands up in the cup and that you have atrocious taste in music. That you won't see a foreign film because the subtitles are too much work and make your eyes hurt. I know that your bedroom is so cold that even Scott of the Antarctic would have asked for a hot water bottle. That you spend loads of money on clothes online but won't take the time from your day to go off the estate to go shopping. Which is also, incidentally, why you insist on cutting your own hair."

"I sound like a prize. I'm not sure why you're even sleeping with me," he says coolly and I swoop down and kiss his nose affectionately, making him give a sound of disgust.

"Beats me," I say cheerfully. "I must be a sucker for hopeless causes." He glares at me and I wink. "However, I also know that when Barb's husband was made redundant you actually told her that employment laws were forcing you to give her a pay rise. I know that when Phil hurt his back and Silas couldn't afford another worker, you did your own and Phil's job so he didn't feel guilty. I also know that you worked for free for years. Silas may have given you this house, but it was derelict when you took it on and you then felt honour bound to renovate it because otherwise, he'd feel like you didn't value the gesture and then it wouldn't make it right and equal between the two of you."

"How do you know this?" he asks darkly.

I sit up and come over him, straddling him and smiling down into his face. "Your staff are very fond of you even with all your faults, more faults, and even more faults." He glares and I smile placidly. "Given any opportunity, they'll wax lyrical about you and it's why you have very little turnover of staff, in case you're wondering."

"I wasn't," he says sulkily and I kiss him, loving the way he chases my mouth when I sit back.

"You're a good friend and a wonderful man, Niall," I say calmly. "So, that's why I'd love to go on a date with you."

For a second he looks confused and almost embarrassed. Then he comes up on his elbows. "You were *always* going on a date with me?" he says accusingly.

I shrug. "Of course."

"Then what was all that about?"

I smile evilly at him. "Do you remember the gravy and how I had to lock myself in the bathroom to get away from Chewwy and Boris?"

He considers it and sighs. "You have a very long memory."

"I'm hung like an elephant," I say modestly. "But perhaps you'd be better off concentrating on the fact that I have a memory like one."

He shakes his head. "Lo, there's more than a touch of the minx about you."

CHAPTER 16

Your past is your past. I mean, yours is more colourful than a bumper box of Crayola, but that's you.

Milo

That evening I come down the staircase at the main house and come to a stop. Niall is there dressed elegantly in a slim-cut charcoal-grey suit with a white shirt. But so are Oz and Silas. Oz has a massive grin on his face and Niall just looks resigned, leaning against the stairwell with his arms folded across his chest.

"What's going on?" I ask.

Niall turns. "I want you to know, Lo, that while I think you're totally worth it, it's at times like these that this belief is sorely tested."

Oz snorts and I shake my head. "Were they taking the piss out of you, sweetie?" I ask, coming up next to him and sliding my arm around his waist.

Oz's eyes flick to the movement and he opens his mouth as if to say something but then at the last minute, he obviously decides not to.

"Are you alright?" I ask curiously, and he flushes.

"Perfectly okay, thank you. Why?"

"I think the fact that your jaw has stopped working is causing us all some concern," Niall drawls, and Oz sends him a fulminating glare.

"Gah! I can't stand it. You're both so cute together and I feel my heart get warm when I look at you."

"Ugh!" I say concisely and Niall shudders.

"You can say that again, Milo. Personally, I think I prefer the acid sarcasm to that."

Oz nods sadly. "I know. You've broken me." He heaves a sigh. "Silas, I'll be watching Hallmark films next and choosing birthday cards that have nice sayings and heartfelt verses on them."

"What, like the card you sent me for my birthday?" Niall says. "The one with the highly touching words, 'Happy birthday, you gigantic twat' on it?"

Oz chortles, his eyes merry. "Niall, you're so sweet at the moment that Barbara Cartland would have denounced you for being too much."

"And on that note, we're out," Niall says quickly, grabbing my arm and towing me after him. We stop as Silas calls Niall's name.

Niall turns. "I would just like to say, Silas, that I appreciate how mature you are being, unlike your small prat of a partner. What do you want?"

Silas smiles widely. "I just want to know your intentions, Niall. Are you able to support Milo in the manner to which he is accustomed? After all, Milo is our own very precious flower and we don't like to think of anyone bruising his petals."

"Oh my God," Niall groans and marches us out, followed by Silas and Oz who are laughing so hard they're having to hold each other up.

"Have him home by eleven o'clock and not a second later, young sir. And no funny business on the way home," Oz shouts, making Silas laugh even harder.

Niall raises two fingers at them, and the last sight we have of them is them clutching each other and laughing like hyenas.

When we're in the car I look at him and start to laugh. He has a slightly jaundiced expression on his face. "You okay?"

He grins wryly and shakes his head. "I was owed that."

I think back to the times he took the piss out of Silas for his dating techniques and nod. "You were owed a lot more than that, actually." I look around at the countryside slipping by, forest green and dun-coloured under the driving rain. "Where are we going?"

"St Ives. There's a gorgeous seafood restaurant there and then I've got a surprise."

"Is it sexual?" I ask huskily, sliding one hand down his thigh.

He makes a noise like an outraged old lady and takes my hand off his thigh. I stare at him and catch the smirk on his full mouth. "Hands off, Milo. This is our first date. I don't put out that quickly."

"I think that's because you've usually put out before the need for a date arises," I say gloomily.

He shoots me a startled look. "Are you okay with that?"

I stare at him. "Are you?"

He shrugs. "I'm fine with my past. I have no major regrets." He pauses. "I've got *some* regrets, obviously. I mean, I'm fine with public nudity, but the Italian police turned out to be alarmingly prudish about it, and I do regret the cell because the seating was very uncomfortable."

I laugh and squeeze his hand. "I'm fine with it. Your past is your past. I mean, yours is more colourful than a bumper box of Crayola, but that's you."

"It was me," he says quietly.

I'm startled. "What do you mean?"

He shoots me an indecipherable look. "I mean that was me. It doesn't mean that it's the present or future Niall Fawcett. He's a different person."

"He's a different person seeking help for mental problems if he keeps referring to himself in the third person."

He bursts out laughing and diverts the conversation to more getting-to-know-you questions. He shoots me a look after a few minutes of discussing our favourite films. "You okay?"

"I'm fine," I say peacefully. "Just surprised that we're doing this. We've known each other for most of my life, not to mention that we've fucked each other countless times. It seems strange to be having the same conversation as people who've just started dating."

"But we have," he says simply. "I'm getting to know you. Milo Ramsay. I want to know everything that makes you tick."

"Why?"

"You know why," he says calmly. "But I'm thinking you're not prepared to talk about it at the moment."

I shoot him a quick glance. "It would take forever anyway," I say gloomily. "As soon as I discuss anything like that, I stutter. The time it takes me to say anything sometimes, we'd be on our first date for a year."

"And I would be just as happy. I don't care how long it takes you to talk to me, Lo, just as long as you keep talking to me and never stop."

I stare at him open-mouthed. That is quite possibly the nicest thing anyone has ever said to me, and the fact that it's Niall should amaze me. Should but doesn't, I think, eyeing him probably not covertly. It still surprises me to have this inbuilt knowledge inside me now that the confident, sarcastic Niall that everyone else knows is actually a big softie who enjoys poetry.

He shoots me a look. "What?'

I shake my head quickly and divert the conversation to something that has happened at Westminster today. We move from that to a footballer moving clubs to an art show that I'd like to see, the conversation never faltering while we eat a superb meal at a small fish restaurant tucked away in a small corner of St Ives.

I push my plate away finally, leaning back and groaning. "God, I'm stuffed."

He smirks. "Not yet, but you will be."

The low voice and the gleam in his eyes make my cock plump, and I stir. "Shall we go home?" I say quietly but to my amazement, he shakes his head.

"Nope."

"What?"

"We have a date to finish, remember?"

"I'm trying to remember how your cock feels in me, but it's becoming a very distant memory."

He bursts out laughing and the rich sound makes people nearby look at him. A couple of people smile, and I can't blame them. He has a really dirty-sounding laugh that's almost contagious. He sobers and grins at me. "Milo, I see I'm going to have to be the chaste one of the two of us. You're far too much of a strumpet."

"Chaste?" I look around and smile an apology because that was way too loud. I look back at him to find his mouth twisted in amusement. "Chaste?" I whisper. "What is happening at the moment?"

"Well, Milo," he says mock seriously. "My milkshake might bring all the boys to my yard, but I'm afraid you're not getting a drink yet because I value my body too much to give it away for free."

"That started awesomely and finished somewhere between Barbara Cartland and Georgette Heyer." I shake my head, trying not to smile. "You're supposed to be the casual shag of the year. Just once I try you, only to find out that you're defective."

He snorts and shakes his head. "Date first, cock after," he says loftily and turns just in time to grab the pad which the waiter bobbles in shock. "Sorry," he says, smiling brilliantly at the man. "It's best to set out one's boundaries early, don't you think?"

I'm still laughing when we leave the restaurant. We pause to button our coats when the cold sea wind hits us. Then he grabs my hand and pulls me along after him.

"Where are we going?" I ask plaintively.

"You'll see."

We wander along after that, taking in St Ives on a cold winter's night. It's a beautiful seaside town known for its surfing beaches and its thriving art scene. In the summer it's murder as cars queue to get in and you practically have to sell an organ to get a parking space, but in winter it's quieter. There are still a fair amount of people about, but the lack of all the tourists makes it easier to admire the slightly raffish charm of the place.

We pass shops whose windows are a golden glowing oasis in the cold night, and I move alongside Niall as he obviously has a destination in mind. Finally, he comes to a stop and I look up at the huge plate-glass window.

"A gallery?" I say, turning to look at him.

For a second, he looks almost embarrassed with his cheeks flushed. "I thought you'd like it," he says quietly.

"But you hate art."

He shrugs. "I like being with you, though, and anyway, when you talk about art it's interesting." He smiles almost shyly at me. "I thought it would be nice and would make you happy."

My heart bangs hard in my chest and I feel hot all over. "I am happy," I say hoarsely, moving into him and loving the way his hands come up almost automatically to bracket my hips, holding me to him. Being with him like this is almost what I imagine dancing with a long-term partner to be. Easy and fluid, our bodies seem to know what the other one is doing and echoes it. "You make me happy." I finally say the words, stumbling a little.

I want to close my eyes in mortification that I can't say that without stumbling, but I can't because his face blazes with happiness and he kisses me swiftly. It's a soft kiss, barely landing before he moves back, but I blink as if he's stunned me. I try to parse what I'm feeling but at that moment the door opens, letting out a gush of warm air, and we both shiver like Pavlov's dogs.

"Come on," he says, tugging me through the door. "It's an art show tonight. Four very successful local artists who got their start here are showing their work. I thought you'd get a kick out of it when I heard about it."

"How did you hear about this?" I ask, handing the woman at the door my coat with a smile.

He grins, looking around curiously. I don't even bother because all my attention is fixed on him. He has a flush from the cold and his blond hair, ever so slightly darker now in the winter, is tousled and glowing under the light. I remember lying in bed the other night, running my hands through the strands as he rested his head on my chest. The strands had gone a light tan colour but I'd found threads of white gold underneath, like a piece of summer had been caught in his hair.

He motions us forward and I look around. The gallery is huge and well-lit and teeming with people. A wave of loud conversation greets us.

I look sideways at him. "How did you find out about this?"

He smiles. "Do you like it?" I nod and his smile gets bigger. Then he leans forward and whispers. "I spoke to Simeon."

I jerk. "You spoke to Simeon? How? When?"

He shrugs. "I met him in St Austell. I'd been to the bank and he was coming out of a pub. We stopped to talk."

I stare at him. "You never said." Jealousy stirs suddenly. Simeon is very good-looking and Niall even more so. "Why didn't you say?"

He immediately looks disgruntled. "Are you bothered that your admirer flirts for a living?"

I open my mouth to say something rude but pause at the note in his voice, and instead I smile and cuddle into his side. "I'm not bothered that he might look at you," I say. "But no one gets to touch you."

He stops dead, stupefaction running across his face, and then a huge smile crosses it. "You're jealous."

"A little bit," I say warily. "Does that bother you?" I have horrible memories of the aftermath of a party when I'd drunkenly accused Thomas of flirting with a young artist. By the time we'd finished, I was under no illusions that I should ever be jealous again. The bruises had taken a while to heal but the lesson is still fresh and I hate that.

However, Niall confounds me as always. Drawing me to the side of the room, he hugs me. "It's nice," he says. "Shows you care." He pauses. "But you know you can trust me, don't you? I would never do anything to damage this between us. It's too precious."

I stare at him, my mouth open to say I don't know what, but the next second my name is called. When we turn, it's to find Simeon walking towards us.

"Hello, you came," he says, shaking Niall's hand and giving me a hug. It's quick and he steps back hurriedly, looking at Niall, but he just smiles happily back at him.

"I said I would," he says. "Milo loves this sort of stuff."

"Not you?" Simeon asks, and my eyes narrow at the way he's looking at Niall. He can stop that right about now.

Niall is oblivious, shaking his head. "Not really. I'm fine looking at art. I just can't stand all the analysing. It's ridiculous. Like looking at page three of *The Sun* and trying to see the real picture behind it."

I laugh and shake my head. "Niall, you're a fucking Neanderthal."

He grins and bites his lip. "You're just jealous because you can't do those picture puzzles."

I groan. "No one can. They just say they have." I shake my head. "All that time spent with your head on one side making your eyes go blurry; I'd have been quicker drinking a bottle of brandy again for those effects."

Niall bursts out laughing, and I see Simeon eyeing us curiously as if we're in the zoo.

"Are you okay?" I ask and he smiles.

"Fine. Just a few impressions I had that have been confirmed. Come and look at the pictures."

The gallery is huge. It's obviously two back-to-back shops that have been knocked through because it stretches far back.

"So these are local artists then?" I ask as we move through the crowd.

Simeon nods. "They've become very successful, but they all had their start here and they've done very well for themselves in London. One is a particular standout. His paintings go for thousands all the time and he's just had his work shown at The Tate, so we're very lucky."

Something stirs in the back of my mind like the warning sound of a bell. I frown but the thought is gone, and I come back to the conversation to hear Niall asking Simeon something but his eyes are fixed on me. When I look at him, I shake my head. "I'm fine," I mouth.

He relaxes, and I look up at the painting we're standing in front of. The artist has painted a young man who's extremely beautiful with long brown hair and big, doe-like eyes. He's dressed in a thin robe that reveals as much as it conceals. The detail is extraordinary in that he looks so real, but the colours are all whites and blues so it actually looks as if he's dead, which adds a disturbing edge. That elusive tug happens again, and I stare at the work. It's perfect and undeniably beautiful but it's cold, as if the artist has imitated feelings that he or she hasn't got. Like a robot making human movements, it just looks wrong.

There's no signature that I can see on the painting, and I'm just looking for the card when Simeon's voice breaks my chain of thought. "I'm glad I've seen you, Milo."

I turn to him, relieved for some reason not to look at that picture anymore. It disturbs me in an odd way. "Why?"

He steps closer. "I have an offer for you."

I feel Niall stiffen at my side and I squeeze his hand. "What offer?"

He bites his lip, looking thoughtful. "I had all this planned out if I saw you again, but now I must admit I'm having second thoughts as to the wisdom of it."

I look at Niall but he's staring at Simeon, his head tilted to one side. However, he won't butt in. I know that as surely as I know that he has a birthmark on his hip and that he's ticklish on his back. I turn back to Simeon.

"Maybe you'd just better get it out," I say, trying for a sure voice which must work because his expression lightens. He shoots Niall a somewhat apologetic look, which makes him stiffen, and then turns to me.

"I want to offer you a job."

"What?"

He nods eagerly. "I'm opening an auction house and I need first-class restorers on my staff, and I can't think of anyone better than you."

"Me?"

He nods. "Yes. You've got a superb touch with art and you're very well thought of in the business."

Warmth kindles in my stomach that people think well of me despite my ignominious exit from the art world all those years ago. It must show on my face because I hear Niall inhale a sharp burst of air and Simeon leans forward eagerly.

"Where is the job?" I ask, feeling excitement run through me.

"London," Simeon replies, and he must see me sag in disappointment because he starts talking quickly. "It would be so good for you, Milo. You could get your career back on track. You'd be working with the best people with access to some of the most beautiful works of art and doing what you're supposed to be doing."

"I'm happy doing what I am," I say, but he shakes his head.

"You're stultifying where you are. It's like suffocating and it's terrible. You should be at the centre of everything. You'll work with the best materials." He names a figure that makes my head spin. He grins at me coaxingly. "What do you say? Do you fancy coming back to where you belong?"

I stare at him. For a wild moment, I want to do it. I want that job. I want people to look at me and not think fuck-up. This is my chance to do what I'd set out to do all those years ago before Thomas and the way he changed me. I could finally make my parents proud. Then I look at Niall. He's staring at Simeon, his eyes hooded and an indecipherable expression on his face.

I take a deep breath. "I'm sorry, but I don't think that's me."

Niall jerks and glares at me, and I gape. *Why is he fucked off?*

Simeon interjects. "Just think about it, please." He hands me his business card. "I'm in town for a few days. That job is yours if you want it."

I go to hand him the card back. "I don't think–"

"Think about it." Niall's voice is hoarse but his eyes are focused on something far away, the way they go when he has a problem to sort out in his head.

"*What?*" My voice is louder than I want and a few people turn to stare before going back to their conversations. "You want me to go?" The incredulity and hurt are clear in my voice and I'm dimly aware of Simeon muttering something and moving away.

Niall turns to me. "Just think about it," he says in a low voice. "You need to think about this because it's an amazing offer, Milo. It gives you back everything you lost because of Thomas."

I shake my head. "You want me to go."

"No," he hisses, dragging me to the side of the picture. "I never want you to go." He pauses, turning to me with an intent look on his face. "Milo, I–"

He's interrupted by a stir in the crowds and I stiffen as I hear a very familiar voice. It's loud and posh with sardonic amusement curling through it, and suddenly it all comes together. The coldness of the artwork and the beautiful man.

"Thomas," I say on a gasp.

"What?" Niall looks offended as if I've called him by the wrong name and for a brief second, I want to laugh. But then air sucks back in and I grab his arm.

"Thomas is here. He's the main artist."

CHAPTER 17

> I'm going to be so fucking happy because I've had the worst and now I have the best.

Milo

He stiffens. "Thomas is here?"

"Yes. Can we go?"

But it's too late. Even as I say the words, I hear Thomas's voice and then he's here in front of us with a sulky-looking young man leaning against him. Wearing a pale blue suit, Thomas's hair gleams golden in the light. When I first met him, I thought there was something angelic about him. He was just so perfect-looking that I couldn't believe he would even look at me.

I only had a few months before I realised that there was a devil underneath. Someone cruel and harsh. It was somehow more frightening when that person poked his head out and showed himself through that perfect exterior. Sometimes I'd wondered whether I was going mad because no one else ever saw anything. Just me.

I look at Niall and swallow hard at the fixed way he's looking at Thomas. *And him,* I tell myself. *He knows.* The thought eases me in some way.

"Milo," Thomas says smoothly, a smile playing along his lips. "How lovely to see you again." He pauses and attempts a sorrowful look. "I somehow didn't think I'd ever meet you again."

Niall stiffens and I squeeze his hand hard, a mute reminder to behave himself. I breathe in slowly and unobtrusively. I won't stutter now.

"Thomas," I say. "I can't exactly say it's a pleasure." It's hoarse but my voice is firm, and I hold my head a little higher. Niall is practically vibrating next to me, and when I sneak a look at him it's to find him staring at me. His face is tight with suppressed emotion but his gaze is fierce and steady, and he drops a quick wink at me before turning back to Thomas.

It's a small movement but I catch the way that Thomas swallows compulsively, that faint click in his throat when Niall turns to him and the way he moves back an inch, and a fierce pleasure runs through me. The young man next to him catches it too and looks uneasily at Thomas.

"You remember Niall?" I say slowly.

Thomas grimaces. "I have certain memories," he says stiffly.

Niall smiles evilly. "As long as they're painful ones, I'll be happy."

Thomas recovers quickly. He always did. "What are you doing here, Milo? Last I heard you'd vanished into the countryside and were cleaning portraits." He sneers, his face alive with malice. "I'd say it was a waste of your talents, but the fact that Barkers sacked you speaks volumes." He laughs. "Unlike you."

I breathe in and look at Niall, worried that he's going to thump Thomas, but instead he's staring at me, his head cocked and his expression challenging. Then he jerks his head at Thomas as if prompting me. For a second I stare at him, feeling all the complicated emotions well up inside me for this wonderful man who I now see is nothing like Thomas. He's brave and fierce but *for* me, not against me. He's on my side but he will never take over. Instead, I suddenly know he will always stand by my side ready to fight anything but alongside me, not in front of me, because he really knows me.

And in a flash my fears of what could go wrong vanish like smoke in the wind because this is Niall. He would never hurt me like Thomas did because he isn't Thomas. He's a much better man, and I feel ashamed that it's taken me this long to work it out. I'm filled with so much love towards this wonderful, irrepressible man that it makes my heart hurt. So much love that I can't keep it in.

"I love you," I breathe and Niall jerks.

"*What?*"

"I love you," I say firmly. "I'm sorry it's taken me so long to know it, to realise that you're nothing like him. You're so different and so bloody precious to me and I love you."

He stares at me, something like jubilation flowing over his face that settles into blazing happiness. "I love you too," he says clearly, ignoring Thomas's huff of disgust. "I always have and I always will because you're bold and beautiful."

"Not always."

He smiles. "Yes always. Just sometimes it was a bit hidden. It took some seeing."

"But you did see it," I say slowly, thinking of him as a young man encouraging me to talk and patiently listening. "You always have."

"He must have had X-ray specs then," Thomas huffs and rage fills me that he's still here interrupting the best moment of my life when Niall Fawcett has finally told me that he loves me. I know it wasn't declared on a mountaintop or in front of my friends like I'd dreamed of when I was fifteen but rather in a crowded gallery in front of someone I hate, but still. Niall Fawcett loves me and I love him and nothing is going to rain on my parade.

I turn to Thomas who, rather unwisely given their past history, is sneering at Niall. "But then you're just what I expected he'd end up with. An ill-educated yokel with nothing between his ears."

"You leave him out of it," I say sharply, rage filling me. "Don't you even look at him because you're not fit to lick his fucking shoes." Thomas inhales a shocked breath but I'm finally on a roll now. I suppose better late than never. "He's wonderful. He's funny and doesn't think that being kind will lead people to assume that he's got a small penis. News flash, Thomas, you have." I look at the man hanging on his arm. "It's the size of a chipolata but they're more useful than what he's got between his legs." The man pouts and moves back and I glare at Thomas. "You're a bully," I say slowly. "A horrible bully who ruled my life for too long. And why?" I look him up and down. "I don't know why I let it happen for so long. You're hardly a catch. Your breath smells, you parrot other people's ideas thinking they make you look clever, and your humour is cruel."

Suddenly I'm sick of him. I've yearned for so long to say what I think, but now he's hardly worth the time when I have a gorgeous man standing by my side with a smile playing on his full lips, ready to take me home.

I take in a bolstering breath. "I'm going," I say. "I'm going home with Niall to a wonderful house in the woods and a sociopathic cat. And I'm going to live there for the rest of my life. We're probably going to have children and definitely some dogs. I'm going to restore paintings and we'll cook for each other. And I'm going to be so fucking happy because I've had the worst and now I have the best. Someone who's clever and funny and who loves me regardless of the fact that I sometimes stutter and lack confidence. Someone who knows that real love takes teamwork. Not a self-obsessed little man whose looks are fading." I look at his paintings and shake my head. "And your paintings are terribly boring. They're so pedestrian that they're practically passed out on the pavement."

Thomas opens his mouth to say something but Niall steps forward suddenly. He's a big man and the move is so elegant that the power in it takes us by surprise, and Thomas makes a funny squeaking noise and jumps back.

"I can't decide what to do with you," Niall says in a very conversational tone.

Thomas looks worried. "Is there a choice?"

Niall hums and smiles. It's not a nice smile. "Lots of different choices. I can't make my mind up on whether to punch you in the balls or push your head through the wood panelling. Or maybe kick you in the arse." He sighs happily. "It's like a tin of Quality Street, mate. So many lovely options."

Thomas stares at him and something like fear runs through his face. I don't blame him. Niall's voice is lovely but there's a wild aggression in it at the moment. Thomas steps back instead and the flinch in his face shows that he knows he's conceded something and lost face. He looks at me spitefully.

"Enjoy your life, Milo. It sounds terribly boring."

"No. Boring was you, Thomas. Niall is so far from that it's actually laughable."

Thomas opens his mouth but Niall shakes his head. "I'm bored of you," he says coldly. "Let's not do this again." Thomas looks at him and Niall leans close. "Let's not *ever* do this again," he says, and there's a chilling quality in his voice. "Don't contact him. Don't ring or email or write. He's gone from your life and I see you, Thomas. I know you've realized what you lost but it's too late because he's mine now, and I swear on my life I will fucking hurt you if you try to touch what's mine. Do you understand me?"

"Can you hear him, Milo?" Thomas says. "Can you hear that he thinks you're his property? Why would you put up with that?"

"Because he does it properly," I say, tugging on Niall's hand to get him moving. He's seemingly stuck staring coldly at Thomas as if he's contemplating dismemberment. "And I own him right back." I look him up and down. "Have a nice life, Thomas. Or not." I shrug. "I really don't care either way."

We push our way through the crowd and all the time we're

getting our coats and manoeuvring our way towards the door I can feel Niall behind me, some deep emotion making his hand tremble in mine.

Finally, we're out and I inhale the cold sea air deeply, feeling it replace the hot staleness of the gallery.

I tug my coat on and pull him to the side of the gallery, following the path down the cobbled street until we're standing in a quiet corner of the quay lit by the glow of light from a house nearby. All around us the air is filled with the sigh and creak of the boats along with the musical tinkle of the rigging. Water slops along the steps and the air is full of the scent of brine. A wind is blowing, catching the edges of my scarf and whipping my hair back, and rain speckles my face.

I turn to face him and he grabs me, pulling me into his arms. "Did you mean it?"

"What?"

"That you love me."

I grab his face between my hands, feeling the sharpness of his cheekbones against my palms. I look at his long nose, full lips with the small scar on the top, and those blue eyes that I've seemingly been looking into all my life and that are full of so much turbulent emotion. "I did," I say softly. "I really love you, Niall, and I know we've come a long way from what we originally said we'd do, but I can't stop it."

"Don't stop," he says hoarsely. "Please don't ever stop." His hands on my shoulders knead the skin almost unconsciously. "I love you too, Lo, so much. I always will."

I lift up to him and he lowers his face at the same time and then we're kissing. The rain splatters harder, cold drops falling on our heads and faces. But it doesn't dull the sense of joy in me that the man I love loves me back. That pure simple thought illuminates my world, and it seems to me that while others might look at this place as unfitting for a declaration of love, to me it's as if we're standing in the most beautiful place in the world. The wind and the rain are just echoes of the most powerful and natural feeling I've ever had in my life.

Finally, he draws back and gives a whoop, lifting me and spinning me. I give a snort of laughter because I have to. It feels like it's filling me. Only he would spin me like an overgrown kid.

"You love me," he says, and he sounds almost awed. "I can't believe you love me."

Blinking in the rain, I cup his face, feeling the cold skin, and laugh. "I can't believe I managed to say it without stuttering."

He puts me down and looks at me steadily, his arms still around me as if he can't bear to let go. "If you had stuttered it would still have meant the same," he says calmly, a wealth of love in his eyes and voice, making me blink back the tears. "What matters to me, Lo, is *what* you say, not how you say it." He laughs suddenly. "And fuck, you gave Thomas what for." He shakes his head, enjoyment written large on his face. "That's the best thing I've ever heard. I wish I'd recorded it so I could play it again and again." He looks at me. "How do you feel, darling? That was a big dragon to slay tonight."

I nestle into him. "I feel good," I say slowly. "I feel at peace for the first time." We stand still for a second and I stir. "It's been a funny sort of night. Got a chance at my old career back and gave my ex a piece of my mind. Like a lot of demons have gone." He stiffens and I pull back. "What?"

"Not all of the demons," he says slowly, reluctance written all over him.

"What do you mean?"

"The job."

I straighten. "Oh yes, the job. You said I should think about it." Hurt stirs for a second. "Do you want me to go?"

"I think that it's your last dragon to slay," he says unwillingly.

"Which I'm perfectly capable of doing," I say sharply. "I slew my own tonight. You were there and you didn't have to help me. Not like before."

"I was, and I couldn't be prouder of you than I am now, but I want a future with you free of doubt and wishful thinking. And sweetheart, a large part of you still somehow sees yourself as less because once upon a time I had to rescue you. And I don't want that to become a problem between us."

I open my mouth to argue but I can't, and he gives a sad sigh and leans down to kiss me.

"Sweetheart, love is a partnership and you can't see that yet. You say you don't want someone to be responsible for your happiness but it's natural in a good relationship when you love the other person. It just has to be with the right person. Thomas was no good because it was like you giving your love to a black hole. He swallowed it up and gave nothing back. Real love goes both ways. It gives back what you give to it tenfold. I might rescue you sometimes, but I know that when I need you you'll rescue me back. I love you, so that means I want the absolute best for you, but I'd also hope that you'd want the same for me."

"I do," I burst out, my voice shaking, and he strokes my hair back with an impossibly tender look on his face.

"There you are then. I will love you right down to my bones until the day we die. We'll argue and fall out and I'm sure at times we really won't like each other, but I will be your fucking cheerleader for the rest of your life because you're epic and I want the whole world to know that shit."

"You should write the verses in greeting cards." He laughs, and I stroke his face. "I'll always love you too."

"I know you will, but that love has to be the foundation that keeps us together and whole. It's what makes a person care more for his lover than he does for himself. It's wanting the best for that person regardless of the personal cost." He swallows audibly. "It's why I'm going to tell you to take that job." He looks hard at me. "Because I love you."

"You want me to go?" I say it slowly, no longer hurt because the sincerity and love are written all over him.

"I want you to go and come back," he says sharply. "Never

mistake that, Lo. You're my boomerang, and while you're flying free, I want it to be with the knowledge that you're on a trajectory that leads back to me."

I sniffle, feeling tears in my throat, and he croons under his breath and hugs me tight. "I don't want you to go," he says fiercely. "But maybe you have to, Lo." He sighs. "You have nothing to prove to me *ever*. I love every single thing about you from your surprisingly thin toes to your very messy head." I snort, and he kisses my head hard. "I love the way you sing off key and completely mangle all song lyrics until they're unrecognisable. I love the way you presume I know what you're thinking and proceed to involve me in conversations that are quite frankly incomprehensible. I even love your habit of reading three books at once and leaving the top off the jam." He sighs. "So, you never need to prove anything to me, but I think that just maybe you need to prove something to you."

I breathe in, feeling love and terror holding onto my heart in a tight grip. I've only just got him and he's so fucking precious to me, but I know deep inside me that he's right.

"I think I do," I say in a low voice. "Niall, I really think I do."

He sighs and pulls me closer, and as we stand on the windswept street as the rain pours down on us, I can almost hear the clock that I've set ticking away my time here.

CHAPTER 18

All I know is that my hands and head are full of him and that's the way it always will be.

Two Weeks Later

Milo

My leaving party is suitably raucous for something that's been organised by Niall and Oz. Everyone I've ever known in Cornwall has seemingly gathered in the Great Hall which has been decorated with a multitude of balloons and streamers. Even the suit of armour has a paperchain boa and a slightly jaunty paper hat.

I look up as Oz falls onto the sofa next to me. "Okay?" I ask, shouting slightly over the window-rattling volume of the music.

He smiles, his blue eyes shining brightly in the light from the tall window. "I'm fine." He shoots me a penetrating look. "How about you?"

I look around the hall filled with all the people eating and talking and laughing. A ray of sun shines through the paned glass, laying a stripe across the worn carpet and highlighting Niall like a spotlight. He's dressed in dark jeans and a black turtleneck and looks gorgeous, his hair gleaming in the light. As if sensing my gaze, he turns his head and smiles at me. It's wide and warm but somehow less than usual, like he's operating a dimmer switch.

I turn back to Oz to find him examining my face as if he'll be tested on it later. "I'm fine," I say quickly.

He hums under his breath as he fits himself into my side, and we sit companionably sharing body warmth and watching my party. After a few minutes, he stirs. "I'll miss you very much. You do know that, don't you?"

I smile at him. "I'll miss you too. I'll miss you all." I pause. "I'm surprised that you haven't had much to say about it." Surprised and a little hurt. He and Silas had taken the news quietly and almost resignedly, and it's never been raised since unless we were talking logistics.

He shakes his head, a frown of concentration on his face. He's watching Mrs. Granger and Molly intently, but somehow I get the impression that his mind is working furiously on something. "What could I say?" he says quietly. "You've made your mind up."

"Isn't it what you originally wanted though? A few months ago, you were telling me to branch out and go out into the world."

He smiles. "I should stop talking, shouldn't I? Silas is always telling me I'll talk my way into trouble."

I shake my head. "You'll never change, and I wouldn't want you to."

"But you *have* changed," he says suddenly, turning to me. "I couldn't see it at first because we spend all our time together, but that time away has made me see how far you've come."

"Still more to do," I say somewhat morosely, and he sends one of his intense quicksilver glances at me.

"There's always something more to do," he says quietly. "We're never finished with our own evolution."

I stare at him. "That's so profound."

He sighs. "I know. People always miss how very switched on I am with my inner being."

"They don't miss how switched on you are about feeding your stomach."

"Three meals a day, Milo. It's only right."

I laugh but he stares at me intently. "Milo, you could work on yourself from here until the end of days and never finish. That's part of being human. But I think it's better to do it with someone by your side. Someone who pays attention to the differences and lauds them. It must get awfully lonely doing something good and having no one to notice."

"I have to go," I say hoarsely. "I need to do something myself, not be rescued and looked after. I need to show people that I'm okay. I don't need him always trying to make me happy. That won't make him happy in the end."

"You don't need to show anyone," he says softly. "Just yourself. That's the person you shouldn't lie to." He cocks his head to one side. "I know Niall is wonderful, but he's not the one who worked through speech therapy. I don't see him struggling most days with getting his words out. I don't see him making his way through every day watching people and making sure they're happy. It's you that did all that." He smiles. "But I do see him cheering you on. I see him so proud of you." He looks intently at me. "You should let him be proud of you rather than making it into something it isn't."

"Something it isn't?"

"It isn't a power that he has on his own," he says simply. "The power here is half yours, but you've never looked closely enough at yourself to know that you wield it. Just remember that while he might be making you happy, you're doing exactly the same to him. That's a tremendous power, Milo, the gift of being able to make the person you love most in the world happy by just being you. It's not given to everyone, so take care of it."

I stare at him, struck dumb by his words. "What do you really think about me going?"

"I don't want you to follow a path that belongs to the past you. I want you to create a path all of your own for the future you. One that takes you to tremendous places." He smiles. "I just want you to be the one who sees the way." He shrugs. "If that leads you away to the bright lights, then so be it. Just make sure that it's what you really want."

His words stay with me all night as the party finishes and when Niall and I lie sated in bed. His even, sleeping breaths skate over my skin as I lie on my back with my arms around him. I can hear the wild wind outside and the scattershot sound of the rain as it's thrown against the window. But inside it's warm and peaceful and safe.

It occurs to me suddenly that I won't be here when the spring comes. I won't see Niall's house in the sunshine when the smell of fresh-cut grass is heavy on the air. I'll be here a lot, of course, but it will be a temporary occupation when my real home will be in London.

The bed moves and a dark shape jumps up next to me. "Dotty?" I whisper and she chirrups, and suddenly her nose is nudging my hand to stroke her. "Oh lovely," I whisper. "*Now* you want to know me. The night before I go away. I was right. You are a tiny tabby psychopath."

She ignores me, her purrs filling the air, and I smile as she curls into my side, her small body warming the side that Niall isn't lying against. And as I lie there on this rainy night with my two people safe beside me, my heart is full and my brain is teeming with thoughts.

Doubt stirs again the way it has for the last two weeks, but I push it aside. I just need to get on with things. This protracted leave-taking isn't good for anyone, and Niall and I will be fine once we're settled into our new normal. It's the last thought I have before I slide into sleep, and I frown because there's a hollow ache in my bones tonight.

Niall

I go to put the bacon on the grill and swear under my breath as Dotty twines around my feet and nearly sends me over.

"What are you doing, silly girl?" I say, bending over to stroke her hard little head, my fingers sliding over the sleek fur. She meows agitatedly and I sigh. "You know something's happening, don't you?" I whisper. "But don't worry. He's going but I know he'll be back."

She gives me a slightly disgusted look before stalking over to her basket as if I've let her down.

"What's up with you?" I hiss, still bent over on the floor. "I can't keep him. You must know that."

"Are you talking to your penis?" An amused voice comes from the French windows and I twist and nearly fall over.

"Oh, it's you," I say sourly.

"Just me and Cora," Silas says happily, stepping into the room and handing me Cora when I hold out my arms for her. She settles into me, her warmth and smell familiar even though I swear she's bigger than she was yesterday. She's like a gremlin with water on her. I hug her tightly until she makes a disgruntled sound, whereupon I ease up and kiss her hair. She seems part of my and Milo's romance somehow. The tiny cog which everything started around.

Silas watches me with a sad expression on his face. "How are you?" he whispers, looking around.

"He's upstairs," I say, thinking of his long body cuddled down in my sheets. "You can talk. Just don't shout." I try a smile. "Oh, I forgot that's your loud partner, not you."

The smile can't be any more convincing than it feels because his face twists in sympathy. "Niall," he says, and I turn back to the counter.

"I'm fine," I say determinedly, grabbing the eggs and cracking them one-handed into a bowl as Cora watches me in a fascinated silence. Reaching for the whisk, I look back at him. "He's only going to London, not the other side of the world, and he'll be back whenever he can. When he can't come back, then I'll go to him."

"And you're okay with that?"

Suddenly irritated, I chuck the whisk on the counter, noting the trail of eggs it leaves on the wood. "Of course I'm not," I say hollowly. "I've only just got him and now he's going again. But I have to be okay with it," I say firmly. "I can't go for what I want this time."

"Why?"

"Because this is too important. *He's* too important. Our whole relationship hinges on the fact that I have to let Lo do his own thing. I will chase him away as surely as if I had a gun and was running after him if I try to lay down the law. And I don't want to lay the law down with him. That's not us."

I sigh and hug Cora close, staring at my oldest friend. "And at the end of the day this might be the best thing for him, and how can I love him if I don't want the world for him?"

He slings his arm over my shoulder and hugs me to him as Cora coos and reaches out for her daddy. "That's how you know it's really love," he says softly. "When they matter more than anyone else."

"Then it bloody sucks," I say sharply. "Why have I done this to myself?"

"I don't think you actually choose love, Niall. It's got its own opt-in clause," he says wryly. "One of those deals that seal you in because you can't read the small print."

"When can you read it?"

"Never," he says softly. "And in the end, you don't want to because it feels both too good and too bad to ever want to leave."

Milo

When I wake, I stretch and send one hand out to find Niall. I crack open my eyes sleepily, but the bed is huge and empty apart from me and the sheets are cold where they aren't wrapped around my body. I lift my head up and hear the sound of the radio in the kitchen downstairs and I sniff at the scent of bacon.

It's enough to get me out of bed, and I stand up, stretching and wincing at the soreness in my arse. I'd begged him to go hard last night, wanting to feel him all the next day, and my wish has definitely been granted. I grab my dressing gown and pause. Today will be the last morning of waking up in the Dower House and *Chi an Mor* as a permanent resident. From now on and for the foreseeable future I'll be a visitor. I frown and then make myself cheer up. I'm going to London, not to war.

Traipsing downstairs I hear the sound of voices, and when I round the corner it's to find Silas seated at the breakfast bar with Cora in his arms. Niall is talking to him in an intense voice and the two men look serious.

"Everything okay?" I ask, and they jump as if electrocuted. I shake my head. "Please don't consider a career in MI5. You'll have spilled state secrets before breakfast."

Silas laughs. "Especially if Oz was questioning me." I walk over and hold out my hands for Cora who waves her arms in excitement. Silas hands her over with a smile and I hug her close, dipping my nose and inhaling the sweet baby scent of her neck.

"I'll miss you," I say to her, kissing her forehead. "I'm sure you'll grow loads while I'm not here." I look up in time to see Niall wince and Silas giving him a sympathetic look. When Niall sees me looking, he puts up his hands.

"No. Nope."

"What?" I ask.

"We're not feeling sorry for ourselves. You're not being deported, for fuck's sake. You're going to London to seek your fortune."

"I'm not Dick Whittington," I say sourly.

"I hope not. You'd never fit all your hair care products in that handkerchief he had."

I shake my head. "Niall."

He comes to me and pulls me close, bending to kiss Cora and raising to take my lips. It's a gentle, almost sweet kiss. Chaste but so warm that I stare at him, seeing a flush on his face. Then his expression clears and he steps back. "Breakfast," he says decisively.

I look at Silas. "Are you staying?"

He shakes his head. "No. I'll leave you in peace. I just wanted to say au revoir."

"Very French."

He shrugs. "I prefer it to goodbye."

I flinch. "It isn't goodbye."

"Of course it isn't, Milo," he says, getting to his feet and drawing me into a hug. "It can't be goodbye because this is your home and it always will be. There will always be a place for you at *Chi an Mor*."

"Thank you," I say, drawing back. "I haven't said it enough, Silas. You took me in when you didn't have to and gave me a safe place. I'll never forget it."

"You're family," he says simply. "That means an awful lot to me." He looks at me and gives me a gentle smile. "When you're ready to come back, we'll all be here."

"How maudlin. Cheer up, for fuck's sake," Niall says in that uber-cheerful way he's had over the last fortnight. It's been like living in an expletive-ridden Disney film and it's getting wearing.

Silas neatly retrieves Cora after I kiss her again and then he's gone, leaving us in a very full silence. I look at Niall and he turns determinedly. "Bacon and eggs and then you'll have to get your stuff together. The train's at ten and we'll have to take the back road."

"Niall," I say quietly. "You know I'm coming back, don't you?"

He turns to me, giving me a sad clown smile that stretches his face but doesn't reach his eyes. "I hope so."

"Niall, of course I am," I say, hugging him tightly, feeling the sharp edges of his ribs and the muscles in his back. "I love you. We're just going long distance for a while."

He turns and hugs me tight in return. "I know," he says deeply.

Breakfast goes too quickly the way time has the last fortnight, bounding forward like a puppy on a lead, eager and searching, and before I know it we're lugging my suitcase to the car. I look around at the woods surrounding the house. The wind is fierce again, blowing the scent of wet wood and earth in my face accompanied by the sharp, tangy smell of the sea.

I feel like I'm taking snapshots every time I move so that I can take them out when I get to London and examine them. Over the last fortnight, I've said my goodbyes to the estate and to my favourite places like the Lime Tree walk where in the spring the snowdrops flourish and the bluebells in the wood that form a magic carpet. But here is the hardest goodbye of all because this has become my home, and it seems odd to me that I've only realised it at the moment of leaving it. Perhaps we never know until we're losing something.

"Milo. You ready?" Niall says quietly and I look round to find him leaning against the car, his hair lifting in the wind. He looks real and full of life and I want to throw myself on him and never leave, and panic fills me suddenly like I've inhaled butterflies and they're spreading through my stomach.

Am I? I think madly. *Am I ready?* Why am I going when I've just found him? Why am I testing this? What happens if the bond between us snaps through the long distance like an elastic band stretched beyond its limits?

I take a deep breath and push it away. "I'm ready."

The drive seems to take no time, and I look out of the window, searching for my last view of the sea. But before I know it, the sea is gone and my time is up as we pull up to the station.

Niall jumps out and retrieves my case for me, carrying it round to where I'm leaning against the car. "Don't come in," I say softly but he jerks as if I've shouted it.

"You don't want me to see you off?"

I shake my head. "I want to say our goodbyes now privately."

"Sweetheart, don't," he says, pulling me into his arms and kissing me deeply. When he pulls back his eyes are warm and loving. "You'll see me in a week. It's hardly any time, and you'll be so occupied with moving into the flat Simeon found for you that you won't have time to miss me."

"I'll always have time for that."

He gives me that tragic-comic face. "I know. But time passes quickly. Now give me a kiss and don't say goodbye. Just say see you soon." I kiss him, twining my hands in his hair, and then force myself back.

"I love you so much," I say quickly.

He squeezes my hand. "Ring me when you get there," he directs. "Don't forget." He pushes a package into my hands. "Open it when you're on the way."

I nod and, taking one last look at him like a hoarder, I turn and make my way into the station. The train is waiting on the small platform, and in a flurry of movement I stow my case and fall into my seat. I stare out of the window, looking to see if I can see the car park, but it's hidden from me by the ticket office. I look around. The carriage is empty, and my hands tighten on the package. I feel lost and suddenly very lonely and the package is like a lifeline.

Without even thinking about it, my hands tear open the paper and a bubble-wrapped object falls out. I open it to find a box of mixed-flavour teas and a red mug. It's obviously handmade, and the squat shape of it is enchanting as is the rich, deep colour. I open the card. Niall's scruffy handwriting makes me smile. It's so him, as if he's too impatient to have proper penmanship.

My darling Lo,

I hope you like the mug. It's one of a kind, like you. When you drink your first mug of tea in the morning in your new place, I want you to think of all the wonderful things that you're capable of doing in the coming day. I want you to also always remember that I'm so proud of you and I'm waiting for you when you're ready to come home. I love you always.

Niall

I stare down at the objects in my lap. *This mug is gorgeous,* I think idly, *but it would look better in the kitchen at home when I redecorate it.* It's the smallest thing but it's like a bomb going off in my head, and suddenly I know with a blinding flash that I'm wrong. I'm so wrong. I hear myself laugh. *What the fuck am I doing?*

I'm leaving my home and my heart behind, to do what? Prove myself to arseholes like Thomas who don't give a shit about me? I'm leaving Niall and all the people who've become my family to strip dirt from pictures in a city that's so foreign to me now it might as well be on the moon. When I could do that at home and still have time to walk the woods with Niall, to wake up next to him and go to sleep in his arms. To decorate his home in vibrant shades, to laugh with Oz and Silas and watch Cora grow up.

"I'm a fucking idiot," I say aloud and grin. "Well, they do say it does you good to know yourself. I'm stupid, but thankfully it's not a permanent affliction." Standing up, I gather my stuff together, moving quickly and feeling for the first time in my life that these decisions are all mine and they're wholly and completely right.

Niall

Unable to stand and watch him get on the train, I head back to the car, sitting on the bonnet so he can see me as the train leaves.

The wind gusts around me, blowing my hair into my eyes and teeth and drawing wetness to my eyes, which is totally the wind, I tell myself. I can't have sunk so low as to cry over a man leaving me.

I slump on the bonnet because of course I have, because it isn't some faceless generic man, it's Lo in all his complicated awkwardness and beauty. It's him with his sharp-boned face and soft full lips, his soft affectionate nature and the fierceness with which he holds me at night. Complicated and wonderful, he's my Lo, and that's how he will always be.

Since the night in the gallery, I've striven to believe that we can make a long-distance relationship work. That some cosmopolitan and arty man won't sweep him off his feet. However, sitting now alone and dampened by the rain that's starting to fall, I remember something I missed. Lo is loyal. He might be quiet and unassuming, but he's the most fiercely loyal person I know.

I let that sink in so that when the train chugs out of the station and past my perch, I'm able to lift my hand to wave goodbye. Although I look hard, I can't see him because of the rain that's starting to come down hard now. Still, I imagine him sitting in his seat looking out at me while he prepares to conquer the world of painting restoration one quiet word at a time. It gives me the strength to smile in case he's watching even though my heart feels torn in two.

The train vanishes, leaving me in the desolate carpark with the scent of diesel and wet leaves on the air. I sit for a few minutes, unwilling to get up and go because it almost feels like I'm abandoning him and us. Finally, when the rain has become a downpour, I recognise the idiocy of my actions and I slide off the bonnet and let myself back into the car and start the engine. I turn on the heater and wait for the windscreen to clear. The blades of the wipers are almost hypnotic, and I stare into the distance, listening to their comforting swish.

They must have lulled me into a stupor which accounts for the reason why, when there's a thump on the window, I squeal like a little girl. The carpark's gloomy now and the window's steamed up, so I use the button to lower the window and then sit in stunned immobility. "*You?*"

Milo peers through the window. His hair is plastered to his face and neck, his skin is winter white, and his teeth are chattering, but his eyes are free from the panic that's been in them since the gallery, and they're steady and soft and warm again the way they always are when he looks at me. The way he's always looked at me, I realise with a shock of recognition. "Me," he says.

There's a short pause while we stare at each other. "Why aren't you on the train?" My voice is rough and hoarse, and his eyes burn into mine.

"I didn't want to go," he says simply.

"Not for me?" I say hoarsely. "Sweetheart, you know we'll be fine."

"I know," he says quietly, cutting through my jumble of words as if he's shouted. He doesn't need to do that, I've discovered. He just speaks and I listen. I always have, even when he was a little boy following me and Gideon around. "I know we'll be fine. I never doubted it. You and I are together now and nothing, no distance, no other person is going to change that." There's a stark simplicity to his words that makes tears form at the back of my eyes.

"Then why?"

"For me." He swipes his hand across his face. "I love you, but if I'd needed to go I would still have gone. I think I needed to test it."

"And you worked out the result when you got on the train?"

He smiles. "I'm a quick study." He grips the window frame. "I realised that I was only going to prove myself in other people's eyes when the only person whose opinion was relevant was me, and I'm happy. To others, I might be wasting my talents burying myself alive in the country. But to me, I'm happy and freer than I've ever been. I'm at home at the Dower House, at *Chi an Mor*. I have friends and a rich, wonderful life and I'm in love. With you. I don't need anything else."

We stare at each other for a long second and then he gives that impish grin that I think I'm the only one who sees the wicked edge to it. "I'm also wondering why I'm standing outside in the pouring rain declaring my love to someone who's dry and warm."

I jerk and fumble to open the door. "Get in here," I say hoarsely. He tumbles in, laughing, and my arms are suddenly full of him. The long slender length of him, the wide gawky shoulders and wild, wet waves of hair. I bury my nose in his neck, inhaling the scent of lemon and rosemary and feeling everything settle inside me for the first time in weeks. "I love you," I say hoarsely. "I'm so glad you stayed."

He kisses me or I kiss him. I don't know. All I know is that my hands and head are full of him and that's the way it always will be.

Finally, we pull back and give each other slightly shaky smiles. "Let's go," I say. "I feel like we've been separated for years. We need make-up sex and lots of it."

He palms my cock, giving a throaty moan of appreciation. "Let's go."

I smirk. "You do know Oz is going to want his present back, don't you?"

He laughs. "He's never going to let me forget this."

I stick the car in reverse but still in sudden horrified shock when there's a dull thud as I back out. "*Shit!*" I groan. "Oh my God, what did I just run over?"

For a second there's silence and then, incredibly, he laughs. "My suitcase. I put it at the back of the car ready to go in the boot."

"And that's what I ran over?" He nods, and I relax and grin. "Just so you know, I'm totally going to go back and forwards over it a few times just to make sure you never leave me again."

"Never," he says happily and gives a contented sigh. "Take me home, Niall."

So I do. With his hand a warm weight on my thigh and his sweet herby scent in my nose, I steer the car towards *Chi an Mor*. Towards the Dower House. But not towards home because my home is riding by the side of me.

EPILOGUE

It'll be epic and romantic as shit and the angels will fucking weep.

Three Years Later

Niall

It's cold outside today, which is hardly surprising as it's mid-October. I stretch my calf muscles idly while listening to the incredibly cheerful woman who is leading the warm-up for this year's mud run. Silas, who is next to me and attending to the warm-up much more enthusiastically, nudges me.

"You awake yet, son? I thought the cold and that twenty-vat cup of coffee you inhaled when we got here would have done the trick."

I turn to smile at him. "I'm awake enough to kick your arse on this run."

He scoffs and smirks. "In your dreams." He cranes his neck. "What are you looking at so intently?" Then he smiles. "Ah, I might have known."

I sneak another look at Milo which once again snags and stays on him. He's talking to Oz with a cup of hot chocolate in one hand and the other hand holding tightly to Cora who is bouncing around more than a Teletubby on speed, her eyes everywhere and mischief written on every inch of her. Milo smiles down at her and says something and she laughs with her curls bouncing around her cute little face like live springs.

My gaze snags on that warm smile on his wide lips. He's flushed with cold and buried under several layers of ridiculous clothing including skinny jeans, shocking pink wellies, and an old turtle-necked jumper of mine which swamps his slender figure. He's topped it off with an ancient brown cord jacket and huge green scarf, and with that attire, he should, in theory, look ridiculous. But he has a bohemian flair with his clothes and with his wavy nut-brown hair caught up in a top knot and his thin face flushed with cold, he looks like a model. I look again at his mismatched clothes. A model dressed like a tramp.

Silas nudges me again, disrupting my memory of how that slanted fey face had looked last night in the moonlight while he hovered over me, rising and falling on my cock in some sort of graceful ballet. I turn to Silas slightly indignantly. "Are you quite alright, Silas, or is breaking people's ribs part of that alarmingly peppy girl's warm-up act?"

He grins. "No, that's just making me feel slightly happier about being dragged along to jump through mud and half drown in the freezing cold pond. It's like going back to school."

I think back to our school days. "You know, you're right. That is why I like it. I bloody loved games, especially the cross country." I smile fondly. "Do you remember old man Masters and how he used to make us run in the pouring rain in our underwear if we moaned about it? So much fun."

He shakes his head. "They should have expelled you for severe mental problems."

I laugh. "It's not my fault that you ripped your shorts playing rugby once and had decided on that day to act out your inner Jezebel and not wear any underwear."

He winces. "How many times have I told you that I hadn't got my laundry back? I had no choice."

"Four thousand times so far, and it's never made a bit of difference."

He grins and gives up warming up in favour of joining me in leaning against the fence and watching my beloved. Because he is that. My beloved. I love every quirky, awkward, and sometimes wilful inch of him. I always will because he makes me laugh and feel more alive than I ever have, like a bottle of champagne that's been shaken up and opened on New Year's Eve. Full of happy possibilities and a wonderful golden reality.

Just being with him feels like home should always do. I never really knew that feeling before. I was at boarding school by the age of seven, and the only real family I had was the one I made with Silas and Gideon.

I'd been bemused when people told me that when love is real, it feels right. To me, sex with lots of different people felt right. Why would I give that up for what sounded incredibly boring? But I've found out that it isn't. Sex with Lo gets better and better. We know each other's bodies so well that anything goes. But I've found lying together afterward is just as sweet. Curling up around him, listening to him breathe and hearing that indrawn breath and slight catch as he talks in the dark and tells me his secrets makes me feel incredibly privileged and intensely happy.

Our lives together have slotted into each other so easily. Coming home to him, knowing he'll be there when I get home or he'll bang through the door later, his eyes bright and alive and his touch warm and welcoming, makes me settle inside. I loved the Dower House from the minute Silas gave it to me. It felt right to me but also as if it was waiting. So we'd both settled down waiting without realising it was for a wild-haired dreamer to come in and make us a home.

Lo is my family now. He's the only one for me, and I will protect him and us with everything in me so we can grow old together in our cottage in the woods.

As if sensing my thoughts, Silas nudges me. "Have you decided when you're going to do it?"

"I trust you're talking about my marriage proposal and not my sex life."

He grimaces. "Definitely the former," he says quickly.

"You sure?" I cock an eyebrow. "Now you're a parent and all, maybe you've forgotten how it works."

He raises an eyebrow in return. "Believe me, I don't need reminding."

I grin and then turn to look at Milo who's laughing at something Oz says and completely oblivious to a city type in new green wellies and a Barbour coat who's eyeing him up lasciviously. The man obviously senses my gaze because he looks back and blanches when he sees me shaking my head at him before hurriedly moving on.

Satisfied, I look at Silas to find him laughing. "What?"

He shakes his head, a smile still pulling at his lips. "You being all caveman. It still surprises me."

"Why?" I ask fairly indignantly.

"Because you very charmingly never gave a shit," he says patiently. "No matter what men and women did to make you jealous, you never moved a hair. Now, Milo manages it without even realising."

"Well, don't tell him," I say hurriedly. "You know what he's like about bossy men."

He smiles. "Somehow I don't think he minds your brand of bossy."

"I hope not."

It's something I've tried very hard to work on with him and I think it's largely been successful. I still have lapses where I'll start to ride roughshod but usually, all it takes is one raise of his eyebrow and I rein it in.

"I hope I'm what he needs," I say fervently, and Silas's smile softens.

"You are because you've worked so bloody hard at it, Niall. He knows that he means everything to you, and out of all of us, you were always the one who heard what he wasn't saying."

I grin. "He's a lot more vocal now."

"Well, that's being in love, isn't it?" Silas says simply. "It gives us the courage to show our full self if someone else loves it, warts and all."

I smile at this gentle man. My brother in all but name. Then I look back at the love of my life.

"I'll know when the right time is," I say, starting to stretch as the countdown begins. "Timing is everything. It'll be epic and romantic as shit and the angels will fucking weep."

"Oh dear," he says faintly, but then the gates open and we're off.

Milo

We stand by the side of the course and wave enthusiastically as the runners go past us, Cora screeching 'Daddy' as Silas jogs past with Niall.

I eye my boyfriend. His hair is in its usual elegant mess, the white-blond strands showing off the denim blue of his eyes that I love so much, especially with the lines that radiate from around them showing a lifetime of laughter. Because that's what I see around Niall. Laughter. He's easy-going and sarcastic and quick-witted, and I love him more every day.

Oz interrupts my thoughts by taking my empty cup and slinging it into the bin. "Next time we'll bring brandy," he says in a disgusted tone of voice.

I smile. "This run business is not your thing."

"You know very well it isn't," he says, catching Cora neatly as she attempts to follow the runners. Slinging her up and onto his hip, he starts to walk slowly and I fall into stride next to him. "Sunday is the one day that we get a lie in and my mother is staying this week. Do you know what that means, Milo?"

I blink. "You're having a nice time?"

"I'd be having a nicer time lying in with my husband while my mother looks after Cora."

"Oh," I say and start to laugh. He throws me a dark look.

"It's okay for you, Milo. In your big old house with just the two of you and no one to hear you scream. Last time I shouted during sex, I had my daughter banging on the door demanding to know if I'd fallen over, accompanied by Chewwy howling." He shudders. "It quite put us off our stride."

I start to laugh helplessly and he joins in, his expression wry.

We walk along for a bit, keeping to the side of the course while Cora jumps and skips alongside while admiring her new flowery wellies.

"What have you got on this week?" he asks.

I narrow my eyes, thinking. "I've got the two portraits from last week to finish. Then they've got to be packed up and shipped off. I've got a few days then before I've got to go to Gloucestershire."

He smiles as if liking that. "How long will you be away?"

"A week at the most. Or at least I hope so."

"I hope so too," he says tartly. "Because Niall will be like a bear with a sore head the longer you're away."

I sigh. "I'll be the same." I shoot him a look. "I know it sounds silly, but I hate being away from him."

"Not silly at all," he says placidly. "You're in love. That's a natural side effect, or it should be."

"I wish he could come with me, but Lord Reid is rather eccentric. He doesn't like his staff to have guests."

"He doesn't want you having a gentleman caller? How very *Upstairs Downstairs!*"

I laugh. "I think that term might be a bit libellous if applied to Niall. A gentleman he isn't."

He laughs, and we lapse into an easy silence while I watch the runners and search for a familiar head and shoulders. I was telling the truth. I will miss him. Far more than anyone could guess.

This tall and effervescent man is my whole heart. I love him fiercely and to the depths of me. He's everything to me. My best friend, my lover, and my biggest supporter. My career has grown in leaps and bounds the last couple of years, now that I'm so much more confident in putting myself forward for jobs. I'll also leave the estate more and it's totally down to Niall. It's as if him loving me both tethers me at his side and sets me gloriously free. I feel happy to show me now because a wonderful man loves that person with all his faults and foibles, and if that person stutters then so fucking what? That little practice that Niall set up in an unused room in *Chi an Mor* for me has now spread to three rooms and I employ an apprentice as well.

I'm totally myself with him and hold nothing back, and we fight and talk and fuck and love and it's wonderful and liberating.

We finally find ourselves by the water jump and I smile.

"What?" Oz asks.

"This is where we were when Niall first kissed me."

"How romantic and muddy," he shudders, but the smile on his lips gives him away.

"Hey, it was romantic, especially the seven-month-old baby in between us and Brunhild the Happy Homophobe to one side."

"Oh my God, is she here?" He ducks around me to look both ways.

"Probably. She's always at these things," I say gloomily. "It's as if when they banned fox hunting she had to pick a lesser blood sport."

"The foxes are probably laughing themselves silly now, having a lie down with a cup of tea." He looks down at Cora. "I remember that," he says. "You had Cora in that sling."

"She wouldn't fit now," I say, eyeing the merry little girl who is jumping around us. She's let her fear of ruining her new wellies be overtaken by the strong desire to jump in muddy puddles, and as such she's speckled with the stuff.

"Sweetie, how do you manage to get it on your face?" Oz says, grabbing a wet wipe from his pocket and cleaning her face despite her screwing it up like she's entering a gurning competition.

All around us are shouts and cheers, and we stand for ages growing colder but joining in the cheers and counting down as the runners jump into the freezing cold pond, grinning like lunatics.

"I can't fathom the British," Oz says, staring at two women who are shrieking at the cold with big grins on their faces.

"*You're* British."

"I'm Irish," he corrects me. "We'd have been in the pub by now shaking our heads at the idjits."

Cora joins in, dancing about and occasionally stopping to admire her wellies or the huge sparkly red ring that Silas bought her from a stand earlier. Oz looks at her affectionately. "She's got the taste of Lily Savage with regards to jewellery," he mutters.

Suddenly he brightens. "There they are," he exclaims, hoisting up Cora so she can see.

Niall and Silas are at the top of the platform. They're covered in mud and already soaking wet, but they're laughing and Niall's grin is white and wide in his muddy face. The crowd starts a countdown and Niall puts a hand to his ear while Silas shakes his head and laughs at him. Finally, holding hands, they jump into the water.

I laugh but it dies away quickly. "She's here," I hiss and sure enough, there she is, marching towards us and dragging her friend rather reluctantly with her.

"I found out today that you're married to the Earl of Ashworth," she says abruptly to Oz.

He blinks. "I'm sorry. Was I supposed to have informed you? I must have missed that memo."

"I think it's disgraceful that a peer of the realm should conduct his affairs so publicly. Married to a man indeed. This is why we need Brexit to get rid of these dreadful new-fangled ideas."

"Oh, Sally," her friend mutters.

"Yes, we should leave Europe and maybe we could get rid of those pesky things called manners too," Oz mutters, bending to put Cora down as she wriggles in excitement at seeing Silas.

She turns her gaze on me. "And you're the one who was kissing a man here last time in front of families and children. What do you say to that?"

"I say I'd do it again," I say, taking a breath at the beginning to calm my breathing.

"I'd certainly hope so," a deep voice drawls next to me. "But only if it's me."

I lean back against him for a second, loving the scent of his cologne mixed with clean sweat. He's hard and warm against my back but also rather wet and soggy, so I move forward again rather quickly, catching the wry quirk of his lips as I do it.

"Nilo," Cora screeches and dances over to him. She's called him this since she could talk, and I love it. It's an amalgam of me and him, so how could I not?

He bends down, pursing his lips for a kiss. "Come and give me a smooch, Cora Bora," he demands, and she screams in delight as she smothers his face in smacking kisses. The old woman tuts, and Niall puts Cora down and stares at her. "Is there a problem?"

"I'll say there's a problem."

"Is it that the food wagon was out of small children for you to eat for breakfast, or are the sweets falling off your house in the wood?"

"*Niall*," I say, trying not to laugh.

"It's disgusting that this child should be surrounded by gay people." She whispers the last words and I stare at her.

"She's surrounded by love," I say quietly. "I don't think there's anything better than that."

I feel Niall's stare on my face and when I turn, he's looking at me with a very fixed and strange look on his face.

"You okay?" I ask curiously.

"Brace yourself," Silas says, looking like he's trying not to laugh.

I stare at him and then stand open-mouthed as Niall drops to his knees in front of me. Cora immediately dances over to him and drapes herself across his shoulder. She loves Niall with a passion.

I frown at him. "What are you doing?" I ask, and Oz starts to laugh.

"Milo," Niall says after giving the old lady a death glare. "Milo Ramsay, you are the love of my life. Will you do me the inestimable honour of marrying me?"

"Oh my God," I say faintly. "Is this actually happening at the moment?"

He stares up at me and the look on his face makes everything else fade away until all I can see is him.

"Not just to piss her off?" I say quietly, and he immediately shakes his head.

"Not even a little bit. I'm glad she's here because maybe if she gets a look at even the teeniest bit of how much I love you it might lessen her sourness." He shrugs. "Either way, I don't care. I've wanted to ask you for ages and it just suddenly occurred to me that we're standing right where we had our first kiss, and I knew that now was the time because that moment changed my life in so many ways, not least of which is having you by my side. And that's where I want to keep you. By my side because you're my home and I love you desperately."

He smiles and all the warmth and heat in his eyes makes me feel suddenly humbled. I don't know what I've done to deserve this larger-than-life man but by God, I'm going to hold onto him. Hold onto him and love him with everything in me.

"I will," I say fiercely.

"Not just to piss her off?" he whispers, and I grin.

"Fuck no. Not even a millimetre." I lean down and whisper into his ear. "I love you so much, Niall. I always will because you're my home too. I'd be honoured to marry you."

For a second his eyes shimmer but then he blinks and pats his pocket, a comical look crossing his face. "Shit! The ring's in the car."

"Why is it in there?"

He shrugs, his grin seeming so big it might take over his face. "I was just waiting for the right time."

"And this is it?" I ask, looking around the muddy field on this blustery day as the rain starts to fall harder, the cold drops blowing into our faces and making the crowd start to move towards the car park.

He nods. "It's right for us, Lo."

I smile helplessly down at him and he looks around as if for inspiration.

"It doesn't matter," I say. "Finish the run and we'll get it when we get back to the car."

"No way," he says stoutly. He looks sideways at Cora, who is watching us with a fascinated expression on her face. "Cora Bora, can I borrow your ring?"

Ever generous, she immediately twists it off her finger and gives it to him. He accepts it with a kiss and, grabbing my hand, he puts the garish sparkly thing on my finger. "And I declare us engaged," he says triumphantly. He winks at the old woman. "Are you waiting to offer your congratulations? We haven't got all day."

Mouthing like a cow chewing grass, she glares at him until her friend pulls her away.

"I think you can borrow that ring for a little bit, Nilo," Cora says but then adds firmly, "And then you'll have to get Daddy to buy you one of your own."

Amongst the laughter, I reach down and pull him up, and he unfolds himself before grabbing me and pulling me into a hug. "Not quite what you were expecting?" he asks after kissing me lustily to a lot of catcalls. The faint worry in his voice makes me pull back and put my hand to his face. It's streaked with mud and rain, but his denim-blue eyes look at me steadily and there's a look in them that says, incredibly, that I'm everything he needs.

"Why would I want that?" I say quietly. "You've always been better than my expectations, Niall. You always will be."

He grabs me close and I cuddle into him on this muddy field, letting him shelter me from the wind which is blowing hard now and giving him my warmth in return. It's our very own brand of teamwork, and I think it's the best way to start our marriage.

THANK YOU

My husband who's my best friend and can always make me laugh. This is for pushing me to write full-time. I love it just like you said I would.

My boys. For being my pride and joy.

Leslie Copeland. For being such an awesome beta reader and friend. You knew just what Milo needed - a prologue!

Natasha Snow. For another fantastic cover. I can't imagine my books without your covers.

Hailey Turner. For all the laughs, encouragement and wonderful friendship. Here's to London!

Edie Danford. My Nanowrimo partner! You make me laugh every day and I would never have got Milo finished without you. Here's to many more Alexander Skarsgard celebratory pictures.

Courtney Bassett. I'm looking forward to many more editing jobs with all your statistics! Your notes are always so encouraging and positive despite the fact that you've had to add one million commas!

The members of my Facebook reader's group, Lily's Snark Squad. They're funny and make me laugh every day. They also cope with my erratic posting schedule. I love my time spent in there.

To all the bloggers who spend their valuable time reading, reviewing and promoting the books. Also, the readers who liven up my day with their messages and photos and book recommendations. I love being a part of this community, so thank you.

Lastly thanks to you, for taking a chance on this book. I hope you enjoyed reading it as much as I enjoyed writing it.

I never knew until I wrote my first book how important reviews are. So if you have time, please consider leaving a review on Amazon or Goodreads or any other review sites. I can promise you that I read every one, good or bad, and value all of them. When I've been struggling with writing, sometimes going back and reading the reviews makes it better.

CONTACT LILY

Website: www.lilymortonauthor.com
This has lots of information and fun features, including some extra short stories.

If you'd like to be the first to know about my book releases and have access to extra content, you can sign up for my newsletter here

If you fancy hearing the latest news and interacting with other readers do head over and join my Facebook group. It's a fun group and I share all the latest news about my books there as well as some exclusive short stories.
www.facebook.com/groups/SnarkSquad/

I'd love to hear from you, so if you want to say hello or have any questions, please contact me and I'll get back to you:
Email: lilymorton1@outlook.com

ALSO BY LILY MORTON

Mixed Messages Series

Rule Breaker

Deal Maker

Risk Taker

Finding Home Series

Oz

Milo

Other Novels

The Summer of Us

Short Stories

Best Love

3 Dates

Printed in Great
Britain
by Amazon